CHRISTOPHER ARTINIAN

The Burning Tree: Book 4
Anarchy

Christopher Artinian

CHRISTOPHER ARTINIAN

Copyright © 2022 Christopher Artinian

All rights reserved.

ISBN: 9798845695000

CHRISTOPHER ARTINIAN

DEDICATION

To Josephine.

CHRISTOPHER ARTINIAN

CHRISTOPHER ARTINIAN

ACKNOWLEDGEMENTS

First and foremost, I want to send a massive thank you to my missus, Tina. She is always there and has never let me down. I am the luckiest man in the world to be with her.

A great big thank you to the gang across in the fan club. I couldn't ask for a friendlier and more engaging bunch of people to hang out with.

Thanks to my great pal, Christian, for another brill cover. Also, many thanks to my editor, Ken – a fantastic editor and a lovely chap. And a massive shout out to Mandi for all the great videos she's created for me.

Last but by no means least, a huge thank you to you for purchasing this book..

CHRISTOPHER ARTINIAN

PROLOGUE

Callie had gone to bed, but as tired as she was, and as hard as she tried, she couldn't drift off to sleep. In fear of waking her mum and brother, who were both in deep slumber, she got up as quietly as she could and slipped through the curtain that acted as the outside wall to her family's current accommodation.

Snores and restless mumbles accompanied her as she walked down the corridor of curtained apartments in the old barn. It was cramped, it was noisy and a little smelly with so many people living in such close quarters, but at least there was a roof over their heads. Who knew how long it would be before the newcomers, who'd arrived the previous day, enjoyed the same luxury?

Callie stepped out of the barn and her eyes were

immediately drawn to the firelight bleeding through the gap in the door of what had become their makeshift infirmary. Despite wanting to know how Harry was getting on, she decided to leave their new friends Nazya and Chloe to it. *Maybe by morning, the news will be better.*

She walked across the farmyard and it was only then that she could make out the outline of a familiar figure in the moonlight. "I thought I saw Debbie coming to get you when I was heading to bed."

Phil turned around, a little startled. "Don't you know it's bad form to sneak up on the elderly?"

"You're hardly elderly, Phil," she said, walking up beside him.

"I'm actually the oldest person here, so I'm the most elderly person you know anyway."

"I don't suppose I can argue that."

"I thought you were too tired to talk anyway."

"I got to bed and I just couldn't switch my mind off."

"Yeah, I get that."

"What was keeping you up?"

"Stuff."

"You worried about Harry?"

Phil turned in the direction of the hut with the slightly open door. "Not at all. Having your leg ripped off by a shark is like mumps. It's good to get it out of the way when you're young."

"People are just beginning to accept you. I'm absolutely begging you, Phil, don't say that to anyone else."

"Is that why Michelle got uppity with me earlier on?"

"You're kidding me. Tell me you didn't."

Phil chuckled. "Of course I didn't."

They stood in silence for a few moments before Callie asked again, "So, what is it? What's troubling you?"

"Other than trying to figure out how we're going to feed all these mouths beyond next week? How we're going to build an irrigation system? How we're going to store the food we grow without it spoiling and in a way that will last us through the winter months? Apart from that, you mean?"

"Yeah."

"Nothing really. Probably Debbie snoring."

"I'll tell her you said she snores."

"Oh, please. Like my life could get any worse."

"You don't mean that."

Even in the moonlight, she could see Phil's teeth as his lips curved into a smile.

"No, I don't, actually. I feel more alive than I have done in years."

"Good, 'cause you need to figure out how we're going to feed all these mouths beyond next week, how we're going to build an irrigation system, and how we're going to store the food we grow without it spoiling."

"Thanks for the reminder."

"So, got any ideas?"

"About what?"

"About what? About that list of stuff for a start."

"None. You?"

"Funny."

"Oh. I didn't get the chance to tell you before you disappeared on me, but Tania brought back mushrooms today."

"Mushrooms? That's good, isn't it? I mean I don't

know much about them, but can't you get thousands of spores from a single one?"

"Yeah."

"So, we'll be able to grow thousands of mushrooms?"

"Technically."

"What does that mean?"

"It means given the right conditions."

"And what are the right conditions?"

"A lab environment so we can grow mycelium from the spores without any other organism kicking the hell out of them."

"Oh."

"Yeah. I'm still figuring all of that out."

"So, that's another one for the list."

"Yep."

"On the upside, the berries and cherries Mum found won't take too much cultivation, will they?"

Phil looked back over to the barn. "Assuming there's anything left of them. I should really—"

"They'll last a few hours until morning, Phil."

He let out a sigh. "I suppose."

"So, we'll be self-sufficient in berries and cherries anyway."

"Then our problems are solved. Listen, I'd really like to head out to this Infinity place as soon as possible."

"Everything works on a barter system there, but I got the impression that our weapons were pretty valuable. We've got an awful lot of them after the quarry."

"Mm."

"What does that mean?"

"It means I'm not convinced it's sensible to give up

our only means of defence."

"I'm not talking about giving up all our guns. Maybe just a few. We could trade for seeds and equipment."

"Possibly. We'll need to think about it."

"It's not like we've got anything else to trade at the moment. Maybe when the crops come in, we'll have plenty, but right now, we need every advantage we can get, wouldn't you say?"

Phil let out another long sigh. "Nobody likes a know-it-all."

"I mean, unless you've got plans for world domination, we're not about to be going to war with anyone in the not-too-distant future, are we?"

"Probably not."

"I bet a dozen or so Q-Eighteens would get us an awful lot in a trade-off."

Phil scratched his whiskered chin. "I suppose with the new arrivals, anything would help at the moment."

"Exactly."

"And like you say, I think we've had our fair share of excitement for a while. It's not like an army's going to invade us tomorrow, is it?"

*

They'd travelled through the afternoon and into the night. They had learnt how to blend into the landscape. They'd learnt lots of things since emerging from the underground.

There they had witnessed horrors that few would believe. There they had committed atrocities few would comprehend. The people they had been before were long forgotten now. Butchers and bakers and candlestick makers, lawyers and cleaners and all inbetweeners living like vermin in the dark, sooty depths side by side, fighting for survival, fighting for every scrap of food, every drop of water.

In London, the asteroid had been the great leveller in more ways than one. Only the strongest survived, but the strongest were no longer the ones with the most wealth. The strongest were the ones willing to do whatever it took, whatever they had to.

When they had taken their first tentative steps back into the light, it had nearly blinded them. For months they lived in the broken bones of buildings like parasites eking out a subsistence on a slowly rotting corpse. But then they had dared to leave the inside-out tomb that had once been their city in search of something else ... in search of this.

Living, breathing, walking breadcrumbs had led them to Infinity. And there they had watched, only occasionally attacking one of the ill-prepared parties who were making a pilgrimage in the hope that they could find the elusive thing they were searching for to give them a better life.

They had sometimes interrogated the people they'd captured before ... doing what needed to be done to survive. It was during one such interrogation that they had learned the people of Infinity referred to them as Ferals.

It was a blanket term, and for some it was more appropriate than others. There were gangs who fell under the moniker but were just people who had survived in shelters only to run out of food and supplies. Having nothing to trade and little hope of returning to civilisation, they lived in the wilds as well as they could, thieving and raiding to exist.

But for Danko and his followers, Feral couldn't

have described them better. They were as much savage animal as human now. Even their language skills had suffered. People spoke a bare minimum in the underground. Sound was not a friend of the hunter or the hunted.

Danko had sometimes gone for days without talking to another person, and if he spoke now, it was under duress. He had little to say to anyone, and likewise, his followers had little to say to him or one another. After all, there were no good times to speak of from their imprisonment in the darkness.

The half dozen or so men and women who were with him all watched the small settlement down below—weighing it up, looking for weaknesses. Studying what resources were available. They had been in position for hours and barely uttered a phrase. But Danko had seen what he needed to. Living in the blackness of the underground for three plus years had conditioned their eyes to see better in the night.

"You two stay out of sight. Watch for the day, come home tonight and tell us what you see," he said, turning to a pair of figures to his left.

No one ever questioned Danko's orders. He had made it clear many times before that he was the alpha leader, and challenging him never ended well for anyone. "Okay," Zeke replied.

"Okay," Rocky added.

"We'll search the rest of area then head home," he said, shuffling back from the ridge.

The others didn't say a word, and they all retreated too. "We'll come back?" It was a woman who asked, but other than the lack of a beard there was little that could distinguish her as such.

"Soon."

They had followed the small group all afternoon. They had witnessed them nearly meet their end in the forest at the hands of the other so-called Ferals, but then they had continued their journey. They had done this many times with many different parties heading from Infinity. But this one seemed like the honeypot.

They had searched for a place, not just to raid but to settle. Somewhere their pack could flourish. Danko was sure this was it. With fields already planted, fresh water at hand and livestock sleeping soundly in their beds, this place would give them a future.

Tens of thousands of people had fled into the underground to avoid the worst effects of the asteroid. Some had chosen their safe havens unwisely and cooked in their own juices as vast parts of the network had turned into smouldering ovens.

Thousands of others had survived the initial impact and beyond, only to succumb to the horrors of the aftermath. The bodies of those who burned to death only fed the burgeoning rat population for so long, but then they began to hunt the living. And as the initial supplies that people had brought into the underground ran out, so the living began to hunt the rats … and the weak … and anything else that could feed them.

Danko eventually led four hundred out into the light. Before they found Infinity, they lost half that number. But now their population had stabilised and they were getting stronger each day. This, though, this settlement would give them the life they had been looking for. The life they had been hoping for.

"We'll need guns," the woman who had spoken before said as the six of them retraced their path back to the caves they currently called home.

Out of the two hundred or so of them, only twenty had guns and a small amount of ammunition to go with them. It was unlikely the people in the settlement would give it up easily, so the more weapons Danko's people could glean the better.

Danko nodded. "We'll get them. We'll ambush a smaller group heading to Infinity."

They had only made the mistake of going into Crowesbury a couple of times. Trying something within the town limits was foolhardy unless you had the numbers to back it up. They had discussed a large-scale ambush of the Infinity security forces in order to gain rifles and ammunition, but in all likelihood, they would lose a lot of people, and to what end? They had managed to pick traders off a few at a time, giving them enough food and supplies to live on, but this was something else. The benefit far outweighed the risk.

"We'll need to plan it," the woman replied.

A smile crept onto Danko's face as his mind drifted back to the times before the world changed forever. Before that fateful day when he'd taken his family down into London's darkest depths, he had been a town planner. He had a level of responsibility that would overwhelm most people. Planning had been something in his blood, something that filled every minute of every day of his life. "Yes," he replied, and he suddenly remembered back to a book his best friend had given him to read the night before he interviewed for the job. It was Sun Tzu's *The Art of War*. An image of a passage highlighted in luminous

DayGlo-green jumped out of the page at him. "Every battle is won before it is fought."

The others all glanced towards one another in the moonlight as they continued their journey down the hill to the remains of the road. "What?" the woman asked.

"Never mind," Danko replied as a wide smile spread over his face.

1

Greenslade and Trunk had been given a tonic and all kinds of shots to make them feel a little more normal. All of Drake's plans were hinging on them, and he couldn't afford for even just a momentary weakness to knock them off kilter.

Drake stood at the door casting frequent looks up and down the corridor while Greenslade and Trunk got dressed. "We've agreed to help. It's not like we can escape this place without you, is it? You don't have to watch over us like some nanny," Greenslade said as he buttoned up his shirt.

"I'm not watching over you, dickhead; I'm watching out for you," Drake replied.

"That's sweet, but I'm pretty certain we can watch

out for ourselves."

Drake looked up and down the corridor once more then stepped back into the room. "You really don't get it, do you? This thing's in motion. Stuff's already happening and has already happened, which means there's no turning back. If they figure out exactly what's going on before we're on our way, it's going to be like a war zone down here."

"Down here?"

"On Level Two, dimwit."

"You've got a great way of talking to people whose help you need."

"We need each other."

"We were doing fine before we met you."

"Oh, sure you were. And how long do you think that would have lasted? As far as they're concerned, you and the rest of them are their property bought and paid for. When you came to Salvation, that was you signing over your lives to these bastards, and the crops you're growing, that little community you've set up, that's theirs too."

"Screw you. Nobody owns me."

"You might think that. There was a time when I thought that. But I know now that me, my family, my friends, we'll never know freedom until we're out from under this place and these people."

"But that's what I'm saying," Greenslade replied. "We were out. We had found freedom."

"No, you hadn't. It would just have been a matter of time before they found you, and then you'd either be brought back here or be dead."

"So why is getting out there going to be different for you? How come you're going to be free when we weren't?"

"Because I understand what's needed to secure

freedom."

A smile cracked on Greenslade's face. "Oh, and what is this magic ingredient that the rest of us failed to grasp?"

"War."

The smile remained on Greenslade's face for a moment before he realised the other man wasn't joking. "Surely, if you were going to go to war with these people, you'd be better doing it from here, from within."

Drake peeked out of the door once more and looked up and down the corridor before shifting back into the room. "We wouldn't stand a chance. Out there, where you are, we're on neutral territory. We could put up a fight."

"Well, it's nice of you to include us in your plans, but it's not neutral territory, it's our home. We're building lives there."

"What is it that you're not understanding? Eventually, they'll find you. It might take them years, but they'll come for you."

"So, you're offering us protection? You're running a protection racket?"

"Something I'm sure you'd know all about."

"How would we possibly be any better off having you and your jackbooted pals as our overlords rather than Bucks and his cronies?"

"We're not going to be your rulers, you idiot. We're going to be living alongside you."

"Said the man in the black uniform armed to his teeth."

"Okay, you have trust issues. I get that."

"That's decent of you."

"I don't want my kids to follow in my footsteps here. I don't want them to become the oppressors, to grow up believing this stuff is normal. Because the more accepted it becomes as a society the fewer people protest when things get worse and worse, until one day, you realise it's all too late and the chance to do something about it has come and gone."

"You sound like a real man of the people."

Drake smiled. "Remind me again, illegal drugs, prostitution, alcohol… How were you a man of the people again?"

"If it wasn't me, it would be someone else."

"The excuse of tyrants since the dawn of civilisation."

"So, now I'm a tyrant?"

"You're a cog, and I'm a cog, and your pal there is a cog," he replied, pointing over to Trunk.

"I've got a name, y'know," Trunk replied grouchily.

"We're cogs?" Greenslade asked.

"Yeah, in a very, very big wheel."

"Do you really think we can win a war against Bucks?"

Drake looked at his watch. His great-great-grandfather had plucked it from the wrist of a dead Nazi soldier after the Battle of Stalingrad. It had been passed down from generation to generation, and he hoped he would live long enough to hand it to his eldest son when he reached eighteen. "Right this minute, I've got more weapons and ammunition than you could believe heading down to Level Three."

"How?" Greenslade asked, confused. "Isn't that stuff guarded to the hilt?"

"This is what I'm talking about. You have no idea about the plans that are in motion right now. We've got people on the inside, but the people who are in the way are either tied up and gagged or dead right now. When morning comes, there'll be an accounting of what this cost, and it will be an expensive day for Bucks and his people, but if this thing comes off the rails before it even gets going, then we're going to be left with the bill."

"Thanks very much. So nice of you to include us in your plans."

"Hey, it's like I said. This isn't just about us. Think of the people you left behind. Every last one of them is at risk. There's one way to secure their future and I'm offering it to you right now."

"Going to war with Bucks? That's the path to safety? Doesn't that sound a little crazy?"

"No, it sounds a lot crazy, but I know what I'm talking about. When we get to where we're going, me and my people are going to turn the settlement into a fortress."

"Err … there's not actually much of a settlement to turn into anything. There's nothing really there other than a farmhouse and a barn."

"Well, with three and a half thousand extra able bodies to help, I'm pretty certain we'll be able to turn it into something else pretty quickly."

"Three and a half thousand? That's how many people from Level Three survived?"

"No. It was about three thousand. The other five hundred are people from Level Two."

"Guards?"

"Guards, their families, doctors, nurses, power plant workers, just decent people who've figured out what's going on and want out."

"And you put all this together since we got here?"

"No, it's like I said. This has been in motion for a long time. Your arrival just acted as a catalyst."

There was a bang as a pair of double doors further down the hallway crashed open. Drake immediately reached for the Q-Eighteen handgun from his holster and a look of concern crept onto his face. A heavy silence hung in the room for a moment before he angled his head out into the corridor once more.

Neither Greenslade nor Trunk could see what he was seeing, but his shoulders and whole demeanour became visibly relaxed and he pulled the door to the room wide open. The woman called Marina, who had left them just a few minutes earlier, wheeled something in on a gurney. She peeled the green sheet back to reveal a weapons crate. Drake released the clasps and opened the lid. "Well, what are you waiting for?" Marina asked, looking towards the two men who, up until a few minutes ago, had been sedated.

"You're giving us weapons?" Greenslade asked. He and Trunk both walked up to the crate and immediately picked out a Q-Thirty rifle each, slinging the straps over their right shoulders in unison. They then grabbed a utility belt, strapping them on as well before finally taking one of the Q-Eighteen handguns.

"The satchels are yours too. They've got stun grenades and spare magazines in them," Marina said.

Greenslade immediately looked inside, and, sure enough, they contained what she said. He glanced at the woman who had brought the weapons, then at her comrade before charging the Q-Eighteen and pointing it directly at Drake's head. "And tell me, what's stopping me from shooting the bastard who put fifty thousand volts through my friend and me then beat the shit out of both of us?"

"The truth," Drake replied, not even flinching.

Greenslade smiled. "What truth?"

"The truth I've spoken tonight. You know everything I said is true. You know that even though you and your people are out there, while the administration still exists you'll never be free, you'll never be safe."

Greenslade let out a long sigh and lowered the gun once more. "We're barely managing to feed ourselves as it is. This could be the shortest-lived revolution in history."

"We're taking supplies, which is another reason we're going to have a target on our backs. Right now, the produce that should be heading to the Level One and Level Two Salmarts is going down to Level Three."

Greenslade laughed. "And the video cameras? Aren't people going to be asking questions?"

"I've got people I trust with my family's lives monitoring those cameras. Before they leave, everything is going to be wiped. The only reason I've got the CCTV running at all tonight is so we can get a heads-up if there's any unusual activity anywhere." Drake snapped his fingers. "As quickly as that, everything could go to hell." He looked at his watch again as the sound of multiple footsteps travelled down the corridor towards them. He and Marina both raised their weapons and backed away from the entrance. Not knowing what else to do, Greenslade and Trunk did the same.

The doors swung inwards, and two doctors, three nurses and a porter entered, all immediately throwing their hands in the air as they saw the weapons trained on them. The porter let out a small whimper of fear until, one by one, the weapons were lowered.

"It's a good job you're coming along because I'm

pretty certain before this night is over, one of us is going to have a heart attack," Marina said, placing a hand up to her chest.

"Those who can handle a weapon, grab one," Drake said, nodding to the open crate.

"If it comes to us fighting, then I'm pretty much guessing that it's game over anyway," one of the doctors replied. Her skin was pale, her face drawn, and it was obvious to anyone that she was a million miles out of her comfort zone.

"If things go south on this thing, Rachael, I'd rather you had something to defend yourselves with."

"If things go south, then there'll be no point. It will be over. We either get out or we don't." Rachael's husband was a Salvation guard. They had a good life on Level Two and were leaving a lot more behind than most. Her nerves were well-founded as one thing going wrong would spell disaster.

The others in her group all reached into the crate for a rifle and spare magazines. "I've never used one of these before," the porter said.

"Marina, show everyone the basics, will you? I'll meet you at the lift in fifteen." Marina nodded and Drake signalled for Greenslade and Trunk to follow him. They left the small private room and headed out into the ward. There were two patients, both fast asleep.

Greenslade couldn't take his eyes off them as they walked past. "What about them?" he whispered. "What about everyone else who's going to be left behind?"

Drake waited until they were out of the ward before he replied. "Those two are Salvation guards, and you don't have to worry about them. They've been anaesthetised. As far as everyone else goes ... well, I'm not a miracle worker. I'm doing what I can. I'm trying to save as many as I can of the people who believe what I believe. It's been difficult. Everything has been organised covertly, and I dare say there'll be a lot of people who would happily go with us if they knew about it but.... Life's unfair." They carried on down the stairs until they reached the street. "Come on. This way."

"So, it's tough shit for everyone else?"

Drake stopped and turned. "Listen to me. I'm doing the best I can here. I'm giving as many people as possible a chance."

"While leaving the others to suffer?"

"What would you have me do? Start a revolt?"

"You could have done that. You could have done that months back. You could have had a lot of the Level Three people behind you."

Drake let out a defeated breath. "Yeah, well, hindsight's a wonderful thing, isn't it? I didn't see you breaking your back to stage a coup. I saw you exploiting those people just like Bucks and the rest of them."

"I was never like them," Greenslade growled, taking a step towards Drake.

The other man didn't flinch. "You keep telling yourself that." They glared at each other for several seconds before Drake spoke again. "None of this is ideal, and if I had my time over, I'd have played things a different way, but unless you know about a time machine somewhere, we're stuck with this here and now and we've got to make the best of it."

Greenslade carried on staring at him for a moment longer and then he relaxed a little. "I suppose I could have done things differently too."

"I don't think there's a person alive who couldn't. So, let's try to make life better for as many as we can, starting now." He looked at Greenslade and then turned to Trunk. Both men nodded and Drake started walking again. It was less than thirty seconds before they arrived at a building very different to the normal accommodation blocks.

A grand brass nameplate hung on the wall by the door stating Salvation Guard Headquarters in large black letters. Without pause, Drake led the way in and took them to a lift beyond the foyer. A minute later, they were getting off once more and heading along the corridor to the CCTV room.

They entered to find two men sitting in front of the screens and another to the right, frantically tapping away at the keys of a computer. They all stopped momentarily.

"Drake," one of the men said.

"Revell," Drake replied. The man at the computer turned back around and continued his work, a little irritated by the interruption. "How goes it?"

"We've got Ludlow and his entire squad in the holding cells."

"I bet that was satisfying."

"You have no idea."

"Trouble?"

"As much as you'd expect."

"Comms?"

Revell looked across to the man on the computer. "PJ, comms?"

The young and painfully thin tech wizard stopped and spun around in his chair. "What about them?"

Drake smiled. "Where are we with them?"

"Where you asked to be. What do you expect?" he replied, spinning his chair back around and continuing his work on the keyboard.

"PJ!" It was Drake's no-nonsense voice, and although the younger tech-head liked to play the rebel, Drake was one man he would never push it with.

He swung back around in his chair and nodded towards a strange-looking radio on the older man's belt. "Analogue only. All mobile comms are down, as is the network for anyone but us. When I pull the plug completely, the walkies I built for you are going to be the only way to communicate."

"I'm surprised you haven't been summoned."

"I have. Paris has been on the phone every five minutes. I'm pretty certain that woman is a vampire. I've never known her sleep."

"So, the hard-wired phones are still working?"

"I thought it best to keep them on as long as possible to avoid any undue suspicion."

Drake nodded. "Smart. And our guys in the plant?" he asked, turning to look at Revell once more.

"All set."

Greenslade and Trunk heard little of the conversation. Their eyes were drawn to the monitors. Hundreds of Level Three inhabitants were lining the streets. They carried bags, rucksacks and bundles of all sorts. Every man, woman and child seemed to be laden with something. Dozens of Salvation guards could be seen on the monitors too as well as many more Level Two inhabitants who seemed completely out of their element.

"How did you get them all down there?" Greenslade asked.

"Carefully," Revell replied. "We've got the only CCTV feed. We cut the mobile tracking and we made sure all of Ludlow's guys were locked up before we did anything."

"Oh shit!" the other guard monitoring the CCTV blurted.

All eyes in the room turned towards the monitor he was staring at.

"Oh shit!" Drake echoed.

A dozen of Buck's own elite guards were entering one of the private elevators from Level One to Level Two. "What the hell are they doing?" Revell asked.

"They must smell a rat, or someone must have tipped them to something going on."

"What do we do?"

Drake looked at his watch. "PJ, you can get word to our people at the plant, yes?"

"Why?"

"We go in twenty."

"What? That's crazy."

"We're bringing everything forward. We go in twenty. Revell, get across to the hospital. Tell Marina what's happening. We've already got everyone in place down on Level Three. The only way we're getting out of here is if we do this now; otherwise, everything's shot to shit. PJ, I need you to wipe everything. All CCTV, call logs, everything."

"That's already in hand. I've uploaded some wicked malware too, but I want to go on record as saying this is insane."

"Duly noted," Drake said, heading to the door.

"Where are you going?" Greenslade asked.

"We. Where are *we* going," Drake replied. "We're

going to make sure Bucks' guards don't get a chance to report back before all hell breaks loose."

"Woah," PJ said, reaching down into the holdall by his feet.

"What is it? I've got about a minute to get to that lift."

PJ pulled out something that looked like a gun with a small silver umbrella sticking out of the end. "This will jam any radio signals."

"What, for real?"

"No, I'm pranking you because I'm bored and we've got so much time on our hands. Yes, for real. Depress the trigger and keep it depressed."

"I thought you said all comms were down."

"Yes, well, I can't discount the possibility that they've got someone almost as good as me working for them up there, can I? There's a slim possibility they might have been given analogue radios, just in case."

"I owe you one," Drake said, taking the device and running out of the door with Greenslade and Trunk following closely behind.

"You owe me a lot more than one." PJ's words followed them out of the room.

"Dwyer, this is Drake. Meet me at Shaft B now. Over." He released the talk button and brought the radio back down from his lips.

"Roger that. Over and out."

"I had a squad on standby in case something like this happened. I was hoping it wouldn't, but you don't always get what you wish for in life."

"So, what's the plan?" Trunk asked.

"We make sure none of them are left standing. We

make sure they don't get the chance to send a message then we get down to Level Three fast—or our lives will take a seriously bad turn."

*

The clunk of the lift arriving down on Level Two told Drake and Dwyer they were already too late to enact an ambush in the shaft itself. They came to a hurried stop as they heard the doors slide open, and instead, they, Greenslade, Trunk and the rest of the squad all pressed their backs against the wall of the accommodation block just around the corner.

The sound of the elite guard marching in formation along the street sent shudders down the spines of all those present. Suddenly, hypotheticals and what ifs were in the past. This was happening; this was real.

Drake turned to the others. "We need this to be fast and clean," he whispered; then he looked at each of the men and women present to make sure they understood. "On my mark," he said, raising his hand. *"Three, two, one. Now!"*

2

The automatic gunfire boomed like thunder in the normally quiet residential street. The elite guard had been sent down to Level Two to take charge of re-establishing communications. They were, after all, Bucks' right hand, and their presence was a reminder of just whom everyone answered to.

The last thing any of them expected was a battle, and that's the last thing any of them got. The twelve men and women did not even have the time to unsling their weapons before being gunned down. Drake had PJ's radio jamming device at the ready, but there was no opportunity to use that either.

"Get them back in the lift. Anyone comes out of these buildings, you tell them it was terrorists posing as elite guards and everything's under control now."

Seven of the bodies were already out of sight by the time the first accommodation block inhabitants dared step out onto the street. Gasps and cries of fear rose from all those who witnessed the aftermath, but they were told to head back inside and stay inside until morning as there was intelligence to suggest that the attack was not over.

It was an easy story to sell. The administration often used terrorists as a cover for their own shortfalls, so people quickly disappeared inside once more, leaving Drake's squad to finish the clean-up.

Once all the bodies had been piled inside the lift, the doors were closed and the control panel was disabled. Under normal circumstances, an engineer would have been able to get it going again in no time, but these were not normal circumstances. Drake looked at his watch and brought the radio up to his mouth. "PJ. It's Drake. Over."

"Well, duh. Who else is it going to be?"

"This kid," he said, looking at the handset with anger before hitting the talk button once more. "Disable the sensors on the hatch and get it open. We're in this up to our necks now. Let's get the show on the road. Over."

"On it. I'm shutting down lift access for Level One as well. There's no turning back now."

"And PJ, make sure everything from tonight is wiped. Over."

"Oh, ye of little faith. They're not going to be able to tell what month it is by the time I'm finished."

"I'll meet you down at the hatch. Be careful. Over and out."

"What now?" Greenslade asked.

"Now we get the hell out of Dodge."

*

"You two hatching a plan that involves more work for me and my crew?" Jason asked, walking up behind Phil and Callie.

"Jesus Christ," Phil said, putting his hand up to his chest. "Doesn't anyone sleep in this place?"

"I'm glad to see you're back safely, Callie," Jason replied, ignoring Phil.

"Thanks. Our trip didn't actually go as smoothly as planned."

Jason looked back towards the makeshift infirmary. "Did you find what John needed?"

"They went one better than that," Phil replied.

"What do you mean?"

"They brought a doctor back."

"What?"

"It's complicated," Callie replied.

"I dare say."

"Yeah," Phil said, "and it gets even better. Callie found a market."

"A market? What kind of market? Who runs it?"

"The kind—"

Callie cut Phil off. "The kind that could help us a lot. The daughter of the guy who runs it came back here with us. She's giving blood to help Harry."

"So, what do they sell?"

"Plants, food, building materials, pretty much anything you can imagine."

"Oh my God."

"Exactly," Phil replied excitedly. "We need to go as soon as we can. Maybe you can delegate to some of your underlings and we can head out at first light."

"Underlings?" Callie asked, shaking her head. "Please, please stop talking to people directly. In future, speak through me and I'll translate."

"For once," Jason replied, "I agree with Phil. This place could be just what we need."

"Okay, there are a couple of reasons why this isn't going to happen," Callie replied. "Firstly, Nazya and Chloe are—"

"Who are Nazya and Chloe?" Jason asked.

"The doctor and the woman who's giving blood."

"Oh."

"So, firstly, they won't be ready to head back. Nazya will need to stay with Harry for a while; I'm guessing Chloe will need to recover after such a long journey and then giving blood. Secondly, we need to be prepared. We need a big contingent to go and we need to figure out exactly what we're prepared to trade."

"Why do we need a big contingent?"

"There are gangs out there."

"Gangs?" Phil asked. "What kind of gangs?"

"They call them Ferals."

"And what do they do exactly?"

"Rob, murder, cannibalise. Y'know, all the good stuff."

"Ooh. They sound fun."

"These people are no joke. We ran into some of them and it could have ended very badly."

"Okay," Jason replied. "So, we go in a big group. How far away is this place?"

"Far enough. We set off back here early afternoon and we got back in the early hours of the morning."

"So, we can write off a day there and back."

"Actually, Eric recomm—"

"Who's Eric?"

"The guy who runs Infinity."

"What's Infinity?"

"Infinity's where the market it. It's the Infinity stadium in Crowesbury."

"Ahh," Jason replied as a big piece of the puzzle suddenly became clear.

"Anyway, he suggests you stay two nights. You spend the first day travelling. Stop overnight. Then spend the day there going around the stalls and trading. Spend another night then head back the next day. He said it's safer."

"Because of the Ferals?" Phil asked.

"Yeah."

"Well, if we go with big enough numbers, what does it matter whether it's day or night?"

"Because they're familiar with the territory and we're not. Because they can set up ambushes. Because nobody in their right mind would want to get into a fire fight in the dark."

"You make a fair point, I suppose."

"Thanks, Phil. That means so much to me."

"So, when should we head out?"

"I think this needs to be discussed. We need to talk to Nazya, we need to plan exactly what we're doing as far as trades go, and we need to put it to a vote," Callie said.

"But—"

"No buts, Phil."

"Why do I suddenly feel like I'm back at school?" Phil asked, and Jason laughed.

"You know I'm right," Callie said, turning to walk away.

"Where are you going?"

"I'm going to go find out how Harry's doing."

"So, I'm guessing that's the end of the discussion

then?"

"By all means, carry on," she said, continuing towards the hut. A smile crept onto Callie's face as she heard Phil begin to mutter behind her, but it didn't stay there long. As she got nearer to the makeshift infirmary, a chill ran through her and she began to flash back to the events leading up to Harry losing his leg.

She paused outside the door, bathing in the warmth escaping through the gap for a moment before finally entering. In the orange glow from the fire, Harry looked so peaceful. Callie couldn't swear to it, but she was sure a little more colour had returned to his face. He was fast asleep, as were Nazya and Chloe, who were propped up against one wall leaning into each other. Tania was the only one whose eyes remained open, and as Harper breathed heavily as she slumbered by her side, she gestured for Callie to sit with her.

Callie headed across, virtually tiptoeing. She settled down beside her friend and a whispered conversation began between them. "Nazya said that she'd given him a strong sedative that should help him sleep," Tania said.

"What's his prognosis?"

"She said that, under the circumstances, he'd been given good care."

"What does that mean? Does she think he's going to be okay?"

Tania's eyes drifted across to Harry as he continued to sleep and tears began to roll down her cheeks. "She thinks yes."

A loud sigh of relief left Callie's lips and a single tear ran down her face too. "So, it was all worth it then."

Tania reached out and took her hand. "It was all worth it, Callie. You did good."

Callie rested her head back against the stone wall. "I think I might just sit here a while."

"Why don't you close your eyes? If anybody deserves to rest, it's you."

A smile crept onto Callie's face and Tania felt the younger woman's hand go limp in her own. A few seconds later, Callie's head lolled to one side as sleep finally found her.

*

The tension in the air was palpable as Greenslade, Trunk, Drake and the others stepped off the lift to Level Three. There was no one in sight for the time being, but a steady hum could be heard somewhere as a thousand conversations continued at once. Marina suddenly came rushing up to them out of nowhere.

"My family. They're here?" Drake asked, concerned.

"All our families are here," Marina replied.

"We've already got people going through the hatch?"

"Ever since you gave the order. Now, come on, it'll be going dark soon enough. Let's make the most of the light while we've got it."

The group set off at a jog, further and further into the underground city. The longer they travelled the louder the hum of conversations became until the source of the noise became visible. A massive crowd blocked the street outside of apartment block seventy-one, and memories of the night Greenslade and Trunk had made their escape from Level Three came flooding back.

"DAD!" a shout came and two young boys and a girl emerged from the periphery of the mass gathering and ran towards Drake. A relieved-looking woman followed. When the children had dispensed their hugs, it was her turn. She held her husband firmly and kissed him on the cheek before pulling back.

"Talk about cutting it fine," she said, looking beyond him to the strangers.

It wasn't until this moment that Greenslade and Trunk relaxed a little. Even though they had seen the mass of faces from Level Three all desperately trying to escape, even though Drake's actions had appeared to be those of a man who matched his words, there was a part of both of them that wondered if it was all part of some giant double-cross. Seeing him with his family, though, allayed these fears.

"I'm going to have to be the last one to go through. You realise that don't you?" he said, guiding his wife away from the children.

"Then we'll stay with you."

"No, Darin!" The words came out more aggressively than he'd intended and his wife's eyes widened.

"There's something you're not telling me."

"There's nothing I'm not telling you. I just need to make sure that no one gets left behind. But I need you to take the kids and go. I'll just be a little while behind you, and when we're on the other side, I swear we'll be together as a family."

"You promise?"

"I promise."

She stared at him before finally gathering their three children and heading back to the crowd.

"Nice family," Trunk said.

"What the hell's that supposed to mean?" Drake snapped back.

"Err ... you've got a nice family. Just surprising,

'cause you come across as a right cock."

Drake fixed him with a stony stare for a moment before a smile finally broke on his face. "Thank you… I suppose."

"Don't mention it."

"So, I'm guessing we're stopping back with you?" Greenslade said.

"No, actually. Ideally, you'd have gone first, but I want you to go with Marina. This whole plan falls apart without you."

"Now you're just trying to make us feel special."

The hubbub continued behind as the desperate did their best to wait patiently for their time to come to taste freedom once more, but Drake made sure he had Trunk's and Greenslade's full attention. "If, for any reason, I don't get out of here, you need to make sure that these people get to safety, do you understand me?"

A confused look appeared on Greenslade's face. "Why the hell won't you get out of here?"

"Listen, we've planned this as well as we can. We've got contingencies and redundancies in place. But there's always that X factor that we can't account for. If it happens, it happens, but if my family's safe, it will have been worth it."

Greenslade stared at the other man for several seconds. Up until a few minutes ago, he had still been suspicious of him, but he could tell that Drake meant every word he said. "Okay." He looked across to Marina. "I suppose we'd better fight our way through this mob and get to the front then?"

More people were joining the massive crowd all the time. Everyone was carrying rucksacks, bags, bundles or all three. Not a scrap of available food would be left on Level Three by the time they left.

"Good luck," Marina said to Drake.

Drake nodded. "Good luck," he replied; then he turned to Greenslade and Trunk. "To all of you." He walked away, leaving the three of them standing there.

"Come on," Marina said, leading the two men towards the crowd. Even though they were all escaping together, even though, after today, they would technically be equals, people cleared a path for the woman in uniform. The trio had entered the accommodation block and just started down to the basement when a tremulous whirring sound began, making the air around them vibrate.

Frightened cries rose as the sound got louder, and when Marina turned to make sure Greenslade and Trunk were still following, there was a look of concern on her face.

"It's the power," Greenslade called out. "That's all. It's just the power going down." No sooner had he said the words than the lights started to flicker before going off completely. More cries and shouts went up, but within a few seconds, dozens of torches flicked on, making some of the panic subside.

Marina handed a spare flashlight she was carrying to Greenslade. "Come on," she said, beginning to barge her way through the crowd once more.

"It's just the power going down like it did before," Greenslade shouted. "It's all part of the plan. No reason to fret." His words began to flit through the horde of escapees, and gradually, the fearfulness began to subside a little more. *This is happening. I'm a part of this now.*

It was obvious he was a part of it. From the moment he had said yes to Drake back in the infirmary, he had been a part of it, but as he tried to give words of comfort to the others, it had finally struck him like a wrecking ball. It had not been that long ago that he had escaped this place with the sole intention of leaving everyone behind. But a lot had changed in those few weeks. He had changed.

It took them several minutes to battle their way down to the basement, but eventually, there was the hatch. In the short time it had been open hundreds had already descended into the mine. Greenslade and Trunk looked around at a few of the torchlit faces. Some were familiar, some not. Some were only too well aware of the men they thought they knew and they struggled to maintain eye contact for anything but the briefest moment before looking away once more.

It would be a long road ahead to win the trust of these people. *I caused a lot of them misery.*

Marina was the first to place her feet on the ladder and climb down into the darkness. The frightened cries were less profound down there. They had already flicked on torches and lanterns, knowing full well what to expect from their journey to the lift.

Greenslade and Trunk followed, and then the three of them kept a lively pace as they overtook numerous Level Three inhabitants where the tunnel allowed. "So, your family, where are they?" Greenslade asked.

"I'm hoping up ahead," Marina replied.

"It's going to be hard, y'know."

"What is?"

"All of it. We're not exactly living on easy street at the farm. We might be escaping the administration, but we could be signing our own death warrants."

"We're taking plenty of food with us."

Greenslade let out a thinly disguised laugh of contempt. "That'll give us another couple of weeks then."

"If you think this is such a bad idea, why did you go along with it?"

"We didn't exactly have a lot of choices open to us. And...." He shook his head, not wanting to continue.

"And what?"

"It's the right thing to do." An image of Callie in front of the Salmart shot into his mind. *Damn that girl.*

"Yeah, well. That's why we're all doing this too, remember." She glimpsed back, and at that moment, he could see the honesty in her eyes. It was true. They could carry on being Salvation guards and lead a good life. All of this was about doing the right thing, about not allowing their children to grow up to become the kind of people they'd hate.

"All I'm saying is that it's not going to be a cakewalk. Today could be a day you look back and rue."

"The only day I rue is the one where I put on this uniform." She slowed down a little and looked back once more. "We'll do what needs to be done."

"What do you mean?"

"I mean if we need to work twenty-four-seven from hereon in, we'll make this happen. There is nothing else. This is everything now." She turned back to her direction of travel and sped up a little more. Greenslade and Trunk cast each other brief glances, both of them thinking the same thing, both of them wondering if the part of the plan after escaping the mine had been reasoned at all.

*

Revell knew they were cutting it fine when they had got into the lift, but now, as PJ's panic began to spread to the other passengers, his mind started to think about the extra seconds he'd taken to tie up a few loose ends and wondered if they had been worth it.

"What the hell are we going to do? What the hell are we going to do?" PJ asked, his breathing already erratic.

Revell was the only Salvation guard among the motley assortment of power plant workers and tech heads who had remained in place until the last possible moment, and now all eyes were looking towards him.

"Okay. Calm down. We're just going to have to—"

"What? Going to have to what?"

"We'll lever the inner doors open and—"

"And what, genius? Everything's locked down. The outer doors won't open for another eight hours. They're specifically designed to stay shut in a situation like this to avoid possible radiation leakage. A problem at the plant is the one thing that causes the ventilation system to shut down too. We're going to suffocate in here."

Revell ignored the younger man and slid his fingers in between the rubber seals of the hefty inner doors before pulling with all his strength. At first, they didn't shift, but gradually they began to move a little for the hulking guard. All he had was the glow of half a dozen mobile phone torches to work by, but it was enough to see what he was doing. "Don't just stand there. Give me a hand."

The gap widened a little more and, one by one, the other occupants began to heave the sturdy doors open until there was a wide enough opening to comfortably fit a body through. "Dammit," one of the women said. "We were so close." All of them stood back and looked towards the bottom of the gap. The top of the external doors came up to knee height. "Just a couple more metres and we'd have made it."

If nothing else, cool air flooded the lift, suddenly making it feel a little less claustrophobic, but other than that, opening the inner doors did nothing to improve their situation.

"Oh great," PJ said. "Now we can see exactly how screwed we are. Great plan, Revell. Got any others up your sleeve?"

Revell took a deep breath. PJ was in his early twenties and irritated most people at the best of times. These were not the best of times. But in this instance, he was right. They were trapped. "Drake, this is Revell. Over." He looked at the radio in his hand and released the talk button, silently praying that the mastermind of this whole operation would have some clue as to how to get them out of there.

"Revell, this is Drake. Go ahead. Over."

PJ grabbed the handset from Revell and hit the talk button. "We're trapped. The power went off before we got down. We're damn well trapped in here and there's no way out. You happy? You happy now? I told you this wouldn't work. I told you."

Revell snatched the radio from PJ and pushed him into one corner of the large lift compartment before raising it to his lips and hitting the talk button. "Drake, we've opened the inner doors, but there's no way we're going to be able to get through the outer ones. Over."

"I'm on my way. Over."

"No," Revell replied. He looked around at the other passengers. The woman who had spoken was in her thirties like him. The others were all considerably younger and their faces seemed to be creased into expressions of perma-panic. "There's nothing you can do here. Over."

"There's got to be something. Is there any way PJ can override it? Over."

Revell turned to look at the computer geek. "What is it you idiots don't understand? There's no power. N-o p-o-w-e-r. Hacking into the panel isn't the problem. The problem is there's no p-o-w-e-r."

Revell brought the handset up to his mouth once more. "He says no. Over."

"Leave it with me. I'll come up with something. Over and out."

"Ooh. I feel so much better now. Our glorious leader is going to come up with something. In the meantime, we're going to—"

"Look, we're all scared," the older woman who had spoken before began, "but behaving like some panicky little bitch isn't going to help anyone."

PJ looked at her for a second and thought about saying something, but instead, he went to the far corner of the spacious lift and slumped down. A handful of others joined him, leaving just Revell and the woman standing by the doors. "Thanks, Addy. I'm not sure I could have put up with that much longer."

Muted conversations began at the far end of the compartment and Addy stepped a little closer to Revell. "Listen. As much as I don't want to admit it, he's got a point. We're going to be stuck in here until the power comes back on, and then aren't we going to need an engineer or something to get this thing going again?"

"In theory. From PJ's little outburst just now, I'm guessing that he's got a way to get around that once the power's restored."

"Hmm. I don't think that'll be much use to us then."

"No."

"So, what now?"

Revell looked at the handset once more. "Now we hope Drake really can figure something out."

*

Drake watched as the Level Three inhabitants continued to file into block seventy-one. *This is on me. If I hadn't screwed around with the timing, Revell and the others wouldn't be in this mess.* Then he caught sight of Darin as she guided their children through the entrance. The torches didn't cast much light, but she was the love of his life and he'd have been able to pick her out of any crowd. He kept his eyes on her until she was through the door and out of sight; then he bowed his head, privately acknowledging to himself what he'd have to do.

He brought the handset up to his mouth and hit the talk button. "Revell, this is Drake. Over."

"Drake, this is Revell. Go ahead. Over."

"The second the power comes back on, you get those lift doors open. I'll be waiting here for you. It won't take the administration long to figure out what's happened and it won't take them long to put a search party together and come looking. Over."

"You've lost me, Drake. Greenslade and his pal are the only ones who know where the settlement is. Over."

"Yeah, well, I'm obviously going to have to be a little more persuasive than I have been up until now. Over."

"You don't have to do this. We knew the risks when we signed up for this. Over."

"I'll see you in a few hours. Get plenty of rest. You're going to need it. Over and out."

Drake took a deep breath and clipped the radio onto

his belt. He scanned the torch and lantern-lit faces until his eyes fixed on Dwyer. He almost ran across to him, pushing others out of the way as he went. "I need you to stay back until everyone's gone."

Without even questioning, Dwyer nodded. "I'm guessing there's a problem."

"You could say that. Revell and half a dozen others are trapped in one of the lifts."

"Shiiit," Dwyer replied, immediately understanding the implications.

"I'm going to catch up with Greenslade and get him to tell me where the settlement is. Then I'm going to hang back and wait for Revell and the others. I'll need you and Marina to hold it all together for me up there," he said with a weak smile on his face.

"Whatever you need. You know that."

"Yeah. I do. Thank you, my friend." He gripped Dwyer firmly by the shoulder before turning and disappearing into the crowd.

3

A thin line of light on the horizon told Phil that they were on the cusp of dawn and a new day. He heard the sound of shuffling feet behind him and turned to see the familiar figures of Wei, Lanying and Jiang. They raised their hands before heading towards the stream.

Another figure emerged from the farmhouse and a smile started inside. *Debbie*. Ever since leaving Salvation, she had been the one constant for him. She'd been the one to make him feel better when it seemed like everything was becoming too much. He watched her silhouette continue towards him until she stretched out her hand, and he grabbed it gratefully.

"Maybe we should see if that doctor's got anything in her bag for insomnia. It's getting to be a bit of a thing with you, isn't it?"

"I'll sleep when I'm dead."

"You won't have long to wait if you carry on like this."

"I just can't switch off right now. There's too much to think about, too much to do."

Debbie squeezed his hand tighter and he pulled her around to face him. Even in what little light there was, she looked beautiful to Phil, and just feeling her hand in his made some of his worries and concerns ease.

She took a deep breath. "Phil, Phil, Phil. We need to talk."

"No good conversation ever starts like that."

"When I saw those people arriving yesterday, I knew this would happen. I knew your mind would go into overdrive. Listen, yes, there are a lot more mouths to feed, and there's a lot to think about, but you took control of the situation yesterday and everyone went to sleep with food in their bellies."

"Yes, but—"

Debbie put her finger up. "Wife's talking. You listen. Tania, Harper, and the group they went out with did a bang-up job foraging. They're splitting up today and taking some of the new arrivals with them. In no time at all, we're going to have dozens of people foraging every day, going further and further afield."

"Yes, but—"

Debbie put her finger up again. "In the meantime, our crops are in the ground. We're preparing other fields for growing; we're planning an irrigation system; we're building houses. We're doing everything we were doing the day before yesterday but just on a slightly bigger scale now."

"Ah, but—"

"And that Greta is an impressive girl. She was rallying

everyone yesterday; she'll be doing the same thing today. You're still in a Salvation mindset. You're still thinking people are working against you. Nobody is working against you, Phil." She paused as the sound of more early risers heading to the stream made them both look. "Y'see, it's not even sun up and people are starting their days wanting to get to work. And do you know why, Phil?"

"Because it smells like a builder's armpit on a hot day in there?"

"Funny. It's because of you. It's because they know that you can help them build a future for themselves and their families, and the reason they're getting up at this ungodly hour is that they know to make it work, they've got to play their part as well." She squeezed his hands again. "It isn't all down to you to get everything done. You can't let things get too much for you, not like before."

Phil let out a long sigh. He understood the *before* Debbie was talking about. It wasn't the before of Salvation and everything that went on there. It was the before during his research when he was putting plans forward to build a multistorey hydroponics farm. The world had seemed to be working against him then. Well, maybe not the world, but certainly the massive food and farming conglomerates and everyone in their pockets, which, for all intents and purposes, seemed to be the world. MPs, local councillors, law enforcement agencies—everybody came out of the woodwork to lodge objections and issue cease and desist orders, all of which he fought, but it took its toll.

He'd had a mental breakdown, and that had been the single scariest thing that had ever happened to him. That was the *before* that his wife was talking about, and as he stood there with her now, he knew he couldn't allow that to happen again. "You're right."

Even in the poor light, he could see her shrug. "Yeah, I know. And?"

Phil chuckled. "And I won't let it happen again."

"And?"

"And what?"

"How are you going to guarantee that?"

He nodded slowly. This was more than just some conversation to make him feel better. This was Debbie needing to feel better too. She realised that without Phil, it would all turn to crap quickly. "I ... I'm going to delegate. I'm not going to take on too much at once. I.... Err.... That's all I've got. Will that do for you?"

"Don't crack wise. I'm being serious. What else?"

Debbie had been the one to drag him back to health before, so she had every right to be asking the questions she was asking. "I'll get more rest."

"And?"

Phil breathed out heavily. "And what, Debs? I don't know what else."

"And you talk to me."

"We do talk. We are talking."

"Yeah, well, I just want to make sure that this line of communication stays wide open. If you're worried about anything or have doubts or get confused or feel like something's becoming overwhelming for you, you talk to me. There is always a solution. Always."

Phil nodded. "Okay. I promise."

"Good," she said, moving in and kissing him on the cheek before pulling back. "I'm going to the stream to wash, and then I may as well start work. All of us have got a lot of long days ahead. All of us, Phil." She turned and walked away.

In the few minutes they'd been talking, the band of light on the horizon had broadened a little and it wouldn't be long before the whole settlement was alive with bustling bodies once more. Phil watched his wife disappear then turned back to the fields. Everything she said was right. *I can handle this. I can do this.*

Suddenly, in his mind's eye, it wasn't dark anymore. And green fields stretched out in front of him as far as the eye could see. A raised pipeline weaved in and out of the rows of crops while dozens of people beavered away, picking fruit from bushes and harvesting vegetables. A smile lit Phil's face. *I can do this.*

*

The Level Two inhabitants still had their mobile phones, albeit with the SIM cards removed. The light cast by them allowed for a steady stream through the mine punctuated occasionally by total darkness or one of the much brighter lights afforded by the Salvation guard torches or the lucky few who had been entrusted with them from the stores. Drake's torch was powerful and it allowed him to move swiftly without the risk of the uneven surface taking him by surprise and tripping him.

He had caught up to his family in no time at all and walking alongside them for just a moment gave him the boost he needed. His heart ached a little as he left them behind and started to run through the tunnel once more. Some let out fearful cries as he seemingly emerged from nowhere, sliding through gaps here, apologetically barging others out of the way there. It took him nearly ten minutes to catch up with Greenslade, Trunk and Marina.

"I thought you were bringing up the rear," Marina

said, looking puzzled as the group had no choice but to continue moving along like twigs in a stream.

Drake had kept himself in pretty good shape. He'd taken full advantage of the gym facilities available for the Salvation guards, but even he'd managed to get a little out of breath in his quest to catch up. It took him just a few seconds to regulate his breathing before he sidled up to Greenslade. "There's been a change of plan."

"Let me guess. You've made nice with Bucks, and me and Trunk are under arrest again."

"Ha." Despite the situation, Drake couldn't help but laugh. "That's actually pretty good. Look, you're not going to like this. I certainly don't like it, but I need your help."

"What, my help beyond leading you and all your friends who helped subjugate us these past four years to safety?"

"Like I said, you're not going to like this."

"Go on."

"I need you to tell me where we're going. I need to know where the settlement is."

"That's funny. I'm guessing you did stand-up before you put on a uniform."

"I wouldn't ask if it wasn't important."

"I'm sure," Greenslade replied, not even turning to look at him.

"I know this wasn't the deal, but—"

"You're damn right this wasn't the deal. Listen, Drake, I really don't care what you think of me. I don't care what you think my intentions are or who you believe I am. There's a part of me that wants to trust you. There's a part of me that's hoping deep inside that I'm not being taken for a mug. And there's another part of me, the part that's talking to you right now, that's thinking this might all be some elaborate set-up to an end game I don't have the foresight to comprehend. Mine and Trunk's families are at our settlement. Other people we care about are at that settlement. What makes you think for a second that I'm going to gift wrap them for you?"

"I don't believe you," Drake said as the four of them continued. It was clear that the escapees in earshot were all intrigued by the conversation as surreptitious glimpses from those in front were becoming more frequent. "You think all of this is some kind of put-up job? You think I'd risk my own family?"

"Like I said, there's a part of me that wants to believe you."

"I'm honoured. A part of the great Blake Greenslade, the nearest thing Salvation had to a Mafioso, wants to believe me."

Greenslade stopped dead, causing the long procession to come to a halt too. "You've really got some nerve. You worked as Bucks' attack dogs and you accuse me of that? The administration is nothing but a bunch of two-bit gangsters with an army of jackbooted thugs laying down the law for them. You want to talk about mafiosos; you just remember who you've been working for these past four years."

The two men glared at each other in the periphery of the torchlight. Each was close enough to feel the other's warm breath on their skin. "Be very careful what you say next."

Greenslade edged a little closer still.

"Are you two going to hit each other or make out?" Marina asked, placing her hand on each of their chests and pushing them back. "Look, Greenslade has a point," she said, looking at her friend. "If I was in his position, I'd find it more than a little hard to trust us too." Some of the fight left Drake's face as the voice of reason prevailed. "Why do we need to know where we're going, Drake? That wasn't part of the deal."

Drake turned to look at her, a little surprised that she seemed to be taking the other man's side. "Revell, PJ and the ones from the plant have got trapped in the lift."

Marina clenched her eyes shut tight. "Shit."

"What does that have to do with anything?" Greenslade asked.

Drake was about to reply, but Marina beat him to it. "It means they're stuck in there until the power comes back on."

The old Greenslade would have said so what, or what's that got to do with me. He ended up saying, "Is there no manual override? Can't the panel be hacked or something?" A brief smile flashed on Drake's face and the other man immediately believed he was being mocked. "Screw you."

Drake put his hands up, shaking his head. "You misunderstand. Those were virtually the same questions I asked. They've got the inner doors open, but, as a failsafe, the outer ones are designed to stay closed for a full eight hours in the event of any kind of problem at the plant. But hopefully, when the power is back on, which fingers crossed will be long before the eight hours is up, PJ will be able to work a hack that can get them open before the guards make it down to Level Three. At least that's what he reckons."

"So, how long until the power's back online?"

"Hard to say. It depends on how quickly they bring

everything under control at the plant. Our people didn't intend it to be something that could get out of hand, but I suppose you never know. Anyway, long story short, they're stuck in that lift and the chances are good that, with the disappearance of those elite guards, there are plenty of people thinking that this is all more than coincidence."

"So, how does this have anything to do with us telling you where our settlement is?"

"I need to stay here with them. I need to be here when they get out of that lift, and then we're going to get out as fast as we can and make our way to you."

Greenslade's brow creased. "That's insane. You could be captured."

"It's possible. But if Revell and the others have no escape, then they're as good as dead."

"You'd risk leaving your children fatherless?"

"Given a choice, I'd prefer not to. But I'd rather they had no father than one who was willing to give up on the people who helped to save everyone."

Greenslade looked across at Trunk, then back to Drake. "Do you have pen and paper?"

"Err ... why the hell would I have pen and paper?"

"How do you expect me to draw you a map?"

"Jesus," Drake said, looking around. "Does anyone have a pencil and paper?" he shouted.

Mutters travelled up and down the tunnel like a breeze until someone shouted. "Here, I do." A woman appeared, plucking a small notebook from her backpack. She handed it to Greenslade and he flicked through, seeing it was full of poems and short pieces of prose. He stopped when he found a blank page, took the pencil and started drawing the map.

"Does this mean you trust me now?"

"Like I said before, if you pull any kind of double-cross, mine will be the last face you see, Drake. But if all of this is on the level, then I hope you get the chance to say, 'I told you so.'"

"Don't go getting mushy on me now, Greenslade."

"What are you going to tell Darin?" Marina asked.

Drake scratched his stubbled chin. "That I'll be right behind her."

"Good luck with that."

"Yeah. I think I'm going to need it."

*

Callie woke with a start. It took her a moment to figure out where she was, but gradually, she managed to piece together the sequence of events. She clenched her eyes tight one, two, three times then leant forward a little. She had dosed off sitting upright against a stone wall. Her back ached a little, and her shoulder blades felt like someone had driven knives through them, but the rest had been much needed.

The sounds of the early morning drifted in from outside as people wearily began to prepare themselves for the day ahead. Tania and Harper were still fast asleep, leaning into each other like two toddlers. Chloe was snoring on the ground, her head propped up by her jacket. Nazya was standing by the side of Harry's bed. "Morning," she whispered, looking across to Callie as she saw her move.

Callie smiled, climbed to her feet and walked over to where she was standing. "Morning," she whispered back. "How is he?"

"He is doing well. He is a fighter. His temperature is down and his colour is much better. He is by no means out of the woods, and he will require a lot of care for some time to come, but things are looking promising."

"Thank you. Thank you so much."

"I did little. He'd been given good care before I got here."

"He'd been given limited care."

Nazya smiled and nodded. "Having the right medication counts for a lot."

"You realise, whenever you want to head back to Infinity, we'll take you. We're not expecting you guys to head out by yourselves."

"This is good to know. I am not really cut out for life on the road."

"Oh, I don't know. You seemed to me to do pretty well when we were facing down those Ferals."

"I think my skills are better deployed in medicine."

"I get that." Callie turned towards the door. "Sounds like people are waking up. I'll be sure to get you and Chloe something to eat when they start making it."

"Thank you, Callie. I would like to have a look around later if that is alright. What you told me about the place yesterday sounded fascinating."

"It would be my pleasure to give you a guided tour. In the meantime, how about some coffee?"

"You have coffee here?"

"Don't get too excited. It's made from dandelions, but it's pretty good."

Nazya smiled. "I would love some."

"Okay, then," Callie said, turning to head out. The cool morning air worked better than a hundred coffees. She took in a deep breath and just stood for a moment as she watched various figures emerge from the house and the barn. There was enough light for people to see what they were doing, and not one begrudged getting up so early.

Even the newcomers, who had initially been made to feel like outsiders by a certain few on their arrival, now wanted not just to prove themselves but to work to build a future, a future that was their own.

Callie turned to her left to see Jason already hard at work piecing together the wall of another house, stone by stone. To her right, men, women and children were heading to the stream. Others were just returning. Several people were already in the farmyard starting the fires for breakfast.

Jason and his crew had erected several large barbecue pits and a couple of crude ovens. The ovens had been to Phil's design and were ugly to look at, but they worked. Once a week, since escaping Salvation, they had baked bread, but flour was in short supply now and in all likelihood the ovens would be used for little more than drying seaweed from hereon in until they were able to start manufacturing their own flour.

Breakfast would be the same as dinner and supper, a soupy vegetable stew padded out with seaweed with a side of dandelion leaves. It tasted marginally better than it sounded. They still had a supply of dried herbs, spices, and other flavourings from the stock taken from the Salmarts, and that definitely helped, but it was hardly haute cuisine. It was, however, nutritious, and that's what mattered.

"I've just been speaking to your mum about what happened to you. I'm glad you all made it back safe."

"Thanks. Yeah, that was some trip."

"How's Harry?" Nicola asked. These three words roused the interest of everyone in earshot, and whether they were breaking up already blackened wood for the fires or fanning flames, they stopped what they were doing and listened with interest.

"Nazya thinks he's going to make it."

"Who's Nazya?"

It suddenly dawned on Callie that most of the settlement had not been privy to the arrival of their guests. "It's a long story, but she's a doctor. Harry's been given a transfusion and antibiotics and things are looking good."

Everyone seemed to let out relieved breaths at the same time. "Oh, thank God."

"I said I'd take Nazya some coffee."

"I think that's the least she deserves, don't you?" Nicola's eyes drifted from Callie towards the small building that was originally destined to be the first family home but was now essentially an infirmary. "There are two people who are going to be relieved."

Callie turned to see Michelle and Ollie heading through the door hand in hand. "Yeah. I dare say."

"Look, it's going to be a few minutes until we get everything going here. How about I give you a shout when we're all brewed up?"

"Sounds good. Is Dani about?"

"I left her sleeping. She was wiped out after yesterday, but look who I'm talking to. Why don't you go give her an alarm call?"

"I might just do that." Callie smiled and walked across to the barn. She made her way down the narrow corridor to the tiny cubicle that was Dani and Nicola's accommodation. It was noticeably darker in there, but the odd dynamo torch or lantern had been turned on, giving enough of a subdued glow for her to find her way. She pulled open the sheet that acted as the front to their apartment and slipped inside, lying down on the makeshift bed. She could see her friend's eyes were already open, but Dani did not move for a moment.

"I was having this beautiful dream. I was dead and I never had to get up in the middle of the night again," she whispered, conscious of the fact there would still be the odd person trying to sleep.

"Don't even think about dying without taking me with you, you selfish bitch," Callie replied in an equally hushed tone. "I thought you'd still be asleep."

Dani let out a giggle. "Fat chance. My mum couldn't get out of bed quietly if her life depended on it. She even makes noise putting her socks on."

"I'd say you could come and sleep with us, but Si snores and Mum mumbles in her sleep."

"I'm going to be nice to Jason and see if he'll build me a place of my own."

Callie giggled now. "I can really see that happening. We've got entire families living outside with nothing above their heads but a bit of cotton and you're going to get Jason to build you a place because your mum makes noise putting her socks on."

"It's for my mental well-being."

"Uh-huh."

Dani remained there a moment before finally edging up onto her elbow. She leaned forward and kissed her friend before embracing her tightly. "There was a part of me that was scared I wasn't going to see you again."

Callie reciprocated the hug and the pair remained like that for several seconds before pulling back. "Ditto. I've got so much to tell you."

"You found the place with the lights?"

"Oh yeah."

"Did you get antibiotics for Harry?"

"And a doctor."

"What, seriously?"

"You won't believe what we found, Dani."

Dani wiped her eyes and leaned up a little further. "What?"

"A market."

The wonder left Dani's eyes and she leaned back to look for a smile on her friend's face. "A market?"

"Yeah. Like nothing you've ever seen before. There were hundreds of people there from all over the place. They all brought stuff to trade. There were plants and seeds and building materials and food, and they have a stage, and people get up and tell their stories and sing and—"

"Okay. Calm down or you're going to stroke out on me. Tell me slower. What is this place?"

"It's called Infinity and it was set up by this guy and his family, and his daughter, Chloe, is Nazya's bestie and they—"

"Okay. Time out. Who's Nazya?"

Callie took a breath. "I can't get my words out quickly enough. There's too much to tell you. Nazya is the doctor. Chloe came back with her to give Harry blood. They're really good people. Finding Infinity is going to be a game changer for us."

"A game changer, how?"

"For a start, we're not alone anymore. None of those people are alone. They share knowledge, and Phil says he wants to build an irrigation system, and from what I saw, they'd definitely have the materials to help."

"Where did all these people come from?"

"Old underground shelters. Eric, Chloe's dad, was telling me that there were hundreds of them dotted all over the country. There's like this network of survivors who've never even had anything to do with the administration."

"Do you think me and Zep will be allowed to go the next time you head there?"

Callie chuckled. "I'm pretty certain you can do what you want from now on. It was really brave what you did yesterday, Dani, bringing all those people back here. All sorts could have happened to you on the road, but you did it."

"I think we had the easier deal. You had the tough part."

"Well, whoever had the tough part, I'm pretty certain nobody would throw up any objections if you're in the next party to go to Infinity."

"When do you think we can go?"

"That's up to Nazya. When she feels happy that Harry can be left, I'm pretty certain she'll want to head back."

Dani reached out again and took her friend's hand. "I'm so glad you're safe."

"You said."

"I was really worried about you."

"It's over now." Callie's mind flashed back to the ambush in the forest. "It wasn't the easiest of trips, but at least we're together again."

"Yeah." Dani sniffed. "I don't suppose there's any coffee on the go yet, is there?" Callie laughed. "What?"

"It's just that in the bunker, if people offered us coffee made from dandelions, we'd have told them where to go. Now we're addicted to it."

"You make the most of what you've got, don't you?"

"I suppose so." Dani peeled back the sheet to reveal she was still fully dressed. "You slept in your clothes?"

"I was too tired. I just crashed."

Callie looked down and realised she had done the same. "I get that."

"Come on then," Dani said, climbing to her feet and offering her friend a hand up. "Let's see what shitastrophe awaits us today."

Callie giggled again, and she took her friend's hand and stood. "Trust me. I think things are going to get an awful lot better from hereon in."

4

Surprised murmurs and questioning looks greeted Drake as he made his way back through the tunnel to the hatch. He held on to the map in his hand like his life depended on it, which, of course, it did.

"Hold on," he shouted as he finally reached the bottom rung of the small ladder. "I'm coming up."

He could see the lights shuffling above as people made way for him. He climbed up and disappeared into the throng of bodies. Eventually, he pushed his way through, up the steps, out of the basement and back onto the street. Dwyer was more or less where he had left him. There was still a mass of people gradually filtering into block seventy-one, but from what he could see, there were no more joining them.

"Let's hope nobody's been left behind," Dwyer said, seemingly reading Drake's thoughts.

"We can only do what we can do."

"You got him to draw you a map then?"

Drake brought the paper up into the other man's torch beam. "Yeah."

"I've been thinking."

"Go on."

"It should be me who stops back."

Drake laughed and shook his head. "I wouldn't put this on anyone. I brought the timetable forward. It's my fault they're trapped in there. It's my responsibility to get them to safety."

"I understand, but—"

"There are no buts. That's the end of the story."

"Listen to me. My family's gone." His words cut through the noise from the crowd and hung in the air for a moment. Drake remembered that day like it was yesterday. Ursula, their daughter, had died from a rare heart defect, and that same day, unable to go on, Mags, his wife, had taken her own life. How Dwyer had continued at all was a miracle to Drake, but here he was still trying to do the right thing. "You have a family, but more important than that, everybody's looking to you."

"Everybody's looking to Greenslade."

"You know as well as I do that he can't be trusted. You need to lead people. You need to be with your family. I can stay here. There's too much at stake for you to be the one who stops behind."

"This is too dangerous. There's no way I could ask someone else to do this."

"You didn't ask. I volunteered." Dwyer reached across and grabbed the radio from Drake's belt. "I'm doing this."

Drake let out a defeated breath. He knew everything Dwyer said made sense. He unfolded the piece of paper and handed it to the other man. Dwyer looked at it for the best part of a minute, memorising every line, every contour, every note. "Looks pretty straightforward," he said before handing it back.

"Don't you want to keep it?"

Dwyer smiled. "If we get captured, the last thing I want on me is a map, isn't it?"

Drake folded the piece of paper and put it back in his pocket. "Thank you for this."

"Good luck, Vad."

The two men shook hands. "And you."

With that, Dwyer turned to leave. Drake lingered for a moment as he watched his friend disappear into the darkness, then finally turned and fought his way back through the crowd.

*

Before dawn had fully broken, virtually everyone in the settlement was up and about. The smell of cooking food filled the air and a line had formed as people waited to be served their breakfast. The news about the doctor and Infinity spread quickly, and for all the trauma and hardships of the previous days, there was a renewed hope in the air.

The newcomers, children and all, quickly learned the routine of the others. Many of them had escaped the Salvation guards' attack with little more than the clothes on their backs. Penny and Greta had organised a feeding rota, as there weren't enough food bowls to go round. The children would eat first—that had been the way ever since their escape. The adults would eat later.

John, Jason, Phil, Susan and Debbie all stood

together by the small hut where Harry still lay. The news from inside was promising and the doctor seemed to have every confidence that Harry would be okay.

"They seem to be fitting in pretty well, considering," Susan said as she watched Penny and Greta marshalling the children.

"I spent time with Greta yesterday. She's an impressive young woman," Debbie replied.

"Callie having a lie in?" John asked.

"Ha. You don't know my daughter. No, she and Dani went foraging."

"Already?"

"Callie's someone who believes in leading by example."

"It certainly seems that way."

"So," John said, turning to look at Phil and Jason, "I suppose we've got some organising to do, haven't we?"

"What you mean in order to feed and house another hundred or so people whom we didn't have to feed and house yesterday?" Phil asked.

"Exactly."

"I say we should just ask them politely to move on."

"Assuming that doesn't work, do we have a fallback plan?"

"Why are you looking at me?"

"Look, I wasn't really in the right head space to think about all of this yesterday. All joking aside, I'm asking you now, where do we go from here?"

Phil let out a long breath. He looked across to Jason and then towards the sun as it continued to slowly reveal itself on the horizon. He was not someone who liked the limelight, but he also knew how much everyone depended on his knowledge to move forward from here. "Things worked out pretty well yesterday."

"Can you stop with the sarcasm for one minute and just—"

"I'm not being sarcastic, John. All things considered, things turned out well. Greta got people working, even the kids. The foraging teams came back with more than I anticipated, and I'm aiming to get even more teams out today. Before yesterday, we'd got to a stage where we were barely touching the reserves we'd brought from Salvation. We need to get to that stage again. Seeing how hard people worked yesterday, I'm fairly confident we can do that within a few days."

"That sounded positively upbeat for you."

Phil smiled. "Well, what can I tell you? My faith in mankind has been reborn."

"Somehow, I doubt that. So, that's the short term. What's the long term?"

"The long term is what we were talking about yesterday."

"The irrigation system?"

"Wait. What?" Susan asked.

"I forgot you weren't here yesterday. Phil's had a plan to build an irrigation system."

"Isn't that really complicated?"

"No, actually," Phil replied. "The concept's very simple. Getting all the materials is the complicated part."

"And do you really think we need one?"

"If you and your daughter could have stopped bringing strays home, we might have been able to manage without one for a while longer, but now I'd say it's essential."

"Somehow, I thought this would be my fault."

"Every time you two leave this place, you come back with more people. I think we should chain you to one of the big rocks."

Susan smiled. "Sounds fair."

"And housing?" John said, turning to Jason.

Jason pointed to the mountain of stones. "Virtually everyone who arrived yesterday chipped in in some way. It's going to take time, but we'll get there. The biggest pain in the arse is that for so many more new houses, we'll have to travel further to get the stones. I really think a visit to this Infinity place sooner rather than later will help all of us."

"How so?"

"Well, getting a barrow or trolley or just some means to cart the stones would mean one person could suddenly do what ten or twelve are doing." John let out a huff of a laugh. "What's so funny?"

"We had self-driving cars, built machines that could make atoms crash into each other at virtually the speed of light, and now we'd give our right hand to have just a barrow or trolley."

"Yeah, well, from what I heard, this Infinity place might have them."

"They do have them," Susan said. "I saw them. They've got a lot more besides."

"That's what I mean," Jason said, taking over once more. "The sooner we visit this place the better."

"I agree completely," Phil replied.

"Okay. When Nazya and Chloe are ready to go back, we'll send a delegation. In the meantime, let's do what we can with what we've got. Fair enough?"

They all nodded. "Fair enough," Jason replied.

*

"I suppose this is what you call facing your demons," Dani said as she and Callie stood on the sand looking out to the water.

"I think that's a pretty accurate analysis."

"I still can't believe it. I can't believe that happened here. I can't believe that those things are still out there somewhere, waiting … lurking."

"Sharks are pretty territorial, but they'll only stay in a place if there's a food supply."

"I'm not going to test that theory out, if you don't mind."

"Yeah, me neither."

The tide was low and dozens of small rock pools lined the cove. During their journey to the beach, the sun had risen properly, and now there was enough light for the pair to see exactly what they were doing. "I suppose we'd better get started then."

"Yeah."

They turned to their right and walked parallel to the sea then followed the cove wall until they arrived at a large pool with plenty of unharvested seaweed. They took off their shoes and socks and rolled their jeans up over their knees before wading in. The black rocks in the centre of the pool were invisible as large crops of sea lettuce covered them.

Callie grabbed her knife and bent over, grasping a handful of the bright green seaweed in her hand before carefully cutting it. She made sure there were at least three or four centimetres of the plant left, and as she brought it out, she gave it a good shake, getting rid of the excess water. It would grow again quickly, and in a couple of weeks, the plants would be ready for harvesting again.

Dani had worked in virtual synchronicity with her friend, and they both straightened up at the same time. Callie swivelled first and Dani placed the handful of seaweed she had collected in Callie's rucksack. Then Dani turned and Callie did the same. Without missing a beat, they bent over once more and grabbed another handful each.

"There's something therapeutic about this," Callie said.

"I know what you mean," Dani replied, straightening up again to place more seaweed in Callie's rucksack before she did the same in hers. They worked in this way for twenty minutes until both backpacks were full to the brim. When they were done, they carefully folded their knives, waded back out of the large, almost circular pool and sat down on a wide rock where they let their feet and lower legs drip dry.

After a couple of minutes, Callie began to put her socks on. "There's going be so much work to do now. I suppose we'd better start heading back."

"There was plenty to do before yesterday."

"True."

"You should have seen the look on Phil's face. I thought he was going to have a breakdown or something."

"There's a lot of weight on his shoulders. Everybody's depending on him."

"I suppose."

"Suppose nothing. All of a sudden, there were nearly a hundred extra mouths to feed. He'd only just figured out how to feed the few of us that there were, but now there's a lot of added pressure on him. We'll have to do a lot more foraging. We'll have to start moving further afield."

"That's what Tania and Harper did yesterday."

Callie nodded. "I'm sure Phil will figure it all out eventually, but life's going to be tough for the foreseeable future."

"I forgot; it was a total breeze before."

Callie laughed. "For everything that's facing us, for all the hardship, I'd still rather be here than stuck in Salvation."

"Yeah. Me too." They finished putting their shoes on and were both about to turn and leave when Callie suddenly stopped. Her eyes fixed on the edge of the shore. "What's that?" she asked, squinting.

Dani followed her gaze and both friends stared for a moment before finally starting to walk towards it. "It's a net," Callie said as they finally reached it. "And it's in pretty good condition, all things considered. Give me a hand."

"What for? What are we going to do with a fishing net?"

"Everything's a resource now, Dani. We could repair this. We could unpick it and use it as twine. I'm pretty certain Jason or one of the others could easily find a use for it."

Dani curled her nose up. "But it stinks." It was knotted in places and old seaweed had wrapped around it.

"Trust me. It will be worth it." Callie crouched down and dragged the net further away from the water before beginning to unhook the seaweed and other detritus that had attached itself.

"Would it be too much for me to have had a normal friend? Y'know, someone who wanted to talk about boys and clothes and things like that?"

"Says the girl who dragged me to an illegal meeting to plot a revolution."

"Firstly, I didn't know what it was. Secondly, it was hardly a revolution. And thirdly, you were the one who wanted to go back."

"Yeah, but you planted the seed, didn't you?"

"So, it's my fault you're this way."

"Exactly. Your actions led us to this moment, here, right now, which is why you're going to help me get the excess seaweed and stuff untangled from this, and then we're going to take it back to camp. You should know by now that virtually everything is your fault."

"Thanks." Dani stood back for a moment. "Err … why are you wanting to get rid of the seaweed?"

"It's half rotted. It'll make people ill if they try to eat this."

"Yeah, but won't it be good for the compost pile?"

Callie immediately stopped what she was doing. "Y'see, that's why I like keeping you around. Occasionally, you come up with a really good idea. Come on then."

Dani grimaced as she grabbed one corner then a second. Callie did the same, and as they picked the weighty, smelly net up, a small mountain of sand slipped through the holes. "This smells awful."

"Trust me. It'll be worth it."

"If this makes my clothes stink, I'm not going to be happy."

"Whine, whine, whine."

"It's alright for you. I've got a boyfriend. He's not going to be impressed when I stink like tuna that's been left out in the sun."

"I'll buy you some lavender water when we next go to Infinity. Now, come on, people will be wondering where we've got to."

THE BURNING TREE: BOOK 4 - ANARCHY

*

Zeke and Rocky were just fifteen and sixteen when they disappeared into the blackness of the London Underground. It had felt like an adventure at first. Their families had taken tents and camping equipment, as had thousands of others. While they were waiting for the strike, a steely resolve had gripped the massive community.

At school, they had read about World War Two and learned of the Spirit of the Blitz. The British people had been stoic despite the onslaught from the German bombers, and although they were not facing a living, breathing enemy now, a similar resolve exuded.

It didn't last long. First came the flood waters washing thousands upon thousands of men, women and children away. Then came the realisation that stoicism alone was not the key to survival. Their families had joined together with Danko and the others early on. They had become strong. They had done the things most others wouldn't or couldn't. They had survived however they could, becoming a little less human day by day. They lived in filth and many succumbed to illness and disease. The ones who survived faced other foes. Rival armies of survivors and ... rats.

They were the most fearsome enemy down there in the darkness. Sometimes they moved like living waves running over each other, jostling for position as they attacked and fought the survivors. It was Danko who taught the others to fight back, and the filthy, foul-smelling, black furry predators became prey.

The flood waters had dragged all sorts into the tunnels, fishing nets among them. Nets they had layered together to trap the filthy vermin. Nets like the one the two girls now carried from the beach.

Zeke and Rocky had followed them as they had broken away from the camp before dawn, curious as to where they were going, what they were doing. They had watched them cut and gather seaweed, and all that time, neither uttered a word.

The chatty ones in the underground were the first to be hunted, the first to die. Like the rest of the survivors, they had learned that economy with the spoken word gave them a better chance of survival, and almost as an evolutionary adaptation, this had continued when they had finally escaped the darkness.

"We should follow them," Zeke said in little more than a whisper.

They had remained in the charcoal forest, using the blackened trees to disguise their equally black camouflaged frames. In the tunnels, dirt and soot had painted their clothes and skin. Out here, they had done it deliberately to go undetected in the charred landscape.

The pair fell back further into the woodland, careful not to move too quickly, always keeping their eyes on the girls as they made their way off the beach.

*

"This weighs a tonne," Dani said.

"Trust me; it's going to be worth it."

"I'm not convinced."

"I mean there are sharks in the sea. Who knows what else we might find? There are probably other fish that survived. Can you imagine what a difference this could make to us?"

"You said it yourself. There are sharks, Cal. How are we possibly going to fish or anything without getting our legs bitten off?"

"I don't mean now; I mean down the line. I mean, y'know, we could build a boat or something."

"Oh my God. You're insane," Dani said, laughing. "You're totally insane."

"We're starting from scratch again, Dan. Eventually, the houses will be built, the fields will be sown, the crops will be picked, and then we have to think about what's next."

They entered the blackened woodland and both of them hoisted the net onto their shoulders a little further. "Well, nobody can ever accuse you of not thinking ahead. I just can't wait to see the look on Jason's face when you tell him you want him to build you a boat." Dani laughed again.

"Who's to say I'll ask anybody?" Callie replied.

"What are you talking about?"

"I'm saying what would stop us from doing it?"

"Err … how about know-how, tools, skill, time—"

"We could learn."

"Learn how exactly?"

"Learn the way anybody learnt stuff originally. Trying and failing until they get it right."

"You're not joking, are you?"

"No. We could get Zep, Jiang and Matt to help us."

"Okay, and how exactly do we make it shark-proof? How do we stop those things from smashing it to pieces and chowing down on us? 'Cause that whole trying and failing until we get it right thing doesn't really work in that instance."

It was Callie's turn to laugh now. "I'm sure we could figure it all out. I'm not saying we're going to build a boat, and bam, like that, it will be done. I'm saying let's think about how we could build a boat right. There's no rush to do this thing, but it's something we should seriously talk about doing."

"You make my head hurt sometimes." They carried on walking for a while. "You're right, though, I suppose."

"About the boat?"

"About all of it. There's nothing to say we can't learn to do stuff, whatever it is. I suppose it makes sense for us all to learn as much as we can."

"Exactly. The wider the database of knowledge in the community the better."

"I suppose. It's just a lot to take in sometimes. We really are starting again, aren't we? I mean it's like—" Dani broke off and stopped walking at the same time.

It wasn't until Callie felt the net tug a little that she realised and turned to look at her friend. "What's wrong?"

For a moment, Dani didn't speak. "I … I saw something."

Callie followed her best friend's gaze. "What? Saw what?"

"I don't know. Movement."

"Like an animal?"

"No. I don't think so. It was—there," she said, dropping the net and pointing.

Callie saw it too, just for a split second—something grey disappearing behind a blackened trunk. Suddenly, the air around them felt ten degrees cooler. "It's probably Jiang or Matt or someone playing a joke."

"I really don't think so, Cal."

In truth, neither did Callie, but the thought of it being someone else, someone not from the settlement, was too chilling to contemplate. "What should we do?"

"You're the one with all the ideas. You tell me."
"Right now, I'm drawing a blank."
"Great."

*

"We'll grab them," Rocky whispered.
"Danko said watch," Zeke replied.
"We'll learn more this way." He pulled two short lengths of rope from his bag. They had captured countless people in the past. Sometimes they had interrogated them as they had left or were approaching Infinity. More often than not, they had hogtied them and taken them back to camp to feast on.

Rocky scratched his chin through the thick, mottled whiskers that sprouted from it. He looked at the spears he and his friend held. "They've got knives," he said, referring to the tools the young women had harvested the seaweed with.

"Spears are better."

Rocky nodded. "Okay." Without any further communication, they broke cover, breaking into a uniform sprint. They almost flew across the ground like birds of prey zoning in for a kill.

*

For a few seconds, Callie and Dani just stood there, barely able to believe what they were seeing or what was happening. Finally, their survival instincts kicked in and they dropped the net. They both turned left at the same time and began to run as fast as their legs could carry them.

Dani turned to see both figures changing course. "They're too fast. They're going to get us."

Callie glanced over her shoulder. *Shit. She's right.* "Back to the beach," she said, veering left.

"We've got nowhere to run on the beach."

"Whichever way we go, we're not going to outrun them."

It was true. The two Ferals seemed to move with unnatural speed and prowess. Dani followed her friend, and within a few seconds, they broke from the tree line. They continued across the sand back towards the rock pools to the right, instinctively slipping off the rucksacks in the hope that discarding the weight would make all the difference.

"What are we doing?" Dani asked, drawing level with her friend.

"We've only got one option. We're going to have to fight."

Dani peeked over her shoulder once more to see the two figures had gained even more ground. "They've got spears, Cal. We won't stand a chance." Callie ignored her, reaching into her pocket for her knife. Seeing what her friend was doing, Dani did the same. "My mistake. I feel much safer now."

Callie carried on, running straight into one of the rock pools. It was deeper than some of the others and the water immediately made both of them slow down. They continued across as the level reached up over their knees. "Here," Callie said. Despite the sand being stirred up, Dani could see several larger pebbles resting on the pool's bed. Callie reached down, scooping up one the size and shape of a large squashed orange.

Dani did the same. "This is your idea, throw stones at them?"

"I didn't really have a lot of time to think."

*

There was something about the hunt that Zeke and

Rocky always found exhilarating. They fed off each other's youthful enthusiasm as they approached the two girls. They'd been in situations like this a hundred times before. Unsuspecting victims backed into a corner, grabbing whatever they could in a vain, last-ditch attempt to try to arm themselves.

The two young men slowed a little as they entered the water, raising their spears towards the girls at the same time. "You come with us," Rocky said as he and Zeke finally came to a stop.

*

"You sure about this?" Dani asked under her breath.

"NOW!" Dani's question was answered in that one shout. They launched their pebbles at the same time, both targeting the smaller of the two figures. One of the missiles flew over his shoulder while the other collided with his nose, mouth and chin simultaneously. There was a small explosion of blood and he staggered back, bringing his left hand up to his lips instinctively. He stared down at his crimson fingers, completely taken aback. Before he could raise his head to look at the two girls once more, another stone smashed into his chest while a fourth crashed against his brow, this time making him stumble back and fall.

*

The attack had even taken Rocky by surprise. *Smart*, he thought to himself as he began to trudge towards the girls once more. In a situation like this, what usually happened, if anything happened at all, was their victims tried to fight everybody at once, but these two had targeted the smaller and weaker of the attackers.

"YAAARRRGGGHH!"

*

The sound that came out of the second Feral's mouth wasn't like anything Callie or Dani had heard before. It was loud and high-pitched at the same time, banshee-like almost. It sent a shiver through both of them as they threw two more pebbles, this time at the taller figure.

"Move away. Keep throwing," Callie said under her breath as she began to wade to her left. One of the missiles hit him square in the shoulder and another bounced off his belly. The pause they caused was almost negligible as they each picked up another pebble.

The Feral continued towards Callie. *Jesus. He barely looks human.* Another involuntary shudder ran through her as she locked eyes with ... him, it, whatever it was.

*

Rocky could hear Zeke splashing around in the water behind him somewhere as he continued towards the girl who almost seemed to be goading him. She held a large pebble in one hand and a knife in the other. He ducked as he caught movement out of the corner of his eye.

Another missile sailed over his head and a sinister smile crept onto his face as he turned towards the girl who was now desperately searching the bed of the rock pool for another chunk of rock. He swivelled and started towards her. She had begun to retreat to a shallower part of the pool and there was less resistance as he stretched his legs wider and faster.

*

"Dani, RUN!" Callie's words echoed around the cove. She threw the pebble she was holding with all the strength she could muster. It thudded against the Feral's back before disappearing into the water. He let out a grunt of pain but didn't miss a step as he closed in on his new target.

Dani straightened up. Terror painted her expression as the larger of the two men closed in on her. She whipped around as quickly as she could and began to charge away, but her foot got tangled in some errant strands of seaweed, and before she could get more than a stride, she fell forwards, splashing down face first.

*

One will do, Rocky thought to himself before taking another couple of large strides and dropping to his knees on top of the young woman who had fallen. He pinned her down under the water as she struggled. His large hand cupped the back of her head, pushing her face down into the sand.

Her arms flailed, and he smiled as he saw Zeke begin to stand and head towards the other girl. "Alive," he commanded as his friend closed in on her with his spear raised.

*

Callie's stomach churned as she saw her friend drowning. The slosh of water as the other Feral climbed to its feet and started heading towards her caused a wave of hopelessness to wash over Callie. She looked down at her hands. In one, she held a chunk of black rock, and in the other, her knife. *No way out of this. Can't save Dani and protect myself.* A small whimper left her mouth.

She turned towards the advancing spearman. His face was bloody and he was still clearly dazed. She quickly glanced back towards Dani, who was desperately trying to throw off the other filthy creature pinning her down as he raised his weapon ready to strike. *Crap! Crap! Crap!*

Callie sucked in a deep breath. She hurled the jagged

piece of rock and watched for a second as it cartwheeled through the air. It cracked against the back of its target's head, and he immediately let out a shriek of pain and toppled forward, plunging face first into the pool next to Dani.

Her friend stopped struggling briefly and Callie's heart nearly stopped too, scared that she was already too late, scared that the damage had been done. But then the pool erupted as Dani shot to her feet, sucking in lungfuls of air as she did.

Callie swivelled back to the other Feral, who was only a matter of three metres away from her now. He kept clenching his eyes shut tight, trying hard to shake off whatever light-headedness remained. She glanced at the small knife in her hand then towards his spear. *This isn't going to end well.*

Suddenly, she crouched. The rapid and unexpected movement caused her aggressor to pause for the briefest moment.

*

Rock. Another Rock. Zeke got ready to duck or weave as he saw the girl's hand plunge into the pool. When she brought it back out, the upthrust caused an explosion of water around her, but there was no rock. Instead, a hand-sized scoop of sand propelled towards him, separating in the air like cloggy confetti. He ducked a little to his left, but still, some exploded in his face.

The gritty, salty concoction made his facial wounds sting as it struck him. He pulled his head away further as more still splatted against his temple. "Ughh!"

A pained, angry grunt left his mouth, and as he opened his eyes once more, it felt like his lids were dragging a thousand tiny rakes over the surface. Reflexively, he staggered back, blind for the moment as he shook his head from side to side, desperate to regain his vision.

*

Dani had never been so convinced that she was going to die. She hadn't heard the crack that had reverberated around the cove as the chunk of granite had smashed against the back of her attacker's head, but a small cloud of blood drifted in the water, and she knew Callie had something to do with her second chance.

The Feral slowly gathered himself, first planting his knees in the sand, then his hands before finally raising his head out of the water once more. *No time. No time to waste.*

Dani looked down. The knife she had been holding was lost for the time being. She grabbed the largest pebble she could find while her attacker continued to right himself; then, with a sudden and violent burst of animation, she brought it down again and again and again. Each time she withdrew it there was more blood in the water, more tissue on the small lump of stone. Within a few seconds, the figure slumped down again. The water turned crimson around his head and his arms drifted out to his sides.

*

Callie stood back for a few beats. She was pretty certain some of the sand had gone in his eyes, but there was the possibility he was faking. *Got to finish this.* Throwing caution to the wind, she lunged.

The slopping, sloshing water made the Feral look up, but he let out another grunt of pain as the cloggy sand tore at his eyes once more. He staggered back, waving his spear from side to side in the hope he could blindly fend off his attacker. Instead, his heel hit a submerged rock, and he fell, splashing back into the water.

Callie leapt forward and dropped down, using the momentum to drive the knife into the chest of the struggling figure. He let out a loud and desperate underwater scream as she pushed further. He continued to writhe frantically, doing everything he could to fight off his assailant, but despite Callie's revulsion, she continued to plunge the knife down harder, dragging it a little from side to side, widening the cavity, causing more blood to erupt from the wound.

Eventually, the scream gave way to panicked gargles as the Feral did everything he could to stop the water from entering his lungs. His body convulsed again and again as Callie continued to bear down on him. Then, finally, he fell still.

For a moment, Callie remained in position, staring at her victim's frightened eyes as they looked back at her from beneath the surface. Then she heard movement behind her and swivelled, withdrawing the knife from her victim at the same time, not sure if it was Dani or the second Feral.

When she saw it was her friend, she dropped the knife in the water and rushed to her. The pair embraced, and both started crying uncontrollably. They were tears of relief, tears of happiness and tears of sadness too. They did not mourn the loss of the two Ferals but the loss of the lives they should have been living. They had been thrust into this post-apocalyptic world and forced to do things that belonged in their worst nightmares. They had won, they had survived, but it was a hollow victory.

They held each other for several minutes until their tears finally abated.

"We should get back," Callie eventually said.

"What about these two?" Dani asked.

"We'll drag them out onto the sand. Hopefully, when the tide comes back in, they'll be taken out to sea."

"I still can't believe this happened."

"No, but let's get our knives and take their spears. The next time we come out, I want to be armed to the teeth."

"Yeah. No arguments here."

5

The news of what had happened to Callie and Dani sent shockwaves running through the entire settlement. Suddenly, their home seemed far less safe. Subconsciously, everyone began to look beyond the fields, into the trees, up to the hills, scouring the landscape for any more boogeymen.

Susan, Si, Nicola and Zep had been glued to the side of the two girls since their return, occasionally hugging them for no reason.

Eventually, people returned to their chores and duties, but a small huddle of the usual suspects, the ones who it always seemed to fall on to make decisions for the settlement, remained outside the farmhouse.

John removed his glasses and gave them a clean before carefully putting them back on. He exhaled a long, tired breath. "I suppose this means we should probably do what they do in Infinity and make sure we go out in bigger groups."

"That's it?" Nicola said. "My daughter was almost killed and that's all you can come up with?"

"What do you want me to do? Raise a posse and go out to hunt the rest of them down?"

"Well ... yes."

John stifled his annoyance, realising how he would feel if the shoe were on the other foot and it had been Emily or Tara. "Look, we can't do that. We don't have the manpower and we don't have the skills. From the little I've heard about these Ferals, they've been living wild since all this began. They'll be more in tune with the environment than we are; they're probably a lot more adept at killing. If we send people out there looking for them, in all likelihood it will be us who end up dead, not them."

Nicola's eyes dropped to the ground for a moment, and then she hugged her daughter a little tighter.

"I understand what you're saying, John," Susan began, "but we can't just wait around for this to happen again."

"What do you suggest?"

"Your idea about going out in bigger groups is a good one. We should double, triple the size of the foraging squads and we should make sure that at least a couple of the people have guns but everyone is armed with spears, knives or whatever we have."

"Okay."

"In addition, I think we should have guards."

"Guards?"

"From dusk 'til dawn. We should have a rotating shift of guards to protect the camp. If nothing else, they'll act as an early warning system if we come under attack."

"How many guards are you talking about?"

"I don't know. Half a dozen, a dozen maybe."

John twitched and scratched his head. He was about to respond when Phil took over. "The biggest problem with that is lost working hours."

"What?"

"Say we have half a dozen guards. They can't be expected to do a full night. You'll need a changeover, so all of a sudden you're talking about twelve guards. They can't work all day and then all night, so they're going to have to rest too. Now we're losing dozens and dozens of working hours. Everything suffers as a result of it."

"So, you're saying we should just carry on? My daughter and Dani almost died today and you're saying we should just do nothing?"

Phil looked at Callie and a brief smile appeared on his face before he turned to Susan once more. "Not at all. I'm saying that everything here is finely balanced and making a decision without thinking about all the implications can have ramifications for everyone."

"And if this was Matt who'd nearly been killed, is this what you'd be saying?"

"In all honesty, probably not, no."

"Well, at least you're being honest."

Tania took over. "Look, we agree that bigger groups need to go out foraging and they need to be armed. I think we're agreed that having guards would be a good idea in principle. Am I right?" She looked around each of the faces staring back at her. Nearly everyone answered in the affirmative, whether with a nod or in words. "Okay, so we just have to figure out a way to do it with minimal impact on everything else."

Everyone fell silent for a moment. "How about rather than having a group of guards patrolling, we just have a couple of lookouts?" Callie said. She'd felt disconnected from everything since arriving back, but the thought of what had happened to her happening to someone who wasn't able to look after themselves was frightening. *What if they tried this with one of the orphans or Scarlett?* She hated some of the choices that this new world forced her to make. She was only sixteen, and a few weeks ago, the thought of harming another human being was horrific. But it seemed to be a part of life in this savage world now.

John smiled politely. "The whole thing with lookouts, Callie, is that they need to be able to see everything that's going on. One lookout at one end of the farmyard and one at the other isn't really going to help us much. There'd be far too many blind spots. My guess is that these guys were watching ever since you got back from Infinity. They're probably used to staking places out and waiting for the opportune moment to strike. So, when they saw two young women break away from the fold, they decided that was it."

Callie nodded. "Yeah, but I didn't mean lookouts at ground level."

John's brow creased and his eyes followed Callie's finger as she pointed to the top of the barn. "Err ... that's an awfully long way up. It would be way too dangerous to have people on top of there, especially at night."

"Jason?" Callie said, looking at him.

Jason stared at Phil. They were both on the same page as far as lost working hours went. They both had mountainous tasks in front of them; one to keep the population fed, the other to house them, and somewhere in between was the water supply. "The fencing we layered for the thatch meshing is pretty secure. I suppose the lookouts could hook themselves up to that. And I could probably erect some kind of platform too."

"And how are they supposed to get up and down?" John asked.

"That shouldn't be a problem. The mesh is a bit like a climbing frame, and me and my gang could probably cobble together something resembling a set of steps to get onto the roof in the first place."

"I don't like it. It would be so easy for something to go wrong, especially at night."

"So, we only use people who are okay with heights," Callie said.

John's shoulders sagged. "What does everyone else think about this?"

"I'll take the first shift," Si said.

"Yeah. I'll join you," added Zep.

John sighed. "Okay, sounds like we've got a solution then, but I really need people to be careful. We can't afford any accidents."

"I'll make sure it's as safe as it can be," Jason said.

"I'll organise more lookouts so we can have multiple shifts," added Zep. "If a few of us do a couple of hours each and rotate across a few days, I bet it won't impact the work day at all."

"Okay then," John replied. "We've got a solution." He clapped his hands together and turned to Jason. "I can trust you to make this happen?" he asked, pointing to the barn. Jason nodded before turning to leave.

The others gradually dispersed too to get ready for the day, leaving Callie and Phil alone. "I literally can't turn my back on you for two minutes, can I?"

"By all means, make fun of the fact that I was nearly murdered. I'm sorry we couldn't get it on video for you."

"Don't beat yourself up about it. Knowing you, there'll be plenty of opportunity in the future."

"Please don't talk this way around Mum. She will literally tear you a new one."

Phil winced. "Why do you think I waited until she left?"

"Always the hero."

"That's me. Seriously, though. Are you okay?"

"I killed someone, Phil. And I'll probably have to kill others. There's nothing about it that's okay." Tears welled in her eyes as she looked at him. "It shouldn't be like this."

Phil nodded, maintaining eye contact. "They were going to hurt you and Dani. It was you or them. It was like that man back in Salvation who confronted Tania and Harper. You didn't have a choice, Callie. And what you have to remember is that they've probably done that many times before, and if you hadn't stopped them, they'd do it many times again."

Callie wiped away her tears. "You're right. But it doesn't make it easier to live with."

"This way, at least you get the chance to live with it."

Callie let out a long breath. "I suppose you're right."

Phil reached out and wiped away an errant tear with his thumb. "I'm glad you two did what you did. Anyway," he said, taking her arm and leading her across to the net that had been left at the far end of the farmyard to dry out. "You brought me a present. It smells foul."

Callie let out a small huff of a laugh. She was one of the few people who ever got to see Phil's tender side. He never revealed it for long, but when he did, it always made her feel better. This was his way of changing the subject and cloaking that side of his personality once more. "I can take it back if you want," she replied looking down at the net.

Phil smiled. "It makes you think, doesn't it?"

"About what?"

"About what else might get washed up. I mean the possibilities are endless. Entire cities were probably swallowed by the sea."

"Yeah, but we've been here a few weeks now and we've found pieces of this and bits of that but never something this kind of size, still in once piece."

"We can live in hope though."

"I thought you didn't believe in hope."

"Okay, we can live in joyful anticipation of the possibility that the currents will shift and something cool will show up on our beach."

"Isn't that just another way of saying hope?"

Phil let out a sigh. "I suppose I could always meet with these Feral people and offer to trade you to them in order to leave us alone. That works out for everyone."

"And how does it work out for me exactly?"

"You like meeting new people."

Callie laughed. The pair stood for a moment in quiet contemplation as they looked at the net. "You look tired."

Phil turned back to his young friend then glanced across to the ovens. "Debbie's making some dandelion coffee. That'll wake me up."

"Err ... it doesn't contain caffeine, y'know?"

"Thank you, Doctor Bridges, I know. But if I close my eyes and imagine really hard, I can fool my body into believing I'm drinking real coffee to give me a kickstart."

"I'm sure you've been told this on many occasions, but you're weird."

Phil smiled. "Look, seriously, with what happened this morning, I don't want you taking risks. If you do go out foraging, make sure it's with big groups. Don't get cocky. Safety in numbers."

"Yes, Dad."

"I'm being serious. If something happened to you, I don't know what I'd do."

Callie waited for a punchline, but when one didn't come, she nodded. "Okay, Phil. I promise."

"Good. Now, to work, and the first thing on today's agenda is the stuff your mum found yesterday. I want to see if I can resuscitate it."

"I told you, she took good care of it."

"Hmm. There is a world of difference between what I consider good care for a plant and what the average peasant off the street does."

"I'm begging you, please, please call my mum a peasant to her face."

"Maybe on your birthday. Right now, just take me to the plants."

*

Greenslade and Trunk headed the long procession. Drake, Marina and their families followed closely behind.

"Dwyer and the others are going to be fine," Marina said. They'd been travelling for a couple of hours, but Drake had barely said a word, lost in his own guilty thoughts.

"It should be me. I should have stayed back."

"No, you shouldn't. Whether you like it or not, you're our leader now. Everybody's looking to you."

"Marina's right," Darin said, taking hold of her husband's hand briefly. "You're needed here with us."

Drake glanced over his shoulder. He could only see to the last bend they had taken. Towering black rocks on either side of the road blocked his view, but he could imagine it in his mind —thousands of sad, frightened people full of questions that might never get answered.

"Absolutely," Greenslade piped up, having earwigged on the conversation. "You're our leader now," he said with a bitter grin on his face.

Drake let go of his wife's hand and cast a glance across to Marina before speeding up a little to join Greenslade and Trunk. "Look, this isn't what you think."

"And what do you think I think it is?"

"I've got no aspirations to be some exalted leader of your settlement. All I want is for my family to be safe and away from that place. I saw an opportunity to make that break and I had to organise it. Trust me; it's not a responsibility I want."

"Ha," Greenslade replied.

"What does that mean?"

"You might not want it, but I'm sure one of your jackbooted friends will be happy to take up the mantle."

Drake didn't reply for a while, but when he did, his words were measured. "I get why you say that. And if I were in your position, I'd probably be thinking exactly the same, but I'll tell you now, I won't allow that to happen."

"Oh, well, that's okay then. You've really put my mind at ease."

"All I want is for my family to be safe and happy and away from that place. I'll do whatever it takes. The only way things are going to work going forward is if we all pull together." Greenslade let out another laugh. "What have I said that's so funny this time?"

"You sound like another idealist I know, except she's only sixteen, so she's got an excuse."

"Thanks."

Greenslade let out a long breath and shook his head. "Look. When you asked us to do this, it felt like the right thing, and, who knows, it might have been the right thing, but...."

"But what?"

Greenslade turned to Drake. "It's not going to work."

A crooked smile appeared on Drake's face. "You've told me where your settlement is. You can't exactly double-cross us now."

"I'm not talking about double-crossing you. I'm saying that I was mad to agree to this. We're all going to starve to death."

"How are your people surviving now?"

"We're foraging while we wait for the crops to come in."

"Then we just do that, only on a larger scale. We're a lot better organised than you were when you left."

Greenslade nodded. Virtually everyone carried a backpack or bag full of food. Shopping trolleys had been disassembled to get them up the lift shaft and then hastily reassembled to cart whatever resources they could. Compared to the original exodus from Salvation, this one was like a military operation. "That food won't last forever."

"But it will help. And we've brought seeds and tools and a thousand other things that you people didn't even have the time to think about. We'll make this work. We'll have to make this work."

Greenslade stared at Drake as they continued walking along. He could tell there was more than a pinch of desperation in the former Salvation guard's words, but there was also something reassuring about them too. He seemed to be as committed to the idea as John or Phil or Callie or ... yes, even himself. He had entered the fray an outsider, and to some extent, he would always be that, but he wanted this to work more than anything. "Okay, Drake. Let's hope, shall we?"

They carried along in silence for a while before the sound of running feet behind them made them all turn. It was a young woman, and they all looked towards her with questioning eyes for a moment before recognition finally dawned on Trunk's then Greenslade's faces. "Sasha?" Trunk said. In Salvation, they had probably passed each other on the street as strangers a thousand times before. But in the quarry, their faces had been etched in each other's minds, like the faces of all those they fought alongside and all those they lost.

"Si? Is he still with you? Is he okay?"

"The last time I saw him, he'd nearly lost his mind looking for you. But I'm hoping Callie and Susan talked some sense into him."

"Oh please, God," she replied, her voice quivering a little.

"Well, we'll find out soon enough, won't we?"

*

Nazya and Chloe emerged from the small building into the bright morning sun. Normally at this time, the market at Infinity would just be getting started. Some groups would be heading home with the wares they had bartered the previous day, while others would be setting up their pitches.

Each individual clan was working for themselves with the goal of bettering their own situation. This was the first time either of them had visited a community starting from scratch. When they had finally ventured out of their bunker, they still had a good supply of food, materials and resources, but these people, they were doing everything with the bare minimum.

They watched in wonder as five men worked on top of the thatched barn to erect some kind of scaffolding or platform. There were already dozens of people in the fields on their hands and knees weeding. Men and women, some with rifles on their backs, were trafficking in large stones to add to the small mountains that already existed, while others went about using them to piece together replicas of the dwelling they had spent the entire night in. Children carried armfuls of reeds from the banks of the stream, carefully laying them out so the sun could dry them.

"Thought you could use some coffee," Debbie said, walking up to them with two cups.

"This is the stuff you make from dandelions?" Chloe asked.

"It is," she replied, a little surprised.

"Callie was telling us about it yesterday." She brought the cup up to her nose and sniffed then took a careful sip. She raised both her eyebrows. "That tastes good." Then she realised how her words sounded. "I'm sorry, I was just—"

Debbie laughed. "No explanation necessary. When Phil first got me to try it, I can only imagine the look on my face. But, as usual, he was right."

Nazya took a sip too. "This is good."

"Glad you like it," Debbie replied.

"We have a stage at Infinity. People get up, and some entertain while others share news and educate. I get the impression Phil could help a lot of people with the knowledge he has."

"Ha! Good luck with that. He's not really a people person. Getting up in front of a crowd would require more alcohol than there is left in the world."

"Oh, I think you'd be surprised how much alcohol is left in the world. We have people at Infinity who make it."

"What, seriously?"

"Woody," Chloe said, taking over. "He makes all sorts, but if you're wanting something with a serious kick, you need to try his potato peel vodka."

"Okay, now I definitely want to visit Infinity." They all laughed as they watched the others immersed in their tasks. Eventually, it was Debbie who broke the silence once more. "How's Harry doing?"

Nazya nodded. "He is doing very well. He has said he is hungry, which is actually why we came out. Michelle and Ollie are with him, but we were hoping we could get some breakfast for him and us."

Debbie reached out, taking hold of the other woman's arm. "Oh my God. I'm so sorry; I thought someone would have been in to ask you. Of course, of course. I'll get some sent in for all of you."

"Also, we would like to freshen up."

"Well, all we can offer is the stream at the moment," Debbie replied, pointing.

"A stream sounds good," Nazya said. "Thank you."

"Okay, I'll go and get the food sorted." Debbie turned and headed back to the outdoor kitchen.

"Hi," Callie said, joining the two women as they walked towards the sound of gently running water.

"Hi," Nazya replied.

"I heard about your run-in," Chloe said.

Callie sighed. "Yeah. It was a bit more than a run-in."

"It's very rare for there just to be two of them."

"Two was all we saw. I'm pretty certain if there were more, they'd have come out when they saw their friends getting squished."

"I suppose. It's lucky you can look after yourself."

"Trust me; it was touch and go. Dani and I could quite easily have been roasting on a spit now if it wasn't for some good luck."

"And suddenly I'm not hungry anymore."

Callie laughed. "Sorry. Err ... not that I'm wanting to get rid of you, but do you have any idea when you'll be heading back to Infinity?"

Nazya leaned forward to look at the younger woman. "I think tomorrow. I want to stay the rest of the day to make sure Harry continues to improve. I will leave antibiotics, painkillers, bandages and some creams, but there is little for me to do. The rehabilitation will be a long one and will take patience and attentiveness, but that is not something I can give when there are so many other patients who may need me. John and his nurses have done a good job caring for Harry, and I think Michelle has the right temperament to follow the job through."

"That's good to know. Thank you."

"I will leave detailed instructions before we go."

"I can't thank you enough for what you both did."

"I am a doctor. This is what I do."

"Yeah, but you both took a huge risk coming here. I'm guessing it's going to be much less of a risk heading back. Virtually everyone wants to see Infinity," Callie said, smiling.

"Well, everybody's welcome," Chloe replied.

"Yeah, I think some people are going to be disappointed. It's not like we can just abandon this place to visit. There's too much to do."

"Will Phil be coming?"

"I don't think a tank division could keep Phil away. I've never seen him so excited."

"Naz was saying to Debbie that it would be good if Phil could share a bit of his knowledge on the stage." Callie laughed, and Chloe's brow furrowed a little. "That was her reaction too."

"Yeah. Phil's not the most socially adept person you'll ever meet. He could climb onto that stage with the best intentions and single-handedly alienate everyone in the audience and start a riot at the same time."

"I thought you were his friend."

"I am, probably his best one, which is why I'm warning you it would be a disaster."

"Fair enough, I suppose. How about you then?"

"How about me what?"

"Get on the stage and talk to people. Tell them about what you're doing here."

"No thanks."

"It would help."

"Help who?"

"Help those who are struggling. Those who just need that little extra helping hand. I mean the dandelion coffee, for example. That might seem like a little thing to you, but it would be a huge deal to someone."

"Well ... I mean ... there are a lot of people who know more than me about that kind of stuff."

"Would any of them be willing to talk about it?"

"I don't know."

"Well, look, just think about it. If a few of you could just chat a little bit about some of the things you do here, you could make a world of difference to someone who's having a hard time. And you might find stuff out that's useful to you."

"I suppose."

"Or you could always just get up there and sing us a song. Nothing gets the crowd going like a good turn," Chloe said, smiling.

"Alas, I have a singing voice that would make birds take flight, but we have got a proper singer here. She did festivals and things."

Chloe stopped. "What, seriously?"

"Yeah. Harper, Harper Kennedy. She's amazing."

"You have to bring her along."

"I'm pretty certain she was on the list anyway."

"Brilliant."

"Chloe fancies herself as a talent scout," Nazya said.

"It's not that," Chloe replied. "It's just when the crowd's watching someone perform a song or a little drama sketch or something like that, the whole place changes."

"What do you mean?" Callie asked.

Chloe thought for a moment. "You can feel the wonderment and happiness in the air. It's like being transported back to the time before the asteroid, to the time when things were normal, or at least as normal as we ever knew them."

"I think I understand, and like I said, I'm pretty certain she'd be on the list to come with us anyway."

Chloe's face lit up. "Good. I look forward to hearing her sing."

"You won't be disappointed.".

6

Tania, Harper and Penny walked along side by side. At least twenty other people, including teens and a couple of younger children, trailed behind them. The original plan had been for smaller groups to head out on multiple foraging trips, but after the events of the morning, this was deemed safer. Debbie, Susan, Nicola, Jiang and Lanying had taken out another group similar in number.

The three of them carried Q-Thirty rifles, as did Matt and Greta, who were bringing up the rear. "Where are we going exactly?" Penny asked.

"We're having a wee bit of an explore," Harper replied. "We've not exactly been this way before."

"Is that safe? I mean considering what happened to Callie and her friend today?"

Harper looked back at the others who were following. Some carried clubs, others spears. "If a couple of little punks want to try to attack us, I wish them luck."

"Yes, but what if it's more than a couple? What if it's an entire gang?"

"We're not heading in the direction of Infinity and I took a good look around when we hit that last peak. I'm pretty certain we're not being followed."

"I hope you're right."

"This looks good," Tania said, pointing to a field up ahead with an area of charred woodland behind it that stretched off into the distance. Even from where they were, they could see yellow flowers amongst the patches of green.

"It looks the same as some of the other fields we've passed," Penny replied.

"True, but I like the fact that there's a forest behind. You find all kinds of things in the forests."

"Even ones that have been burnt to a crisp?"

"Trust me. We'll find something."

They carried on until they reached the dry-stone wall that surrounded the field then, one by one, climbed over. They carried on towards the blackened woodland, careful not to trample the vegetation, instead skirting around the edge of what once would have been a field of crops or maybe pasture for cattle.

They entered the woodland, and despite the lack of foliage, the heat from the sun wasn't quite as strong all of a sudden. "Okay," Penny said. "I get dandelions and nettles and all that kind of stuff. I mean it's not something I'd order from a restaurant if I was going out, but it helps fill a hole. What are we going to find in here?"

Tania and Harper slowed down to a stop. Their entourage halted too and formed a semicircle around them. "Okay," Tania began. "Some of you have been out before, some of you haven't. Penny's just asked me why we've come into the forest when there's a field with all sorts in it just over there."

"Why do I suddenly feel like a kid in a classroom?" Penny asked and laughter rippled around the small crowd.

Tania and Harper laughed too before Tania continued. "Sorry, force of habit. We'll still find dandelions and nettles, and recently we've discovered ground elder and a few other plants too. They're not in the same sort of abundance in a wooded area as they are in the field, but the protection that the woods give, even in this state, means that we might discover something new. Yesterday, we found mushrooms while Susan found blackberries and cherries."

"So, you're saying that even though we might not fill our rucksacks in the forest, we might discover something that will allow us to grow a new crop."

"Exactly," Tania said. "Remember, we're starting from scratch. There will be hundreds of thousands of plant species that didn't make it, and if we can find just one plant, then we can grow more."

"You seem to know a lot about this."

"I didn't used to. Phil taught Harper and me a lot in a very short time."

"Sure," Harper said. "The hours learning about the different types of wild plants we can put in our stews just flew by." The small audience laughed again. "And don't even get me started on seaweeds, 'cause I'm getting hungry just thinking about them."

"I understand. It's not very exciting, but right now, this is the difference between us starving to death and surviving. And every little thing we find that adds to the menu is a big deal."

"Joking aside," Penny said, "I get it now." She turned to the men, women and children she had survived with since the Salvation guards had raided the forest by the mine. "Tread lightly. If you see anything you don't recognise, find Tania, Harper or Matt. You heard what Tania said. This isn't just about filling our bellies tonight; this is about the future too." They all nodded, separated into smaller groups and began to scour the forest methodically. "And stay within sight of us and one another. Don't go wandering off. You all know what happened to Dani and Callie this morning."

Tania, Harper and Penny all watched for a moment before they began their search too. "Now who sounds like the teacher?" Harper said, smiling.

"More like Mother Hen. That's what it's felt like since all this happened."

"You did amazing to keep them all safe this long."

"To be honest, if we hadn't found Si when we did, I don't know how much longer we'd have survived."

"Well, thank goodness you did."

"Thank you both for agreeing to bring us this morning."

"No thanks needed. The more knowledge we share the better for everyone, right?"

"I suppose."

"I know things have been like a rollercoaster for all of us," Tania said. "And I can't imagine the horror of what happened to you. But things will get better. Every minute of every day, we're building, planting, foraging. It's hard to envision a rosy future sometimes, but I know it's there."

"I look forward to the day I have that kind of faith. It just feels like we're hanging on by a thread at the moment."

"Trust me. Better times are on the horizon."

*

"This thing weighs a tonne," Callie said, placing the end of the blackened, rusted bathtub down on the ground. "And tell me, why the hell would they have two old bathtubs in the middle of a big field?"

Phil put his end down and looked towards Dani and Wei as they did the same with the second tub. "In rural communities, there used to be very little waste. These baths probably came from abandoned properties. They were sturdy and well-built and why get rid of them when they'd make good feeding or water troughs?"

Callie wiped her brow. "Fair enough. And what possible reason could we have for wanting them? Have you got a flock of sheep you've not told me about?"

"No, these are going to be for our special little projects."

"I don't know if I dare ask the next question."

"Then don't. Come on," Phil said, wiping his forehead and picking his end up once more.

Five more gruelling minutes passed before they finally reached the farmyard. Phil carefully guided Callie to the spot for the first tub, and when that was in position, he directed Dani and Wei to put theirs down. All four of them stood with their hands on their hips for a moment in order to catch their breath.

They looked towards the barn where Jason, Zep and several others were on the ridge of the thatched roof, carefully erecting what looked like a scaffolding frame made from bound-together boughs and branches. The wood was black, like most of the wood they used, but Jason was a perfectionist and they all knew he wouldn't employ any materials that didn't pass muster.

When they'd finally caught their breath, Callie spoke again. "So, are you going to reveal the big mystery or not?"

"We're going to fill them with soil and use them to grow the plants we find that need a bit more nurturing."

"That's it? You made us drag these things fifty miles so you could have a little hobby garden?" Dani asked.

"It was hardly fifty miles. Forty-nine at the most."

"That's funny. And why did you recruit me and Callie for this and not anyone else?"

"Because I like you."

"Oh well, that's okay then. I feel much better now."

"I thought you might. Liking someone is an honour I don't bestow on most."

"This is to do with the blackberries, isn't it?" Callie said, raising an eyebrow.

"I doth my cap to thee, ma'am."

"It's because you're paranoid Mum damaged them in her rucksack even though you can plainly see there's nothing wrong with them."

"I just don't want to take any risks."

"And the cherry branch too. Are you going to plant that in there?"

Phil looked at her with a look of bewilderment on his face. "You may as well ask me if I'm going to plant some kelp in the hope of growing a seaweed tree."

Wei chuckled. "I shall get back to the fields now," he said, nodding politely.

"Thanks, Wei. We'll carry on our chat a little later."

"I look forward to it."

Wei departed and Callie turned back to Phil. "Chat? What chat?"

"Oh, I'm sorry. Did I not get the requisite permission from you to have a chat with my friend Wei?"

"Fine. Don't tell me if you don't want to."

"Don't pout. We were having a discussion about the materials we'll need and the length of time it will take to build the first section of the irrigation system."

"In which case, I'm eternally grateful that you left us out of it."

"I thought you might be."

"So," Dani said, "other than liking us, why are we here helping you rather than out foraging?"

The smile disappeared from Phil's face. "I've decided it's important that I share as much of my knowledge as I can."

"Okay, and why us?"

"You seem to be far less dim-witted than most of the others."

"Far less dim-witted? Wow. Thanks."

"You're welcome. Seriously, though, you're bright, and you communicate well with others. You're both capable of retaining the information I give you and passing it on."

"Passing it on?"

"We're going to need to pass on all our knowledge. That's how things will work from now on."

"And you want to pass all your knowledge on to us. What about Matt and Jiang and some of the others?"

"Jiang already knows quite a bit. Wei and Lanying have an incredible breadth and depth of understanding.

Matt's someone who will learn when he's ready. Right now, his head's into foraging. He's a quick learner and a good communicator and I'll show him what I need to when the time is right."

"So you're not going to show him what you're showing us?"

"I think the best way forward is if I give a little knowledge to a lot of people. It reduces the burden on them and on me. There'll be a pool of individuals whom others can go to."

"I'm not sure I understand."

"Well, today, for example, I'm going to show you how to grow a new plant from the limb that Susan cut and we're going to plant the two blackberry saplings, giving them the best chance to thrive before we relocate them on the farm."

"And you chose us for this," Callie said. "I'm touched."

"As well you should be."

"So, what's first?"

"Well, while I go get a cup of coffee you two are going to three-quarter fill these bathtubs with soil."

"You're serious?"

"Well, they're not going to fill themselves, are they?" he said, shrugging his shoulders and walking away. "Oh. And make sure the last few centimetres are sieved."

Callie and Dani looked at each other. "He wouldn't pick on me if I wasn't friends with you."

"So, this is my fault?"

"Well, it's not mine, is it?"

"Come on. The sooner we get this done the better."

There was a small collection of tools leaning up against the wall of the barn. The pick-axe head they'd found in the burnt-out shell of the house on their journey to find the settlement had been fitted with a reasonably sturdy handle, thanks to Jason. Callie picked that up while Dani grabbed the folding shovel that had once belonged to

Greenslade. Both girls cast each other a sad glance. For all the bad he'd done, he and Trunk had saved their lives, and for that, they would be eternally grateful.

Despite both of them complaining about the tasks Phil had demanded of them, secretly they were grateful. They were grateful to be occupied and grateful to be together after the events of the morning. Having something to do and focus on took their minds off what they had gone through ... what they had done.

They looked around. The fields, the farmyard, the roof of the barn, the patch of land that had been designated for building, there wasn't a single still body. Men, women and children were all busy with their tasks. The work was hard and unending, but there was an upbeat mood that brought small smiles to each of their faces without them realising.

"This place is special, isn't it?" Dani said.

"I don't think it's the place. I think it's the people, the feeling of freedom. I think it's not being slaves anymore," Callie replied.

"Aren't you done yet?" Phil asked, reappearing from around the corner.

"You were saying?" Dani said.

*

"How are you feeling?" Rachael asked, catching up to Greenslade and Trunk.

Greenslade stared at the diminutive figure for a moment before answering. "You're one of the doctors."

"That's right. Rachael's my name."

"Is this your version of a house call?"

The younger woman smiled. "Sort of. Both of you had quite a cocktail of drugs yesterday. I just want to make sure you're feeling okay."

"Well, aren't you sweet?"

"You should keep hydrated. You're perspiring quite a bit."

"It's a warm day."

"True enough." There was a pause of a few seconds before Rachael continued. "So, what's it like this place of yours?"

"And there I was thinking you were just coming to make sure we were both okay."

"I'm sorry. I did want to check on you though."

They carried on walking for a short while before Greenslade continued. "It's bare bones. We've got people living in two buildings, an old farmhouse and a barn."

"They were still standing?"

"Kind of. They were shells, but they were built from stone, and enough of them survived to give us something to work with. We put roofs on them and they give us somewhere to bed down while we get to work building more houses."

"How did you put roofs on?"

"We've got some clever people among us. They thatched them."

"Thatching. Wow." Rachael had seen pictures of houses with thatched roofs, but she'd never seen one up close.

"Yeah, we're doing that for the new builds too."

"The new builds?"

"We're building more, smaller ones so each family can have their own."

"How? What are you building them out of?"

"There's lots of stone available and we've tweaked the design they used for the Highland Blackhouses."

"I'm not sure I know what they are."

"The Highlands and islands in Scotland used to have a lot of them. They're small stone dwellings that used to have an open fire in the centre of the room. There was no chimney and, subsequently, the interior of the thatch turned black. That's how some people think they got their name."

"You seem to know a lot about them."

"No. Like I said, we've got some clever people among us. I just listened. Jason, he's the brains behind the building side of the operation, opted to build chimney stacks instead, so they're a little bit of a step up from the original design. Although, it's like I was saying to your pal earlier, I really don't know what the hell's going to happen now. We're going from a few dozen to a few thousand people overnight." Greenslade shook his head despairingly. "I don't know what the hell I was thinking. I've probably just signed the death certificates for all of us."

"Everyone will do whatever it takes."

Greenslade laughed bitterly. "Course they will."

"Didn't you? Didn't you do whatever it took to survive? I mean, no offence, but from everything I heard, you were hardly a team player when you were stuck in Salvation. Now you sound like a cheerleader for the new settlement."

"You don't know what you're talking about."

"I know that you could have tried to escape with the others. I heard what you did, what both of you did. That seemed like a pretty selfless act to me. I don't think the Greenslade I heard about from Salvation would have done anything like that."

"What's your point?"

"My point is I think freedom has changed you. I think this place, your new home, has changed you, and I think it will do the same for a lot of people."

"My mistake. When you said you were a doctor, I didn't realise you meant you're a psychiatrist."

Rachael smiled. "That's funny. Well, I'll get back to my husband. I'm sure you boys have got plenty to talk about between you." And just like that, she was gone, leaving the two friends to continue their long march home.

"Did you mean what you said, chief?" Trunk asked when she was out of earshot.

"Which bit?"

"About signing our death warrants."

Greenslade inhaled deeply then slowly let out a long breath. "I think ... I ... I didn't think it through. You should have seen what those bastards had done in that forest, Trunk. Kids … they'd murdered kids, shot them in their backs, in their heads. They'd executed them. When Drake came to us, I think there was part of me that wanted to help the Level Three people, but there was a bigger part of me that just wanted to piss off Bucks and his minions. I don't think I saw beyond that."

There was a time when other people would have been the last thing on Greenslade's mind. Trunk knew that Callie's actions had played a big part in changing that. He knew that it was for Callie that he had been willing to sacrifice himself in that tunnel. Maybe not just for her benefit but because she was the future of the settlement, her and the people around her. She was the best chance Grace, Theo, Lydia, Stef and the rest of them had. Now Greenslade seemed to hold himself up to the young girl's standard, turning his life and Trunk's life around completely. Trunk reached out and put his hand on the other man's shoulder. "It was the right thing to do. Whatever else happens from here, it was the right thing to do."

"I hope you're right, Trunk. I hope you're right."

7

Callie and Dani stood back from the two bathtubs. Both of them had worked up a sweat but carried out Phil's instructions to a T. "That took you long enough," he said as he returned from a conversation with John.

"I'm holding a shovel in my hand, Phil. I really wouldn't advise you to continue down that line," Callie replied.

Phil smiled. He put down the rucksack with the two plants and the limb from the wild cherry bush hanging out of it. "I told you. I told you that you should have let me have these sooner," he said as he looked at the blackberry plant with snapped branches.

"I'm sure my mum would apologise in person if she were here. But considering that happened when we were being attacked by an army of Ferals and she'd just fallen into a massive ditch, I think she had a pretty reasonable excuse."

"Meh. I suppose." He slid on the gloves that Debbie had lovingly crafted from a thick imitation suede jacket. It had been Zep's favourite, but in the end, even he had to admit that it was barely wearable anymore. There was zero waste in the community now and every fibre of it had been put to good use.

Phil carefully scooped the damaged plant out of the bottle holder compartment it had been shoved in and placed it on the ground. He then proceeded to create a hole in the sieved soil in one of the tubs before gently taking the plant once more and lowering it down. Ensuring none of the exposed roots were compressed too much, he carefully mounded the earth back around the base of the plant.

"That's it?" Dani said. "That's the great trick you were going to show us?"

"I never said it was a trick. I just said I was going to show you how to nurture young plants, so we could give them the best opportunity to thrive."

"Anyone could have figured that out."

"We're not finished yet, impatient one." He proceeded to gently snip the squashed and broken limbs from the sapling with a pair of sharpened kitchen scissors before planting the healthier one in an identical manner further along in the tub. "You need to make sure that you give them plenty of room. You don't want the roots of a stronger plant stifling those of another and restricting growth."

Callie was less impatient. She watched carefully as Phil worked. "Okay, I get the blackberry saplings," she said, "they've got their roots, they're viable plants. What about the cherry branch?"

There was still a small handful of cherries attached to the limb and Phil picked even amounts off, handing them to the two girls and keeping a few for himself. "Make sure you don't swallow the stones." The two girls looked around guiltily as they ate the sweet-tasting fruit.

"If we could grow these, that would be amazing," Dani said.

"We can and we will."

"So, we're just going to grow them from the stones?" Callie asked.

"Well, yes. We're going to plant them and replant the saplings once I'm happy they're viable. That's pretty straightforward, but what I wanted to show you was how to grow a plant from a limb like this," he replied, holding up the bare cutting. "That actually takes quite a bit of care and know-how."

"Okay," Callie said.

Phil looked to each of them before continuing. "Okay, what we're looking for is something like this." He pointed to a small branch protruding from the main limb. "We need to cut it at a diagonal close to the joint where the growth has taken place." He carefully snipped it with the scissors and pointed to the green part at the top of the cutting. "We need to get rid of this bit as well," he added before removing that section too.

"So, you're basically left with a twig?" Callie replied.

"Kind of. Y'see these little nodules?" He pointed to small growths along the fifteen-centimetre cutting. "If we can get this to take, that's where new branches are going to form, but before that happens, we need to get it to root."

"How do we do that?"

Phil smiled. "Well, this is the cool part." He placed the scissors down and removed a small, sharp triangle of metal that resembled a blade from his pocket. "We need to wound the cutting around the base until we see what's called the cambium layer, which is basically this green stuff," he said, showing each of the girls in turn.

"Then we plant it?"

"I'd dip it in a growth hormone if I had one, but in the absence of that, yes, we plant it. Dani, can you make a small mound for me and then poke a hole right down in the centre?"

"Okay." From being blasé about the whole thing, suddenly both girls were fascinated by the process. Dani did as she was asked, and Phil carefully inserted the cutting before compacting the earth around it.

"And is that it? Will it grow now?"

"In all likelihood, yes, but we can do something to increase its chances further, and I'll come on to that in a minute, but first of all, you two are going to do what I've just done." He handed Dani the rest of the branch, the scissors and the blade and watched as she mimicked his actions before she passed the mantle to Callie, who did the same. "Excellent," he said with a proud smile on his face. He reached into the rucksack and pulled out a collapsible bottle. "Come on," he said, heading off towards the stream.

"Are we going to water them now?" Dani asked.

"Kind of." They walked downstream for a minute or so and then Phil guided them behind a large growth of scrub grass. A piece of charred panelling lay on the ground behind it and Phil turned it over. A potent smell struck all of them at the same time and the two girls took a step back.

"What the hell is that?" Callie asked, horrified.

"This is one of my other little projects," Phil said with a smile. They had found lots of flotsam and jetsam washed up on the beach. What they were all staring down at now were the remains of large marker buoys, which had been sawn in two to make vessels to hold whatever foul concoction Phil had created. They had been positioned in a dug out section of earth beneath the metal panel. Phil grabbed a blackened piece of wood that lay next to them and gave each one a stir. All four contained the same brown liquid with what looked like rotting weeds floating in it.

"Okay. Do we need to get worried or is there a justifiable reason why you've been making this weird stuff … whatever it is?"

"This is seaweed tea."

Dani laughed. "I'll do your digging, I'll plant your saplings, I'll cart around a load of earth, but there's no way you're going to get me to drink that. No way."

"Okay, I take back everything I said earlier about you being less dim-witted. It's not for drinking. It's for feeding to the plants," he said, bending down and filling the collapsible bottle.

"I thought you wanted to nurture them, not poison them."

"Get used to the smell because as my newly appointed plant nurturing tsars, you're going to have to start using this stuff on a regular basis."

"I am never going to get used to that smell."

"So, what is it, Phil?" Callie asked.

"It's basically a super fertiliser. I know it smells and looks pretty repulsive, but the difference this makes is astounding."

"And how do you make it?"

"That's the beauty of it. It's just water and seaweed. You thoroughly rinse the seaweed off in fresh water then put it in the containers, fill them with water and stir it every couple of days. In a few weeks, you get this." He put the bottle down and slid the panel back into place. "There were all sorts of products on the market before that helped spur growth. This will do the same as the best of them, and the great thing is we can make it ourselves."

"Actually, that is pretty cool."

They returned to the tubs, and Phil lovingly poured a generous amount of the liquid around the base of each of the freshly planted saplings and cuttings. "And here endeth the lesson," he said, replacing the cap on the bottle and straightening up.

"So that's it?"

"In a nutshell. Other people would probably show you slightly different methods, but that's what I want you to stick to. Oh, and there is one other thing."

"What?"

"Well, obviously, we've found that our climate seems to have become a lot warmer. Assuming this is a permanent change and not just some freak occurrence, we'll be fine sticking to this method. But if we find it becomes cooler again, here's a trick to help the cuttings anyway." He lifted the bottle up once more and moved his finger across the top horizontally. "Cut this off and carefully put it over the top of the plant. It will act as a mini greenhouse, protecting it from the cold."

"That's pretty ingenious."

"Not really, but it's effective."

"Okay, so what's next?"

"What do you mean? That's it. I'm all teachered out."

"I heard Tania and Jiang found some mushrooms yesterday. Aren't you going to show us how to plant those?"

"Plant them? What is wrong with you? You don't just plant mushrooms."

"Well, whatever it is you do with them."

"Follow me," he said and began walking around the house. The three of them entered and walked along to the end room that acted as Paul's family's accommodation.

"Are you sure we should be in here?" Dani asked.

"They have more room than anyone else and Paul said he was fine letting me have a corner." The shutters were open, letting in the sun, so there was plenty of light for them to see. They weaved around the folded blankets that were their makeshift beds to the wide stone sill. On it were four sheets of Tania's notebook. In the centre of each of them was a mushroom minus the stem. Plastic drinking glasses, borrowed from one of the families, with a stone to weigh each one down had been placed over them. "I put these here last night."

"Err ... why?" Dani asked.

Phil removed one of the glasses and delicately lifted the cap off the paper. It had been trimmed and finagled a little to make it as flat as possible. "See?" he said, gesturing to the page.

Both girls looked carefully and saw the pattern of the mushroom gills on the page. "Is this like an art project or something?"

"Yes, Dani. I've cut up the first mushrooms we've found since leaving Salvation to create an abstract piece, which I call 'Just for Simpletons'."

"What is it then?"

"It's what's called a spore print. On that one piece of paper are tens of thousands of individual spores."

"And we're going to be able to grow them into mushrooms?" Callie asked.

Phil winced. "Eventually ... I hope. It's a lot more complicated than growing vegetables or plants or trees. Kept in the right conditions, these spores will last a long time. I'm going to do the same with the other mushrooms, so we'll have literally millions ready when I can figure out how to get us to the next stage."

"The next stage?"

"Like I said, it's complicated, and it's a long time since I've done this, so I'll need to get everything right in my head first."

"Getting everything right in your head? Good luck with that," Callie said with a grin.

Phil smiled too before placing the cup back over the spore print. "But all that will be a lesson for another day." He looked towards the glasses one last time before turning back to Callie and Dani. "Right. I'm an important man. I have things to do and people to see. You'd better revise everything I've taught you today. I'll be testing you on it." He started to leave.

"Phil," Callie said, causing him to stop and turn.

"Yes?"

"Thank you."

"Yeah. Thanks, Phil," Dani echoed.

Phil nodded. "Remember. This isn't just for us, just for now. This is information we'll need to pass on to the next generation and the next." He fixed them both with a long stare once more before exiting.

They both watched him leave before turning towards each other. A broad smile was painted on Callie's face. "What are you smiling about?" Dani asked.

"Everything's coming together. Bit by bit, everything's taking shape. The housing, the food, Infinity. We're going to be okay, Dani. We'll hit setbacks, that's just life, but I've got a feeling in my gut that tells me our biggest problems are behind us and there's a good future ahead … for everyone.

*

It was mid-afternoon when the two foraging teams arrived back at the settlement within about fifteen minutes of each other. Many of the adults carried two rucksacks each, conscious of the extra burden on their supplies now they were having to feed so many more mouths. Both expeditions had been fruitful, and, as always, Phil was among the first to greet them as they entered.

He watched as rucksack after rucksack was unloaded on the banks of the stream. "Sorry, Phil. Nothing exciting today," Tania said as she and Harper joined him.

"Susan said virtually the same words when she arrived," Phil replied. "Am I really that predictable?"

"You can't complain too much. I mean you got mushrooms, blackberries and cherries all in one day."

"Yes, but that was yesterday."

The two women laughed before Harper pulled a piece of paper from her pocket. "We got a good haul and we've checked out another forest," she said, showing it to Phil. It was a map that had been crudely drawn on a page from Tania's journal. "We're going to try this area tomorrow," she said, pointing to a section a little further to the west.

Phil nodded slowly. "Good."

"Y'know," Tania began, "we've found more than enough sources in the area without us going further afield."

Phil nodded again. "I know and that's a good thing, but I'm keen to find out what else is out there."

"I get that," Harper said. "There's only so long you can eat soups and stews without pining for a little variety."

"Variety's good, we need a well-balanced diet, but that's not all I'm thinking about. If we're going to start trading with Infinity, the more surplus and the greater diversity of surplus we can grow the better."

"Well, yeah, but don't we have to think about feeding ourselves first?"

"I am thinking about that, but not just for next week and next month and the one after that. We need to think long term. We've been very fortunate since we left Salvation."

"Tell that to Harry," Tania replied.

"I wasn't meaning that."

"I'm sorry. I was just being glib."

"I mean we haven't experienced any harsh or problematic weather conditions. We haven't lived through a full year yet, so we don't know what issues the changing seasons are going to bring us. We don't know what's going to face us. We might have a bloody monsoon season for all we know. We might get twisters or hurricanes or we might get prolonged droughts or winters with ten feet of snow that make it impossible to leave our homes until the thaw."

"Well, aren't you just Mister Happiness today?"

"I'm just saying that we have to plan ahead. And yes, I'm aware that you can collect more than enough leaves and roots and weeds for us without travelling as far as I'm asking you to go, but it's all about anticipating what might happen."

"I suppose that makes sense."

"Hopefully, but the time...."

Tania and Harper looked at each other with confused expressions as Phil just stopped talking and gazed away into the distance. "Err ... Phil? Phil, are you okay?" Harper asked. "Phil?"

"Phil!" Tania almost shouted, and just like that, he was back with them.

"Hmm?"

"You were in the middle of a sentence and you just zoned out." He continued to look at her for a moment before turning and walking away, leaving the two women just standing there.

He carried on towards the makeshift infirmary, oblivious to everything that was going on around him.

"Don't say hello to your wife then," Debbie said as she watched him walk straight by her.

He stopped and turned back, looking at her for the briefest moment with little recognition in his eyes. "Sorry. Hi, Debs."

"I know that look. What's going on?"

"Syringes," he said before heading off once more.

Debs stood with her hands on her hips for a second. "Okay. Good talk, as always. See you at dinner," she called after him.

Phil stopped in the doorway to the small infirmary. Harry was awake and Michelle and Ollie were on either side of him, holding his hand. Even from where he was standing, Phil could see the boy's skin appeared a healthier colour since the last time he had checked in. The sombre atmosphere had dissipated too. Nazya was standing back from the family and a self-satisfied smile adorned her face. It was a few seconds before she saw Phil standing at the door.

"Hi." She walked across to greet him. "He's doing better," she said, guiding Phil into the sunlight once more.

"Hmm?"

"Harry. He's doing much better. He's on a lot of pain meds, but the wound, his vitals, everything is much better than it was when I got here last night."

"Oh, that's great."

"Wasn't that what you were coming to find out?" she asked.

"Well, no, actually."

"Okay. What can I do for you?"

"I don't suppose you've got such a thing as a syringe in that medical bag of yours, do you?"

"Well, yes. Why?"

"Do you have a spare one?"

Nazya's left eyebrow arched upwards. "Well, nothing's really spare. We have to use and reuse everything. Nothing is disposable these days."

Phil scratched his cheek pensively. "You just have the one then?"

"Well, no, but they are a valuable resource as I'm sure you're aware."

"Mm. I'm sure they are. Okay, no matter. I'll think of something else." He started walking away.

"What are you wanting it for?"

Phil stopped and turned back. "One of our foraging teams found mushrooms yesterday, and—"

"You want to make a spore syringe?" Nazya replied with a smile on her face.

Phil nearly took a step back in surprise. "Yes. That's it exactly. How do you know about spore syringes?"

"When I was at university, I had a housemate who had a serious interest in growing mushrooms."

"I bet that saved you a fortune."

"Err ... not quite. The kind of mushrooms he grew didn't really make for a healthy diet."

"Aha. Your friend grew magic mushrooms?"

"He did, for a while, until he was caught dealing them. They were a class A drug. Needless to say, he never finished his degree."

"I dare say he didn't."

"What type of mushrooms did your people find?"

"Oysters."

"Hmm. And what substrate were you thinking of using to grow them?"

Phil's face cracked into a wide smile. "You seem to know an awful lot about this stuff."

"I never partook in his wares, but I did find the process interesting."

"Oysters are pretty adaptable. Logs, straw, coffee grounds."

"You have a lot of those things?"

"Err ... no. But I was thinking about cutting some of the scrub grass that's growing everywhere, letting that dry out and using that."

Nazya nodded. "How many mushrooms did your friends gather?"

"Quite a few."

"Quite a few what?" Chloe said, seemingly appearing out of nowhere.

"Mushrooms," Nazya replied. "They found mushrooms yesterday."

"Cool."

"Cool?" Phil said.

Nazya smiled. "I'll make you a deal," she said.

"You're more than welcome to my firstborn. He's a little dim but strong. He'll make a good worker," Phil replied, and Nazya laughed.

"I will give you a syringe in return for half a dozen of your mushrooms."

"We're not going to be able to cook a lot with six mushrooms," Chloe said.

"I will explain in a minute," Nazya replied.

Chloe shrugged and disappeared as quickly as she had arrived.

"You're going to try to grow them too?"

"Try being the operative word. Maybe we can compare notes each time you come to Infinity."

"I'd like that."

"So, we have a deal?"

"You're sure I can't interest you in my firstborn instead?"

Nazya laughed. "I'm sure."

"Oh well, you can't blame a man for trying," he said, extending his hand. "Deal." They both shook.

"What's a deal?" Matt asked, walking up to them.

Phil placed his arm around the teenager's shoulder. "Nazya, this is my son, Matt."

"Your firstborn?" she asked with a wide grin on her face.

Matt's brow creased. "I'm his only son."

"I see. I'm pleased to meet you, Matt."

"So what's a deal?"

"I believe we have just completed the first trade between my settlement and yours," she replied, smiling at the teenager once again.

"Oh, okay. Have you seen Mum?"

"Err ... yes. A couple of minutes ago. She's back there somewhere," Phil said, pointing over his shoulder.

"I am happy it was your people who found the mushrooms."

"Why?"

"Because most would only think about eating them. This way, they may once again become a regular part of our diets. Not just us," Nazya said, gesturing around, "but us as a species." She looked out to the fields where lots of people were still working. "You are doing something impressive here. I see many people come to Infinity only thinking about the here and now, but you are thinking about and planning for the future."

"We're trying. You never really know what the future's going to hold though. Y'know, we could do with a good doctor. You'd be more than welcome to join us here."

Nazya smiled. "That is very kind, but I think I am not quite ready to give up some of the luxuries we still enjoy where I come from."

"I get that. If you ever change your mind, though, it's an open invitation."

"That is good to know. As you say, you never really know what the future is going to hold."

8

There was a bone-trembling whirring sound that echoed down the shaft causing all the occupants in the lift to jump to their feet. A few seconds later, the lights flickered on. It had been five and a half hours since they had gone off, and the safety system was designed to keep the lift shafts and staircases locked for eight, but there were workarounds for those who knew what they were doing.

"You got light?" asked Dwyer. "You got light in there? Over."

"Just come back on. Over," Revell replied.

"They have out here too. Can you get the lift moving again? Over."

"Let's hope. Over." Revell hit the button for Level Three, but nothing happened. He hit it again and again and again. "Shit."

"Move out of the way, you moron," PJ snapped, grabbing a small screwdriver from his pocket and beginning to remove the front of the control panel. "You opened the inner doors between floors. The safety override will have kicked in. This isn't going anywhere until we reset it."

"PJ's going to try to hack into the panel. Over."

"Roger that. Over."

PJ took the facia off and immediately slid a computer only slightly bigger than the Salvation-issued phones out of his satchel. He plugged it into one of the waiting sockets and began to type. His fingers blurred as he worked. There was a shrieking sound as the inner doors jolted from their unnaturally forced position and clunked shut. Three seconds passed and the lift descended the remaining few feet before juddering to a stop once more. The doors opened and the relief in the air was noticeable as they all saw Dwyer standing there with the radio in his hand. "Okay. Let's get the hell out of here," he said, starting to turn.

"Wait," PJ replied.

"Wait? What the hell are we waiting for? We're probably just a few minutes ahead of them if we're lucky."

"That's why I'm disabling the elevators completely, you moron."

"I swear to God, kid. You call me a moron again and you're going to be gargling your teeth." PJ looked up from his terminal briefly before continuing with his frantic typing. The lights suddenly went off in the lift compartment. "Shit, what's happening?"

"I'm happening," PJ replied with a self-satisfied smile before pulling the cable out and sliding the small computer back into his satchel. "Now we can go."

"What did you do?"

"In terms that you can understand, I disabled the lifts. It will take them hours to sort that out."

"There are still the staircases."

"I'm aware of that. That's why I've changed all the access combinations. That's as much as I can do unless you expect me to halt gravity."

"How you've lived this long is completely beyond me."

PJ just gave Dwyer a look. "Shall we save trading insults until later and just get to the hatch?" Addy said.

The eight men and women all began to sprint at the same time. Dwyer and Revell led the way, turning left, then right, then left down street after street in the giant labyrinthine underground city.

Even though the lights were on, the absence of people made the whole place seem creepy. They finally arrived at block seventy-one. Dwyer and Revell had barely broken a sweat, but the others all had fairly sedentary jobs that didn't require high levels of physical fitness and they were barely able to catch their breath by the time they reached the entrance.

"Come on," Dwyer said as PJ and three of the others slowed down to a walk on their approach to the building.

"I need a minute," one of the power plant techs said, bending over and resting her hands on her knees.

"You can have a minute in the tunnel."

She waved her hand. "You go. I'll catch up."

Dwyer marched across and pulled her upright. "What don't you understand about this? If they haven't figured out what's going on already, they're going to very soon, and then the entire Salvation guard is going to be down here hunting us—"

His words were cut off by the sound of an explosion. "Ohhh shit!" Revell hissed, taking hold of Addy's arm and forcing her through the door. "Everybody get down to the basement, now! We'll be right behind you."

"What was that?" PJ cried.

"My guess is somebody's figured out a way around you changing the codes."

"They've blown the doors open?"

The sound of shouts travelled through the streets towards them. "No more questions. Move!" Suddenly, PJ and the others got their second wind and charged through the door leaving Dwyer and Revell alone. "I thought we'd have more time than this," Dwyer said.

"Someone must have found Ludlow and the others. I was hoping, with everything that was going on, checking the prisoner holding cells would have been the last thing anybody did."

"What do you want to do?"

"We don't really have a choice. We run. We run as fast as we can and hope we can escape."

The shouts became louder and more numerous and both men slipped into the building and sprinted along the corridor. They ran down the stairs two at a time, jumping the last few and joining the others in the laundry room. A couple of people had already disappeared through the hatch and another was just making his way down as they arrived.

"Are we going to make it?" Addy asked.

"I hope so," Revell replied.

"You're not exactly giving me a lot of confidence."

One by one, the escapees entered the tunnel. "I need to go last," PJ said.

"What? Why?" asked Dwyer.

"I've got one last little spanner to throw in the works."

The sound of a door crashing against a wall upstairs made both men look to the ceiling. "Jesus!"

"Come on." The arrogance was gone from PJ's voice now, being replaced by pure fear. Dwyer disappeared through the hatch and the younger man followed. He shuffled down a few rungs of the step ladder and paused, looping his left arm around one of the horizontal bars and pulling out his screwdriver once more. With lightning speed, PJ removed the front panel of the keypad and slid the tiny computer from his satchel once more, hooking it up and immediately beginning to type, this time with just one hand while his other held the small terminal.

The sound of pounding feet as what sounded like a small army descended the stairs gripped all of them with terror. "Oh shit! Oh shit," one of the women cried, shining her phone light further down the tunnel.

"Go. All of you go," PJ said. "If this doesn't work, some of you might make it anyway."

There was the briefest of pauses before several men and women began to sprint into the darkness with only their phones to guide them.

"I hope you know what you're doing, PJ," Dwyer said.

"I know exactly what I'm doing, but by all means, try to undermine my confidence and make me feel more pressure than I already do. That really helps," he replied as the heavy hatch door slowly began to close. He continued to type frantically, and even in the fading light, Dwyer, Revell and Addy could see his left eye twitching repeatedly.

"You're doing great, PJ," Addy said.

The sound of the basement door bursting open travelled through the diminishing gap as the hatch continued to close. "Oh crap," Revell said under his breath as he and Dwyer both aimed their Q-Thirties upwards. The outline of a figure appeared above them and they both opened fire. The sound was deafening in the tunnel and the figure vanished from view as quickly as he had arrived.

"CLEAR!" came the shout as the hatch door lowered the final few centimetres. Revell and Dwyer looked at each other with confused expressions on their faces for a moment until the sound of something rolling across the floor above stopped and a black fist-sized object dropped through the gap.

Addy's phone light followed it. In that split second, they all realised what it was. *SHIT!*

Dwyer's hand reached out instinctively, taking the weight as it fell before turning and flinging it down the tunnel. The hatch lid closed with a loud metallic thump and the sound of the locks engaging filled the air as the grenade disappeared out of the arc of light cast by the phone.

"GET DOWN!" Dwyer yelled, hoping the ones who had already fled were out of danger but warning them just in case.

PJ whipped the lead from the control panel and jumped to the ground. *We're dead. We're dead. We're dead.*

The four of them dropped down, covering their heads, and a deafening explosion made the air around them quake. A searing heat followed, and each of them was convinced in that instance that they would be burned up then and there. The initial explosion diminished then another rumble began as the walls and ceiling of the tunnel around the point of ignition began to cave.

The quartet remained down on the ground with their hands still covering their heads as the frightening sounds reverberated around them. Their own collective silence was broken as, one by one, they started to cough as the cool atmosphere of the tunnel whirled into a hot, dusty cloud.

Addy angled her phone up, illuminating the dense, grey particle-filled air. Just the sight of it made them cough even louder. She climbed to her feet and the others followed, slowly edging towards the cave-in. The odd rock still fell, and the whole area felt like it might just crumble at any second, but they had no options.

"Shit," Dwyer said, holding the back of his hand up to his mouth and launching into another coughing fit as they saw the small mountain of rubble reach up to the ceiling of the tunnel.

"That's it. We're dead. We're dead," PJ cried hysterically before spluttering and coughing once more. "My lungs are burning."

"Here," Revell said, handing an administration-issued torch to Addy. "Keep this on us." The two guards carefully scaled the debris, continuing to cough and splutter as they went.

"There's a gap!" Dwyer called out. He immediately began to claw and dig at the slag that had collected around it, and, bit by bit, the gap got wider and deeper.

"Dwyer? Dwyer, is that you?" called a voice from the other side.

"Yeah. We're okay, but—" He descended into another coughing fit.

"Are you alright?"

"There's not much air in here."

"Hold on."

"Be careful. I don't know how secure this tunnel is. It could come down on all of us any second."

The man on the other side began coughing too. "No offence, mate, but you really need to work on your motivational technique." Dwyer let out a huff of a laugh before coughing again.

He and Revell worked on one side while the remaining escapees worked on the other. After ten minutes, there was a gap big enough to fit a body through. The man who had been talking took his phone light and shone it. "We'll pass you our rucksacks first; then we'll come through," Dwyer said.

PJ and Addy passed their backpacks up to the two guards who shoved them through the narrow aperture. It was about fifty centimetres wide, a little less than that in height and just over a metre in length, but with the knowledge that there could be another cave-in at any minute, the short shuffle to freedom tied knots in all of their stomachs.

"You first, Addy," Dwyer said, stretching out his hand and helping her up the hill of rubble."

"I don't want any preferential treatment because I'm a woman."

"You're not getting any. If this thing collapses, you won't turn into a panicky little pissant like PJ, so we want you to go first." They all laughed, even PJ, before the laughter degenerated into coughing once again.

"Okay," she said, stretching out her arms and reaching into the narrow gap. Two hands grabbed hers from the opposite side, and she felt Dwyer and Revell gripping her belt securely, pushing her through, willing her to freedom. She could feel the debris shift around her as she moved. Up until this moment, she had never considered herself claustrophobic. Even when they were stuck all that time in the lift she had not flinched, but now, as the possibility of an even bigger cave-in awaited them, her palms began to sweat.

Centimetre by centimetre, she shuffled and was dragged to the other side. The cold glow of LED lights beckoned her as she wriggled through like some slow-moving worm. Addy's head finally popped out of the other end, where she began to cough once more. The air was a little less polluted by the dust from the cave-in there, but it was by no means clean. She slid down the heaped debris, arms first, before two strong hands grabbed her and helped her onto her feet and firm ground.

PJ was next and, despite several fearful pleas for people not to let go of him, he made it to the other side in much the same way. The two soldiers were the last to head through the gap, and once everyone had made it, the entire group turned and shone whatever lights they were carrying in the direction of the rubble mountain.

"Jesus," PJ said.

"Yeah," Addy replied.

"Okay," Dwyer said, clapping his hands. "We've got a long way to go before we rest. Let's get out of this tomb."

One by one, the lights turned in the opposite direction illuminating the otherwise black tunnel that stretched out in front of them.

"Amen to that," Revell replied as he and his friend began the march to freedom.

*

Debbie, Susan and Nicola all gathered around one of the stone ovens as the wire grills were brought out. Jason and his team had built these ovens. They were simple but effective and designed to cook in bulk.

Others were still working, getting on with the various duties they had been given, but soon, the whole settlement would begin to wind down. It had been another hard but productive day. It would not be too long until dinner, and that would herald the beginning of the rest period before the next day when it would all start again.

The three women looked at the shrivelled green-brown strips spread over the metal racks. "I can't say they look that appetising," Nicola said.

"Are you sure Phil got this right? It was definitely this type of seaweed?" Susan asked.

"That's what he said," Debbie replied, looking as unconvinced as the other women. "I suppose the proof is in the testing."

"He's your husband. You test it."

"Who'll look after Matt if I die?"

"We all will. That's what a community does. He can stay one night with us, one night with Nicola, one night with Lanying and so on."

"I suppose it's best to try this while we've still got a doctor here."

"That's the spirit."

"Okay. Here goes nothing." Debbie picked up one of the strips and examined it for a moment, turning it from side to side. Without realising, her nose had curled up some seconds before.

"Are you going to eat it or what?" Nicola asked.

"Look, it's one thing when seaweed's in a stew and it looks like a piece of spinach. It's another when you've actually got to ... y'know ... look at it and taste it." She turned to Susan. "This is the right one, isn't it? He did say it was this one?"

"I'm the one who asked you that."

"I know, but...." She let out a long breath. "Okay." She closed her eyes, opened her mouth and took a small bite. The other two women heard the light crunching sound as Debbie's teeth bit into the strip of sugar kelp. She closed her mouth and slowly began to chew. With each rotation of her jaw, the crunch dissipated a little further until she finally swallowed.

"Well?" Nicola said as she and Susan looked towards the other woman in almost fevered anticipation.

Debbie opened her eyes. "Holy crap!"

"What? What is it?"

"That tasted so good," she replied.

"Now I know you're taking the piss."

"No. Seriously." She took another bite, and this time, a smile decorated her face as she chewed.

The other two women looked at each other before they each grabbed a strip too. They eyed them suspiciously for a moment before tearing a corner and placing it in their mouths.

"Holy crap," Susan said, nearly laughing in delight as she ate. Nicola's face lit up too.

"I don't need anything else. I can just live on this from now on," Debbie said, finishing off the rest of her piece. "It tastes like junk food."

"Okay, tomorrow we need to hit every rock pool on this stretch of coastline," Susan said, and the other women laughed. "I'm not joking."

"Actually," Debbie said, "it's not a bad idea. Phil said that when this stuff is cooked, it'll last for ages."

Everyone else was completely oblivious to what they were doing, still getting on with their allotted tasks, and the trio guiltily grabbed another of the crispy snacks from one of the baking trays, immediately taking big bites. "This is divine," Susan said, letting out a long, satisfied breath as she ate.

"What's divine?"

"Agh!" All three women jumped as they turned to see Callie and Dani standing there.

"Don't you know it's dangerous to sneak up on people like that?" Debbie said.

"What's that? What are you eating?" Callie asked.

"Err ... just something we were road testing before we unleashed it on everyone."

"Can I try?" Dani asked.

"I doubt if you'd like it," Nicola replied.

Dani and Callie both picked one of the dehydrated strips up and gave them a sniff. Their noses curled as

Debbie's had done at first before they tentatively took bites. Smiles crept onto both of their faces as the texture and taste tantalised their senses.

"What is this?" Callie asked.

"Sugar kelp," Susan replied.

"We need to find as much of this stuff as we can."

"Way ahead of you, kiddo."

They all laughed apart from Debbie, who had stopped eating and was staring into the distance with a perplexed frown engrained on her face. The others turned too, and now the wonderful new culinary discovery was the last thing on any of their minds as they watched first a handful, then dozens, then seemingly countless figures appear over the brow of the hill that led down to their settlement.

"Oh ... my ... God!" Dani said.

"WEAPONS!" Susan shouted at the top of her voice. "EVERYBODY GRAB A WEAPON."

Suddenly, the whole camp saw what they had seen and panic seemed to become a living, breathing thing as everyone scrambled to hide children in the buildings and lay their hands on guns, spears or whatever they could to face the massive advancing army.

Everything was starting to come together. Callie's single thought was drowned in sadness. Life hadn't been easy since leaving the bunker, but they had taken small victories where they could. Despite the tragic events that had befallen Harry and subsequently the rest of the camp, they had found Infinity as a result and thus a whole world of new possibilities, but now this.

From this distance, no one could tell who these people were. Frightened words travelled around the settlement like rustling leaves in the wind. Ferals, cannibals, administration were just three that sent even greater waves of apprehension through the ragtag band of survivors.

Before Dani had found something to fight with, Zep was by her side, armed and ready to protect her come what may. She reached out and squeezed his hand while others awaited instructions from John or Jason or whoever would take the decision-making out of their hands.

"Find cover where you can and don't open fire until we know what we're dealing with," John shouted out, pushing his glasses up his nose. It was clear to everyone that he was a universe away from his comfort zone, but in the absence of anyone else taking charge, he felt compelled to say something.

Everybody paused. The realisation that they were all looking at him was suddenly jarring. He was their unelected leader, an intelligent, kind and caring man, but he wasn't someone people would follow into battle. In the absence of an alternative, though, they eventually broke rank and went to find sheltered positions.

"Stay with me, you two," Susan ordered as Callie and Si stood by her side.

"Yeah, and you two stick with me," Nicola said less convincingly as Zep and Dani remained glued to each other's side.

Callie searched out the frightened faces to see Phil, Debbie, Matt, Wei, Lanying and Jiang. They were all together. The two men held rifles, but neither looked like they had any idea how to use them or indeed possessed the want to use them. Her eyes moved back to the approaching army, which was now clearly in the hundreds.

"There's something not right. If they meant us harm, they wouldn't just march over the ridge. They'd spread out ... they'd charge or something."

"They're probably just thinking that we'll all put our hands up without a shot being fired."

"I don't know, Mum. Something's not right."

*

"We need to stop," Greenslade said.

"We're nearly there," Drake replied.

"Well ... yeah. I brought you here. I can see that. But we need to stop. They don't know that it's us. If you're willing to risk a fire fight breaking out and people losing their lives without reason, by all means, carry on."

"They'd be massacred. No one's going to start a fight with us."

"I know these people. I know that some of them will never give up while there's a breath left in their bodies, no matter how hopeless it seems."

Drake brought his hand up and the massive procession gradually slowed to a stop. "So, what then?"

*

"They're getting ready to charge." An alarmed cry came from someone at the far end of the farmyard.

Other frantic shouts flitted around and the sound of children's screams could now be heard from within the house and the barn.

Callie shook her head. "No. This is something else."

At least a dozen people remained in the centre of the farmyard, just watching. They had not run off vying for a good vantage point when John had given the order. They had been joined by Chloe and Nazya now as they all stood staring at the vast horde. Holy cow!" Chloe said, her eyes widening to the size of golf balls.

"Err ... you guys might want to get back into the infirmary. The walls are thick. If you stay down, you should be okay," John said as his face suddenly turned a shade paler.

"I'm telling you," Callie replied. "Something isn't right here."

"No offence, Sis," Si began, "but I think it's what it looks like. I think they're about to charge."

*

"Let me get this straight. You two are going to head over there and explain everything to them and I'm meant to trust you?" Drake asked as Marina and some of the other soldiers gathered at the front of the massive convoy.

"That's exactly what I'm saying you should do."

"Why?"

"Look. I had you pegged as someone who was reasonably bright, but the longer you talk the more I think that initial assessment was wrong. What the hell do you think I'm going to do? You think we've got another three thousand armed people hidden away that we can just summon up to make a fight of this? Our families are down there, Drake, and I'd prefer it if this didn't turn into more of a shit show than it's already going to be."

"They've got a point, Drake," Marina said, casting her eyes towards the settlement.

Drake looked back at the vast line of people following him then turned to Greenslade and Trunk once more. "Okay."

*

"I'm guessing that's them coming to negotiate our surrender," Phil said as he, Wei and the others walked up to join the small group who remained in the centre of the farmyard. "What's the plan?"

"Err … it's not like we can realistically put up a defence against that many people, is it?" John replied as he squinted towards the two approaching figures as they slowly made their way down the road to the settlement.

"So we lay down our guns," Phil said grimly.

"Or go out in a blaze of glory," Zep replied.

"Either way, we're screwed," Nicola said. "If it's the Ferals, we know what's going to happen to us. If it's the administration, they're probably going to take us back to the—"

"It's not either of those things," Callie said. "The Ferals tend to be smaller groups, and even if they all banded together, I doubt there'd be that many. And the administration … there are hundreds … thousands maybe. The Salvation guards don't have those kinds of numbers either." The entire procession had come to a standstill. The line disappeared over the brow of the hill, so there was still no way of seeing just how many people there were.

"So who are they then?" Debbie asked.

"There's only one way to find out, isn't there?" Callie said, laying her rifle on the ground.

"What are you doing?" John asked.

"Going to see what they want."

"No, you are not," Susan said, taking hold of Callie's arm before she could leave.

"Mum. Think about it. They're coming, whoever they are. Fighting isn't going to save us. Talking is all we can do."

"She's got a point," John said reluctantly.

Susan let go of her daughter and placed her own rifle on the ground too. "Well, you're not going alone." She looked towards John. "I think, as our leader, you should come too."

John looked uncomfortable as he nodded. "Yeah. I suppose I should."

Si's shoulders drooped. "I don't understand how you always end up at the centre of all this stuff," he said, looking at Callie and placing his Q-Thirty down on the ground as well. "It's like you're a magnet for trouble."

"Err ... is it just me or does the one on the left remind you of someone?" No sooner had the words left Dani's mouth than a shout rose from the other side of the barn.

"It's Dad. It's Dad!" Before anybody had time to react, Stef, Trunk's daughter, had broken into a run and was heading over the scrub-grass-covered field towards them. Lydia wasn't far behind and, putting two and two together, Grace and Theo joined them.

Callie and the others watched for a moment. "I thought you said they were dead," John said as everyone's eyes fixed on the two figures.

"We heard gunfire," Susan replied. "I don't understand how they could have survived."

"I suppose we'd better go find out, don't you?" He, Susan, Callie and Si all set off at a more sedate pace and in a state of complete bafflement.

*

Trunk sniffed loudly and Greenslade looked across towards him. In all the time he had known the man, he had never seen him emotional, but now tears ran down his friend's face as he saw his wife and daughter running to him.

Behind them were Grace and Theo and a breath caught in Greenslade's throat. Suddenly, stinging tears filled his eyes too. He reached up to wipe them away before anyone saw, and as hard as he tried to quash his own feelings, he couldn't deny how happy he was to be back home with his family. Both men sped up a little, changing direction and heading across the fields instead of along the road. Within ninety seconds, they were in the warm embrace of their families' arms, and now hiding tears was the last thing on any of their minds. No one said a word; instead, they just held and kissed one another.

Finally, Lydia spoke between quivering breaths. "We thought you were dead."

"We very nearly were."

"What's happening? Who are all these people?"

"That's a longer story," Greenslade said, hugging Grace and Theo again. For the first time since taking hold of them, he looked up to see Callie, Susan, Si and John walking in their direction. He wiped his eyes once more, kissed Grace then Theo on the head and started towards the advancing quartet. Trunk remained with his family, unwilling to let them go for even a moment in fear that this was part of some dream that would end if he did.

John extended his hand as he approached and Greenslade, although surprised, took it, shaking it firmly. "How's Harry?" he asked.

"Doing well," John replied.

"Good." He turned to Si, who nodded respectfully. Greenslade reciprocated the gesture. There was a part of him that wanted to say that Sasha was okay, that she was with them, but he pushed that particular ace a little further up his sleeve for later.

"I see you made it back then," he said, smiling and looking at Susan and Callie.

"I never thought I'd say this, but I'm happy to see you," Susan said.

"Well ... that goes for me too."

He and Callie looked at each other for a moment. "So, what's going on?" she finally asked, nodding towards the massive horde.

"We kind of mounted a jailbreak."

"That must have been a pretty big jail."

Greenslade felt a presence and looked to see Grace standing there with Theo right by her. "There's no easy way to say this, but we agreed to help these people escape."

"Who are they?"

"They're the ones the administration recaptured along with some Salvation guards and some others from Level Two."

"Salvation guards? You brought Salvation guards here?" Susan asked, horrified.

"It's complicated."

"Well, it must be."

"Look. The guy who's running things is called Drake. Why don't we get him down here and we can have a proper talk back at the farm?"

"A proper talk about what?"

"I don't understand what there is to discuss," John said. "We don't have the resources to help this many people. They're going to have to find a place of their own. It's madness to think anything else."

"Look, let's just get together with Drake, yes?"

"What have you done, Greenslade? What the hell have you promised?"

"I promised I'd help them."

"And did you think for a second what that meant for the rest of us?"

"So, I should have just turned my back on all those people?"

"Would it have been so hard? I mean that's all you did when we were all stuck in Salvation."

Suddenly, the friendliness and the hopes of a happy and warm homecoming were gone, replaced by the bitter reality of what lay ahead. "Look," Callie said, "however we ended up here, we're here now, so let's talk and figure everything out from there."

John shook his head and cast his eyes once more to the massive procession still waiting to descend upon them. "It's all over." He turned and began to head back to the farm once more. "It's all over," he said again to himself more than anyone else.

Susan and Si followed him. The dark clouds of doom that had gathered with the prospect of doing battle with this massive army somehow seemed darker still, knowing that the weight of saving them would lead to a longer drawn-out death for them all.

"Nice to see that I haven't lost my knack for making people regret knowing me."

"You shouldn't put yourself down. I doubt that you'll ever lose the knack for that," Callie said with a straight face.

"Thanks. I knew I could rely on you to bolster my ego. Well, I suppose I'd better go and get Drake and the others." His face was grim as the impossibility of the task ahead finally bore down on him with its full weight. He, Grace and Theo all turned to leave.

"Blake," Callie said, causing him turn back.

"This was the right thing to do."

Greenslade let out a short sharp laugh and glanced towards the massive procession before looking at Callie once more. "It felt like it at the time, but now I feel like a bloody fool for ever thinking we could make this work."

"We'll make this work. We have to find a way to make this work; otherwise, what was the point of us ever escaping Salvation in the first place?"

He gestured towards the farm. "There are something like three and a half thousand people in the crowd. Where the hell are they going to live? What are they going to eat?" He shook his head again and Grace grabbed hold of his arm lovingly.

"We'll figure something out."

"We'll see." He turned and the trio started walking away once more.

"Blake," Callie said, and he turned again.

"I'm glad you're safe. I'm glad you're back with us. This place is better for having you around," and this time, it was Callie who turned.

Greenslade watched her as she headed back to the farmyard, and now there was a tiny part of him that wondered if the task ahead was as impossible as it seemed.

9

Drake looked long and hard at Greenslade, Trunk and their families. "So you're saying that after a full day of travelling, everybody should just wait here until we send a delegation in there and hash all this out?"

"Maybe it would be a good time to rest and eat and have—"

"This is bullshit. These people need to know what's going on."

"That's the point of this. We need to meet and work out the logistics."

"The logistics? The logistics are that there are a hell of a lot more of us than there are of them."

"Drake!" Marina said. "That kind of talk doesn't help anybody. We have to find a way to make this work and we have to find a way for everyone to co-operate."

Drake turned back to Greenslade. "And who should be in this delegation exactly?"

"Well, I suggest her," he said, pointing to Marina. "The doctor." He pointed to Rachael. "You, for your people skills, and Sasha."

"Sasha? Who the hell's Sasha?"

"She's the girlfriend of one of the people we need to convince that all this can work out hunky dory."

Drake let out a long, tired breath, and now there was a big part of him that wondered what he'd gotten himself and his family into. "Okay. Let's do this."

*

People lined up with their bowls for their evening meals outside with no fervour, no pleasant anticipation. A hard day's work had come to an end, but what loomed over them could drown out any prospect of future happiness.

Inside the farmhouse, John, Susan, Jason, Tania, Harper and Si waited for the arrival of the others. "By any chance has anybody seen Phil in the last few minutes?" John asked.

"Callie's gone to look for him," Si replied.

"I wouldn't have thought he'd want to miss this under any circumstances. Where's Debbie?"

"Not seen her either," Susan said.

"That's a little concerning."

"On the upside, we made sugar kelp crisps today, and they were delicious, so there's that."

"Uh-huh. And is there any way we can feed the five thousand with those?"

"In fairness, I think Greenslade said that there were only about three and a half thousand."

"My mistake."

"And no, to answer your question. Probably not."

"Well, it's pointless having a sit-down or a meeting or whatever you want to call it without Phil here. Everything depends on him."

"Maybe he's just psyching himself up," Tania said.

"Yeah. I'm sure that's it."

*

Phil was sitting down with his legs crossed and his eyes closed when Callie finally found him in the forest. His back was pressed against what had once been a magnificent oak tree but was now just a charred impersonator of its former self.

"Everybody's waiting for you," Callie said as she sat too, leaning her back against a neighbouring tree.

"Uh-huh."

"I knew you'd be here." She looked across to the sapling they had discovered a few weeks before. It still seemed a little like a miracle that something so green and full of life and hope could sprout up in the middle of a charcoal forest.

"I came here for peace and quiet." There was none of the usual good humour in his tone or on his face.

"It wasn't like Greenslade could just leave all those people, especially after what happened, after the massacre." Phil didn't respond. "I mean ... what would you have done in that position?"

Finally, he turned towards Callie, and to her shock, she could see that he'd been crying. "Me? If it was me? In all honesty, I'd have chosen to live. I'd have chosen not to condemn my friends and family to a drawn out death. I'd have chosen not to commit suicide."

"It's not like we weren't facing something much more daunting than this a few weeks back, is it? Over eighteen thousand of us escaped from Salvation remember. We were going to set up a community and you were up to the challenge then."

"It's as simple as that to you, isn't it?"

"Well, yes. What's changed since then and now?"

"A lot. A lot's changed, Callie. We've learnt just how few resources there are out here. We've learnt just how hard life is. We've learnt what lengths we have to go to if just one of us gets injured and needs help. We've learnt that it's not just the lack of food and the environment that we've got to contend with, that there are other people out there who wish us harm." Phil shook his head disbelievingly and fresh tears rolled down his cheeks. "Even after everything, even after nearly going extinct, we're still at war with one another.

Like an asteroid nearly wiping us out wasn't enough of a wake-up call."

"But—"

"No. There are no buts, Callie. There's a manufacturing fault with humankind. It goes back to the very first one that came off the production line, and it's never been fixed."

"I've never heard you speak like this."

"Maybe…. Maybe before we put the seeds in the ground, we could have searched around for a better spot, for somewhere more sustainable. When the others showed up yesterday, I managed to keep all my shit together. By bringing plans forward for the irrigation system and mapping out the clearance and preparation of more fields, we still had a viable future. It would be hard, but it would have been possible. But let me tell you, there is a universe of difference between another hundred people showing up on your doorstep and another three and a half thousand."

"Phil. Please. You need to get out of this headspace. You are the one person who can—"

"Who can what, Callie?" He shook his head again. "You're all just like the administration."

"What?"

"You think I'm this miracle worker that can come out and clap his hands and make all your worries about food disappear. I'm nothing to anyone except a goose that keeps laying golden eggs. Well, guess what; the goose has run dry."

"You can't give up now. Not when people need you the most."

"No. This is exactly the time to give up." Phil wiped his eyes and stared at the sapling once more.

"Well, what's the answer then? What do we do?"

"We don't do anything. I can head south with Debs and Matt in the hope we can live off the land and find enough viable crops to plant, to build our own smallholding."

"That sounds like a lonely life."

"Yes, but it's a life, though, isn't it?"

"And what about Matt? You just want him to exist with no friends, no future?"

"It's better than watching him suffer and starve to death here, isn't it?"

"This could be an opportunity, y'know. This doesn't have to be the end of everything, but it seems like you've got it into your skull that it is, so I don't know why I'm sitting here wasting my time talking to you."

"Hallelujah." Phil raised both his hands into the air. "Praise Jesus, she finally understands."

"I expected more from you, Phil. I thought we were a lot alike."

"In some ways, we are, Callie, but you've got this big up with people flaw running right through you, and that's the difference between you and me. I'm a realist."

Callie climbed to her feet and dusted herself off. "I'm a realist, Phil. When I went charging down into that quarry, I knew there was probably a good chance I'd die, but my brother's life was at stake, and I'd do anything for the people I love. When those guards were coming after us in that tunnel, I was pretty certain we were finished again, but Greenslade and Trunk saved us."

Phil shrugged. "And? What's your point?"

"If I'd have given up back then ... if we'd have given up, it would have been a very different story. Giving up before you even try always leads to nothing. But fighting? When you fight, sometimes the unexpected happens. The improbable happens. The impossible happens. You want to take Matt and Debbie and get out of here, fine. But I'm not giving up. I'll never give up. Like I said, we could turn this into an opportunity. I'm just sad you don't have the vision I thought you had." She turned and started walking towards the farm. "And FYI, you were wrong, by the way."

"Wrong about what?"

"I didn't ever see you as a miracle worker or a golden goose, but I did think you were my friend. I thought we'd always be friends." Without another word or another look, she carried on out of the woodland.

*

Sasha had tried to contain herself, but in the end, she had bolted towards the encampment while Greenslade, Drake and the others were still talking. It was almost like a sixth sense had driven her to Si. Half-recognised and half-remembered faces looked in her direction as she entered the settlement, and then there he was.

He had emerged from one of the buildings and just stood there like a statue looking back at her. Without realising it, she had stopped moving, and she was just standing there too until both of them launched into a run towards each other.

When they met, Si lifted Sasha into the air and twirled her around. They kissed and they cried and their salty tears mingled. Nothing else mattered at that moment. The hardships of what was to come and the pain that Si had lived through when he had searched that Godforsaken graveyard looking for her were all but forgotten now.

"I thought I was never going to see you again," he said, beginning to sob.

"You and me both." They continued to hold each other tightly. It was difficult for others not to watch; after all, it was happening in the middle of the farmyard while people were waiting in line to be fed. But with all the uncertainty that lay ahead, the sight did raise spirits. These were their people, and, yes, Preacher had somehow managed to hoodwink them into believing he knew best, but how many times had charismatic zealots done that in the past? They had all started off in the same place.

"We're together again now. That's all that really matters." They finally broke their embrace and Si took Sasha's hand.

"Greenslade said you came looking for me."

Si nodded. "I'm so glad I didn't find you."

"What?"

"Back there in the woodland near the mine. I'll never get those images out of my head. I turned over body after body convinced that it was you but praying each time that I was wrong, and, thankfully, I was."

"There hasn't been a day when I haven't thought about you."

"Ditto." He squeezed her hand a little tighter. "Your parents. Are they okay?"

"Yeah. But things have been hard. As soon as I arrived back with them, I knew I'd made a huge mistake. I just wanted to be with you. I only felt safe with you."

Si smiled broadly. "We're together now. Everything else was just leading up to this. We're together now," he said again.

For the first time, Sasha looked around her. She looked from the farmhouse to the barn to the other small house and the mountains of stones and reeds that had been gathered. "I was so excited to see you again, so grateful to be out of that place once more, that I didn't actually think about the practicalities of how this was going to work. How is it going to work, Si?"

On cue, Greenslade, Trunk, and their families as well as Drake, Rachael and Marina entered the farmyard. "I'm guessing that's what we're all about to find out."

*

Brief introductions were given as the newcomers entered the farmhouse. Greenslade joined the others for the meeting, but Trunk remained with his family.

"Is this everyone?" he asked, a little surprised at the assembly.

"We're still waiting for Callie and Phil," Susan said.

Drake knew only too well who Phil was. Everybody worth their salt in Salvation knew who Phil was. "Who's Callie?" he asked.

It still seemed strange for Susan, John, and the others to be standing opposite administration guards. Greenslade had briefly explained what had happened back in Salvation, but there was a natural air of mistrust lingering. These people had put the Level Three inhabitants through trials barely to be believed, and it was hard not to hold grudges, but for the sake of the three thousand or so Level Three escapees and their own future, they buried their animosity for the time being.

"Callie's my daughter," Susan said.

Drake shrugged. "And why are we waiting for her exactly?"

"Because none of this would exist without her. Nobody would have got out of Salvation. This place would never have been founded. If it wasn't for that girl, we wouldn't be talking right now."

Drake looked taken aback by the voracity of Greenslade's words, as were the rest of the small congregation. It was rare for him to speak at length about anyone, but praise rarely left his lips. Suddenly, he went up a notch in Susan's estimation.

"She sounds like she's worth waiting for then," Rachael replied with a smile, desperate to diffuse the obvious simmering tension.

"This place is smaller than I envisioned," Drake said, casting his eyes out to the fields through the unshuttered window.

"It was big enough yesterday," Harper said, fixing him with a stare. She had more of a grudge to hold than most. She still remembered that night at the Pig and Whistle like it was yesterday. Just the thought of it sent goose bumps running up and down her arms as the true brutality of the administration was unleashed on her, Jiang and others in just a few minutes of unbridled violence.

"There's a boy here who lost his leg?" Rachael asked, looking at anyone but Harper, desperate to change the subject once more.

"There's a doctor with him now," John replied.

"A doctor?" Drake replied. "Who?"

"No one you know."

"I don't understand."

"I dare say there's a lot you don't, won't and can't understand," Harper said.

"This is going well," Drake said, looking at Greenslade.

"I said I'd get you here. I can't make them like you."

"Shame. I'm a likeable guy when you get to know me."

"Yeah. I remember how much I was thinking that when you put ten thousand volts into Trunk and me."

"We're back to this again?"

"This isn't doing anybody any good," Marina interrupted. "What's in the past is in the past. Let's leave it there."

"That's easy for you to say," Harper replied. "Were you there that night? Were you there when they raided the pub and beat my friends? Were you one of the ones who bludgeoned a sixteen-year-old boy until he was barely recognisable?"

"Harper!" Everyone turned to see Callie standing at the entrance. "Whatever happened back then was unforgivable. The fact that these people are here now puts them in just as much crap as the rest of us, more even. If we were recaptured by the administration, they'd put us back to work. They'd probably kill them and their families just to make sure that the other guards didn't step out of line. Nobody's expecting anyone to forgive and forget. Trust is something that's built over time, but I think the risk they've taken proves that they're willing to make those first steps, don't you?"

Silence shrouded them for a moment and even though Harper did not reply, the tension eased. "Glad you could make it," Greenslade said.

Callie looked a little less sure of herself as she walked up to join them. She'd mediated a small conflict in what she was sure would be a long line of such battles, but the biggest problem still lay ahead. Without Phil, their long-term strategy was virtually non-existent—small patches of flesh on the skeleton of a giant.

"Where's Phil?" John asked.

Callie flushed red as she felt all eyes upon her. "Err ... he—"

"He can't get a minute's peace to think no matter how hard he tries," Phil said, appearing at the entrance to the largest of the cubicles in the house.

It was as if a massive weight had been lifted from Callie's shoulders. She felt almost euphoric and a wide grin lit up her face. "I'm sorry to get in the way of your valuable you time, Phil, but we've got a bit of a situation here," John replied.

"Yeah. I guessed you'd be panicking by now. I thought I'd better head over here and bring my own inimitable blend of reason and serenity to the decision-making process."

"Reason and serenity?" Callie asked with a smirk.

"Sorry, do you need definitions? I forgot not everyone has the same grasp of the language that I do."

"No. I'm good, thanks."

"Excellent. Shall we proceed then?"

The others all turned to look at John, but Callie couldn't take her eyes off Phil. She could see the worry behind the façade he'd put up for the others. She could see the fear in his eyes. She reached out and squeezed his arm for the briefest moment before turning to John too.

John scratched the back of his neck and pushed his glasses up his nose. "Well, everybody's looking at me, but I don't have a bloody clue where to start. I suppose we need to discuss the short term and the long term."

"Before that," Tania said, "I think we should figure out what we're dealing with exactly."

"I don't understand."

She turned to the three newcomers. "Are all these people free to come and go as they please or are you guys like a watered-down version of the administration?"

"Now look—"

"It's a fair question," Marina said, interrupting Drake. "I suppose we're better starting this discussion so you know exactly what we're bringing to the table."

"Actually," John said, "That would be useful."

"Over to you, Drake," Marina replied.

"Okay. Well, we've brought just over three thousand Level Three inhabitants with us. There are seventy-eight Salvation guards plus their families. We've brought about another three hundred or so Level Two inhabitants ranging from farm, powerplant and tech specialists to doctors, dentists and everything in between. We siphoned off weapons, ammunition, food, seeds and medical supplies. We've probably got in excess of two weeks' worth of food for every man, woman and child out there without rationing. We've brought tools and trolleys, which, by the way, is no mean feat when you look at how the roads have completely disintegrated in places. We brought whatever we could to help … to help build what we need to."

"Two weeks' worth of food?" Phil said.

"Without rationing."

"And seeds?"

"Bags of them."

"What kind of seeds?"

"You choose."

Phil let out a long sigh. "You do realise it takes time for seeds to grow, don't you? You don't just put them in the ground and pick the produce the next day."

"It's a good job you're here; I'd have been scratching my head without that little nugget of advice."

"I don't suppose you've brought any prefabricated housing with you, have you?" Jason asked. "'Cause we were struggling before. Now I really just…." He ran his fingers through his hair. "I really don't know how we can…." Jason had only just managed to wrap his head around providing accommodation for the refugees who had arrived the previous day, but this was something else. "I don't know how you can possibly think that we can do this. You can't just spring three and a half thousand people on us and expect us to carry on."

"I knew none of this was going to be easy," Drake said. "But—"

"Man, you've got some talent for understatement."

Sensing the rising tension once more, Marina took over. "I think what Drake's trying to say is that everybody is prepared to work for this."

"You reckon, do you?" Jason said. "'Cause it was only a few weeks ago that these bastards high-tailed it back to the mine looking for an easier option. You really think that they're all going to work for the greater good?"

Marina's shoulders sagged. "I'm sure after what they've been through they'd do anything to avoid going through it again."

"Well, kumbaya. Preach, sister. You've obviously got the pulse of everything that's going on here. I'm sure you and your jackbooted friends can whip them all into shape."

"This is getting us nowhere," Drake said.

"No, actually, it's helping me a lot," Jason replied. He turned to John then to Phil. "This idea of ours ... what we hoped this would be. It's over. If we even think about going along with this madness, we're as good as dead. It will be a slow, drawn-out death for us, and when it comes down to fighting over the last scraps of food, I'll let you guess who'll have the upper hand."

Drake rubbed his hands over his face. "Look. I've had just about enough of this shit. It's been a long, long day, and I'm—"

"That's enough. THAT'S ENOUGH!" All eyes turned to Callie as her raised voice even made the muted conversations that were drifting in from outside stop.

"Callie. Calm down, sweetheart," Susan said.

"No! I won't." She turned to look at Phil. "You're right. There is a manufacturing fault, but we can put it right if we work together."

"What are you talking about?" Susan replied.

"Listen to me. We can either let this snowball out of hand and pit ourselves against the guards, against the people who left with Preacher, against the people who we think had it easy on Level Two or we can forget about all that and start thinking about solutions and about working together."

"It's that simple to you?" Jason said.

"Yeah. It really is. Remember in the Pig and Whistle, Jason, when we were talking about helping people, when we were talking about doing positive things to counteract all the negative stuff that came down from the administration? Well, even though we're out of that place now, it's still going on. They kept Levels One, Two and Three separate for a reason. They kept the people separate and they made sure everyone knew there was a hierarchy. They created divisions. And right through history, that's how governments have taken attention away from all the treacherous stuff they've done to screw people over. They pitted us against one another and the threat of hardship for our families if people fell out of line loomed over all of us like the Sword of Damocles."

"The what?"

"Never mind. The point is you're still thinking the way they want you to think."

"In fairness, Callie, Jason has a point. You've seen what the Salvation guards can do ... have done," John said.

"Yeah, I have. And what I'm saying is that we have to draw a line; otherwise, we'll never be able to move on."

Harper stared at Callie for a moment. "That's a big ask for everyone who's suffered at their hands."

"I know. It's a huge ask. And building relationships is going to be hard, and it's going to take a long time and not everybody is going to get on with everybody else, but we're all here now and we need to figure this out or we're going to tear ourselves apart."

It was Tania who spoke up next. "Say we do that, Callie. What then? We're still in this mad, impossible situation. How are we going to feed people and house people?"

Suddenly, Callie felt like she was at war on all fronts. *I thought at least you'd be on my side.* "Well ... we—"

"There are two ways to look at this," Phil began and all heads turned towards him. "We can either see it as a disaster of monumental proportions or an opportunity that could give us what we need to bring all our plans forward."

"Plans?" Drake asked, a little confused. "Like what?"

"For a start, the building of an irrigation system and the preparation of more fields." He turned to Jason. "With this many people, we could gather massive amounts of materials to build more houses and I can't believe for a second that there aren't more than a few skilled labourers among those three thousand people. We can have dozens of scavenging teams and salvage teams. With this many people, we'll be able to send delegations to Infinity every day to trade."

"Infinity?" Rachael asked. "What are you talking about?"

"The Infinity stadium in Crowesbury," Callie said, taking over once more. "It's a huge marketplace for survivors."

"Survivors? What survivors?"

"There were other bunkers. The old-fashioned type. There's a network of them and they all congregate at the stadium to trade."

"Salvaging? You said salvaging?" Drake asked.

"Apparently, they have salvaging teams at Infinity who have gutted buildings and collected all types of materials. They have the busiest stalls there, according to Callie," Phil said.

"That's right. There are the remains of houses and all sorts just in this general area that we haven't had the time or the tools to explore. We could get teams of salvagers working, and the stuff we don't use for our own building projects we can trade."

"Exactly," Phil said. "This many people at our disposal means we have a real chance of developing this settlement into something substantive and something sustainable."

Jason let out a short laugh and scratched his head while shaking it at the same time. "You still haven't explained how we're going to house everyone, how we're going to feed everyone in the interim."

"We don't send out two foraging teams tomorrow; we send out thirty or forty or fifty. We go further afield while more teams still prepare the fields for planting. We sow the fast-growing, high-yield crops first, like spinach and kale, broccoli, peas and so on. We get those in the ground fast while we prepare the other fields."

He turned to Drake. "All the food you brought with you. Collect it, inventory it. We have communal meals here that we've been stretching out with what we've foraged. They're not the tastiest dishes, but they're balanced, and nobody goes hungry. We'll use the food you brought, we'll use what we've still got left, and we'll use what we forage to last us until the crops start coming in. The first few months are going to be hard, and there are going to be times when we all want to throw in the towel, but I know that, if we work together, we can do this."

"You're serious, Phil?" Tania said. "You really think we can do this?"

He looked towards Callie then turned to Tania once more. "Yes. I do."

10

After Phil's short speech, the meeting took on a far more positive tone. Susan and Callie talked about Infinity. They talked about the Ferals and Callie went on to discuss what had happened that morning to her and Dani.

Phil explained in more detail what an irrigation system would mean for the settlement and Jason spoke about his building plans. Drake did most of the talking for the others. He gave a brief outline of the supplies other than the food that they had with them and Jason nearly broke down in tears when he spoke of the trolleys that they had brought.

The meeting went on for over two hours, but long before it was over, it had been decided that the newcomers should set up camp in the charcoal forest for the time being. That would give them some small modicum of extra shelter and it wasn't too far removed from what a lot of them had been living in during their brief first escape from Salvation.

"So, I think that leaves us with just one issue to discuss before we pick up again tomorrow," Drake said. "Security."

"Ah, well," Jason began. "We've built two platforms on top of the barn for lookouts. We should be able to—"

Drake put his hand up, cutting him off. "That was for before. Yes, this small settlement would be alerted, but if we've got civilians in the woods who could be picked off one by one, we need something a little more substantial, don't you think?"

"So, what are you suggesting?" John asked.

"Well, for tonight, I'll have roaming guards and I'll position lookouts on the ridge," he said, gesturing in the direction of the brow of the hill that they had marched over a couple of hours before. "Tomorrow, we need to come up with a proper plan and probably discuss something longer term. Turrets even, maybe."

"Turrets?" Jason asked, laughing.

"I want to be prepared."

"Prepared for what?"

"Prepared for anything."

"We've told you about the Ferals," Susan said. "They're not that well organised and they certainly don't have the kind of numbers to launch a full-scale attack on us. I think it's a good idea to have roaming guards, it's a very real possibility that they might try to pick people off, but turrets?"

"He's not thinking about the Ferals," Callie said, and suddenly she had Drake's attention. "You're thinking about the administration, aren't you?"

Silence hung in the air for a moment. It was his single biggest concern. He knew what Bucks was like, and he knew he wasn't a man who forgave. "There's always that risk. They may come looking for us. To be honest, it's a long shot that they'd ever find us, but whether it's them or someone else, I don't think there's any harm in being prepared."

"Do you have any reason to believe they'd come after you?" John asked, suddenly looking ill at ease.

"Other than the fact that we stole food, sacks of seeds, weapons, ammunition, tools, equipment, and medical supplies and freed their entire Level Three workforce, you mean?"

"Yeah. Other than that."

"Because Bucks is the most vengeful piece of shit I've ever come across in my life."

"Well, isn't that a cheery thought?" Susan replied.

"But look," Drake continued. "I've got no reason to think that they're going to find us down here, but I'm someone who's always erred on the side of caution."

"Well," John said, looking at the others. "All things considered, building a couple of turrets might not be a bad idea after all."

*

"Oh my God! How much farther?" PJ whined as the small group continued along the road.

"Like I said the last time you asked," Dwyer replied, "we get there when we get there."

"I mean are you sure we're even going in the right direction?"

"Once again, yes, I'm sure, PJ."

Dwyer took a deep breath. "That's good. Deep breaths are good," Addy said.

"Yeah, not as good as wrapping my hands around the little bastard's throat," he replied, "but good enough for the time being."

He, Addy and Revell headed the small band of escapees while the others shared their woes behind them. Nobody had walked this far in a long, long time and it was debatable whether the tech heads like PJ had ever travelled this kind of distance on foot.

"Y'know, there'll be no need for computer geeks where we're going. We could just dump him in a ditch somewhere," Revell said, and the other two laughed.

"No. I can't wait to see the look on his face when someone gives him a shovel or a hoe and expects him to do some real work."

"Oh, man. That's going to be sweet."

"If he bleats and moans when he has to do a little walking, can you imagine what he's going to be like when he's got to do a day of hard labour?" The three of them laughed again. It felt good. There was a time earlier in the day when they had thought they weren't going to make it. Now, to be outside breathing fresh air and feeling the gentle breeze against their skin visited a level of happiness on them that none had experienced for the longest time.

"Now that's funny," Addy said.

"What's funny?" PJ piped up from behind.

"In-joke. Don't worry about it."

They walked along silently for a little while before Revell spoke again. "I hope my girls are okay." The girls he was referring to were his wife and his two daughters. Even though they had been fully primed and prepped for the evacuation, he had not laid eyes on them since his shift had started the previous evening.

"You've got nothing to worry about. Drake can be a hard arse, and sometimes a downright pain in the arse, but there are few people I'd feel safer entrusting my family to." Dwyer closed his eyes as the thought of his own family suddenly stabbed him in the chest like a cold blade.

Addy reached out and placed a comforting hand on his arm. "They'd have been proud of what you did today. Most people wouldn't have stayed back with us."

"It was the right thing to do."

"That's what I mean. People are willing to do the right thing when there's no risk involved. But when it means sacrifice or danger, you don't see them for dust. I'll never forget you stayed back with us. Thank you."

The pair looked at each other and warm smiles decorated both their faces for a moment. "Where is this place, London?" PJ's voice piped up again and Addy's smile turned into a laugh as Dwyer shook his head despairingly.

"The longer this journey takes the more I wonder if I did do the right thing," Dwyer whispered, and Addy laughed even louder.

*

By the time the refugees had disappeared into the charcoal forest across from the farm the sun was getting very low in the sky. Campfires could already be seen blazing here and there and memories of that first night when they had escaped Salvation came flooding back to everyone.

The road ahead would be a long one, but at least there was a road. "I'll give you this," Chloe said as she, Nazya and Callie leant against the cool stone wall of the infirmary staring towards the blackened woodland that seemingly flitted with life now its new inhabitants were settling in. "Life's never dull with you around, is it?"

Callie laughed and took a sip from her bowl of soup. The other two women did the same. "At least we're going to have a proper armed guard when we leave here tomorrow."

"We're still going?" Nazya asked.

"Well ... yeah. Why wouldn't we be?"

"I thought things would be hectic, to say the least."

Callie smiled. "Well, yeah, you could say that. But you need to get back home and Phil, Drake and a few others are dying to see Infinity. Judging by the stuff that came out of Phil's mouth when we had the meeting, it's going to play a pivotal role in this place succeeding."

Chloe almost beamed. "I knew it. I had a feeling about you and this place. I knew we'd be on the same page. All of this is the start of something bigger."

"All of what?"

"You finding us, us coming here, your newcomers, your plans for the future. It's all part of a much, much bigger picture."

"But you've already got that with Infinity. You've already brought people together; you've already done so much good."

"Yes, but there's so much more we can do and I know, with you and this place, we've found kindred spirits. I knew it the first time I met you."

"Well, like I said, I think we're going to be seeing a lot of each other."

"Hey, I can talk to my dad and we can get a lock-up for you like we have for Woody and some of the other traders."

"That would be good, but I really don't know what we're going to be trading at the moment."

"I'll speak to him anyway. Consider it a zero deposit reservation."

Callie giggled. "Thank you."

The sound of movement made them all turn and Michelle appeared from the doorway. She stretched her arms and arched her back a little before turning to see the other three. "I can't thank you enough for what you've done," she said, joining them. She leaned forward and looked at Callie. "All of you."

Callie shrugged. "You'd have done exactly the same if the shoe were on the other foot."

"That's nice of you to say."

"It's true."

Michelle rested her back against the wall and stared towards the forest. "I wonder if my boys are in there."

"Your boys?" Chloe said. "I thought…."

"Long, long story."

"I guess it is. So they left and you stayed?"

"They were always closer to their father."

"Oh."

"Like I said, long story."

"I suppose you'll find out soon enough," Callie said.

"I'm a horrible person."

"What?" Callie asked, but Chloe and Nazya also turned to look at Michelle. "No, you're not. What you've done for Harry and Ollie proves you're not."

"When Dani and Zep came back with the others and told us about the massacre; when they told us about you carrying on your search to look for antibiotics and anything else that could help Harry, it didn't even register."

"What didn't register?"

"That my family could have been among the ones murdered by the guards. All I was thinking about was Harry, whether you'd be successful, whether he'd be saved. What kind of a mother does that? What kind of a person does that?"

Callie was about to say something, but Nazya beat her to it. "You were and probably still are suffering from PTSD. Your thinking, your decision-making processes, everything could conceivably be affected. Our brains cope as best they can, and sometimes that means focusing on the present moment and blocking out everything else. You are not a bad mother or a bad person. You are just human. You were thrown into a terrible situation and you were doing everything you could to stay strong for Ollie. Don't be hard on yourself, Michelle. Tomorrow, you can go and see if your family are here. And if they aren't, there is no statute of limitations on grieving."

Michelle looked at Nazya for a moment. "You have a kind heart."

"It is not kindness. It is the truth."

Michelle turned to the forest once more and gazed at the flickering fires for a few seconds before nodding to herself. "I'll go look for them tomorrow." With that, she headed back through the doorway.

*

Drake ran his fingers through his hair and let out a long breath. There had not been a minute's respite for him since their arrival at the settlement. Now, with the sun going down even further, he was standing with Marina and the four guards who would be the evening's lookouts. They were on the ridge of the hill that overlooked the encampment to the north. From here, there were plenty of vantage points where they would be able to see if any potential threats were heading towards them.

He looked at the four men in turn. Cribbs, Surnow, Chester and Landis, the latter being Rachael's husband, were the first to volunteer when he had asked for lookouts for the ridge. Rachael had been busy all day walking up and down the long procession of escapees, making sure people were okay. She and her husband had barely been able to spend any time together and Drake had offered to find someone else, but Landis had refused. Drake already held him in fairly high regard, but that one selfless act notched him up a little further.

The six of them looked down at the forest and the neighbouring settlement. "Okay," Drake said, "Dwyer and the others might decide to rest up somewhere for the night. If they don't, they should be the only people you see coming down this road. If you're unsure about anything or even if you just get a bad feeling, come and find me. I'm going to be in the farmyard so everyone knows where I am. We've got half a dozen guards patrolling the southern end of the forest too, just in case anybody tries to come at us from another direction, but from what I've been told, these Ferals are to the northeast, so, in all likelihood, we'll see their approach." Drake had given everyone a briefing about the Ferals soon after his meeting with John and the others, so the term wasn't foreign to them, and the guards were primed and ready for a face-off.

"Anybody have any questions?" Marina asked. The other four men all shook their heads. "Okay. We'll see you in the morning." Marina and Drake headed back down the road leaving the others to seek out their respective vantage points. "What are the bets we head up here tomorrow and find them all fast asleep?"

"I wouldn't blame them. I can't even remember the last time I slept."

"Yeah. I'm with you there. So, these Ferals; are you worried about them?"

"I'm not exactly worried. I think we need to keep our eyes peeled. I was speaking to that girl and her mother about them. Ferals is a pretty apt description. They seem to have more in common with wild animals than people, but it's better to be safe. They'll get a bit of a surprise if they come back tonight."

"You can say that again." They carried on down the road, lost in their thoughts for a moment, until Marina spoke again. "And the administration?"

"What about them?"

"How worried are you that they'll find us here?"

"I'd be lying if I said I hadn't thought about it."

"I know."

Drake laughed. "From everything I've gathered, they picked this place purely from an agricultural point of view. Trainor saw that the forest would provide good wind resistance, that it was close to a water supply and the rest of it, but strategically it's a good spot too. The ridge," he said, pointing back over his shoulder, "gives us a good view of what's going on. The sea isn't far beyond the woodland to the west, and speaking to Greenslade, he reckons the terrain is pretty hilly to the east too. In addition, it's in the opposite direction to where the administration planned on starting the new settlement, and it's a hard day's walk."

"So, you think we're safe?"

"No. Not for a second. But they'd have to be really committed to finding us. It would use up a lot of manpower and resources, and let's face it, after taking away their workforce, stealing so much food and so many supplies and pretty much shutting the whole shebang down for eight hours they're going to be stretched to the limit. As pissed off as Bucks and the rest of them will be, I think they're going to be doing everything in their power to maintain order, keep food on the table and services running."

"When it comes out of your mouth, somehow it makes me feel better."

"You think otherwise?"

"I don't know, Vad. I honestly don't know."

Drake smiled. Marina was one of the few people other than his family who called him by his first name. She only ever did it when they were in private but also when something was worrying her. "Look. I think it's unlikely. That being said, with the weapons we have and the people we have, we vastly outnumber what's left of the Salvation guard. It would be foolhardy for them to come after us, but if they do, they're going to get into a fight that they can't win."

"I suppose you're right."

"Suppose nothing. If they show up here, we'll send them straight to Hell."

*

"I've been looking all over for you," Callie said, finding Phil nestled down behind a pile of rocks that had been collected for the ongoing building work.

"I've been busy."

"Oh?" she replied, sitting down next to him. "You going to pull another all-nighter?"

"Ha. Not this time. I'm struggling to stay awake. I just wanted a few minutes' peace to finish my list and then I was going to get a relatively early night."

"I think the boat's already sailed on that one."

"Well, early for me, anyway."

"I'm guessing that's a list of materials for your irrigation system."

"Nothing gets past you, does it?" he said, scribbling out another line.

"How are you feeling?"

Phil placed the pencil and paper in his shirt pocket and turned to look at his young friend. "How am I feeling?"

"The last time we talked, you were ... stressed. Great performance in the meeting, by the way. You even had me convinced."

He let out a small laugh. "Y'know, my life was a lot simpler before I met you."

"How do you figure?"

"I could have a rant and a virtual breakdown and nobody would hold me to account and make me feel guilty about it. That's the thing about being perceived as a genius.

People don't question any abhorrent behaviour; they just accept it as part of the package."

"And I've spoilt all that?"

"Yes. I can safely say that you have ruined my life, Callie Bridges."

"I've ruined your life? In what way exactly?"

"In every possible way. I can't sleep a full night without a thousand things flashing into my head about what we need to do, what we need to plan for. I can't eat a meal without thinking about foraging the next day, the next week, the next month, but all of that, all of it, pales into insignificance compared to the other thing you're responsible for."

"Oh, and what was that exactly?"

"You gave me an air of approachability."

"Oh, God, not this again," Callie said, rolling her eyes.

"Because other people see you speaking to me, they think they can come up to me too and just start random conversations. It happened again just this afternoon."

"That must have been traumatic for you."

"You have no idea. And … they don't seem to get sarcasm or nuance. It's completely wasted on them."

"What happened?"

"I don't want to talk about it. It's too painful."

"Okay then."

"Well, if you must know, one of the surfs who drifted in yesterday walked up to me and said in what sounded like some west country dialect, 'I used to have a vegetable patch at the end of my garden, y'know?'"

"And?"

"Exactly."

"No, I mean what did you say?"

"Well … I didn't. I just looked at him. I wasn't quite sure if he expected a response or if he just randomly walked around stating things about his past to anyone who was standing still long enough to listen."

"And that was it? That was the whole conversation that got you so upset?"

"No, he went on to say that if ever I wanted to talk to a fellow green fingers, I knew where to come."

"And what did you say?"

"Well, I just looked at him for a while, but I eventually said, 'Being responsible for the cultivation of what must conceivably be hundreds of thousands of tonnes of produce over the years, I can't tell you what a relief it is that someone's finally arrived who understands what's involved. Thank you for reaching out.'"

Callie giggled. "And what did he say?"

"'Anytime.' Then he just walked off."

"I see."

"I mean … what if he comes to talk to me again? How do you deal with someone like that?"

"Oh, I don't know, Phil. You could humour him for a couple of minutes. Ask him what he grew; ask him about himself. He was obviously just trying to be friendly."

"And so we go back to the point that you've ruined my life. No one ever tried to be friendly with me before. I was unapproachable and aloof. I was happy and, subsequently, through avoiding conversation with me, they were happy too. And now this … it's anarchy. Any second, from any direction, someone could just come up to me and start talking without any point or purpose."

"I don't know how you manage."

"No, neither do I."

"So, anyway, going back to what we were talking about. How are you feeling?" Phil let out a huff of a laugh. "What's funny?"

"It's usually the adult who asks the kid how they're feeling."

"That should tell you something right there."

"I feel better than I did. I thought about what you said and it actually made a lot of sense."

"I said a lot. Which bit?"

"The bit about it being an opportunity. You were right."

"Words I hear a lot, but somehow they always sound like music to me." Callie paused a moment before continuing. "I saw you having a long conversation with Wei earlier."

"Do you actually do anything other than stalk me?"

"You call it stalking, I call it disaster management."

Phil laughed again. "Funny. Yes, I was giving him instructions."

"Instructions?"

"Well, I'm going to be gone for three days at least, and there's a huge amount of work to be done."

"My God, Phil. It sounds like you trust him."

"Wei and Lanying almost seem to commune with the earth. We're lucky to have them here with us. They're passing on their skills to Jiang as well, and in all seriousness, yes, I trust him. There isn't a doubt in my mind that what I ask him to do will get done."

"Wow! I'm impressed. That's actually a big thing for you."

"Facetiousness doesn't suit you, Callie."

"I'm not being facetious. That is a big thing for you."

Phil shrugged. "I suppose."

"Now, if you could just develop that relationship with the other three and a half thousand people we have here, you'd be all set."

"I'll get my pencil out and add that to my list of things to do."

"Now who's being facetious?"

They sat for a while as the sounds and conversations around the rest of the settlement gradually quieted more and more. "Thank you, Callie," Phil said eventually.

"For what?"

"I'm sure it's no surprise for you to learn that I struggle sometimes, that it all begins to seem a little too much."

"That's why I keep a close eye on you."

"I'm being serious now."

"So am I. The success of this whole place depends on you, Phil. I can't even imagine the pressure that puts you under, but I'm here to lend my ear when you need it, as I'm sure Debbie is too."

"Debbie's my wife. She has to. Why do you do it?"

"Because you're my friend, Phil. And it's what friends do."

"How old are you again?"

"Sixteen, but when I'm around you, I feel sixty."

Phil laughed again. "Well, thank you, anyway."

"You're welcome." Callie climbed to her feet. "Now, we've got a long journey ahead of us tomorrow, so I'm going to turn in. "I suggest you do too."

"Yeah. I will in a minute. I just want to sit here and ponder a little while longer."

"Okay. Night."

"Night, Callie."

Callie had only taken a few steps back towards the barn when she ran into Debbie. "I don't suppose you've seen Phil anywhere, have you?"

"Can't I get a minute's bloody peace in this place?" he called out and both women laughed.

"Does that answer your question?" Callie replied.

"Thanks. I'll see you in the morning. Sleep well."

Although a fire was still burning in the middle of the yard, there was no sign of anyone around it. It had been another long day, and there would be plenty more of them to come, but as Callie stepped into the barn, a small candle of hope burned inside her.

11

Revell and Dwyer had started a fire. They weren't quite sure how far there was left to travel, but everyone in the small party was both physically and mentally drained. Darkness had fallen a couple of hours before and the road they were on had deteriorated since then, making the risk of sprains and other injuries possible, if not likely. So, the two guards deemed it prudent to rest until daybreak.

They had shared out the small amount of food they'd had with them and, one by one, the rest of the party had curled up, using their rucksacks for pillows, and drifted off to sleep. Revell, Dwyer and Addy were the last three left awake, but only barely.

They sat in the warm, comforting glow of the flames. "I don't know what I expected out here, but I can't say I expected this," Addy said, gesturing to the patch of blackened woodland to their left. "I can't even imagine what it must have been like for the people left behind."

"I think it's for the best that you don't try to imagine. Let's just hope it was quick for anyone who wasn't in a bunker," Revell replied.

"Somehow, I doubt that."

"Like I said, it's best not to think about it."

"I wonder what the settlement's going to be like."

"If Trainor's there, it's going to be different to everywhere else. That's for sure."

"I only know what I've read about him."

"I've heard lots of stories. He's a little eccentric, a little misanthropic, but a genius. The administration would have executed him a long time ago if he wasn't. He was a constant thorn in their side, but they had no option but to keep him around."

"I still can't believe we're doing this," Revell said. "I can't believe we're out here."

"It's going to take a lot of getting used to, that's for sure," Addy replied.

"And it's going to be a hell of a lot of hard work."

"But it'll be worth it."

"Let's hope."

"It already is. We all knew what that place was, what those people were. Welcome to Dystopia. We're your hosts, the administration. Today on the show, we have the enslavement and subjugation of generation after generation, but first, we'd like to turn you against your neighbour, causing conflict and hatred in a way that will make you take your eyes off the bigger picture."

Revell and Dwyer both laughed. "You should do stand-up," Dwyer said.

"I used to."

"Really? I thought you'd always been a tech head."

"Well, yeah, I was. That was my day job, but I used to do comedy clubs now and again. I did the Edinburgh Festival once."

"Seriously?"

"Yeah. Let me tell you, there is no buzz in the world like making a big crowd of people laugh. Just knowing that every last one of them is tuned into your wavelength at that moment. It's magical."

"I'm guessing people are going to be in need of laughter where we're going, so maybe you could revive your old routine."

"Why do you think I wanted to come?"

"PEACH TREES."

All three of them were immediately jarred from their conversation and looked at PJ with alarm. The others were still asleep, but his eyes were now wide open and his chest was heaving up and down wildly.

"PJ, are you okay?" Revell asked.

"Err ... yeah. I had a nightmare ... I think."

"Something to do with peach trees, I'm guessing."

"What?" PJ said, finally blinking and turning towards the other man. "What are you talking about?"

"You shouted, 'Peach trees.' I'm surprised you didn't wake the others up."

"Why the hell would I shout peach trees? You must have misheard."

"Nope," Addy replied. "You definitely shouted out peach trees."

PJ shook his head dismissively. "You all must be smoking something. I wouldn't shout out peach trees for no reason." He shuffled to his knees and then his feet. "I'm going for a piss."

"Thanks for the update," Addy replied.

She, Dwyer and Revell all looked at each other and giggled quietly. "Peach trees," Dwyer said again, shaking his head.

The trio returned their gaze to the flames and listened to the gentle pops and crackles with contented smiles. It sounded clichéd, but they had faced a fate worse than death and come out at the other end able to laugh and smile. If they had not been able to escape the lift, the administration would have stopped at nothing to get information from them.

Their thoughts were disturbed once more as PJ's shuffling feet roused them. They could tell instantly that something was amiss. His back was turned to them and his eyes were cast out somewhere into the darkness beyond as he continued to edge backwards. "PJ? PJ, what is it?"

For a moment, he didn't answer. Then he finally stopped moving and spoke. "I saw someone."

"It's probably just the darkness playing tricks on you," Dwyer replied.

PJ turned to look at him, and despite the orange glow, they could all see how pale his face was. "I'm telling you; I saw someone ... six people in fact."

Dwyer and Revell cast concerned glances towards each other before grabbing their weapons and jumping to their feet.

"Where? Where were they? Did you get a good look?"

PJ pointed. "They weren't close, but I saw them. I saw six distinct figures in the moonlight."

Dwyer and Revell both moved forward, well out of the glow of the fire. They continued walking a little further into the darkness until they were out of earshot. "What do you think?" Dwyer asked.

"I don't know. I mean he seems pretty convinced."

"Maybe it was a couple of peach trees he saw." They both started laughing again.

They scoured the night, peering as far into the distance as the light would allow. "I don't see a thing."

"Me neither," Dwyer said, turning back to look at PJ, who was standing by the fire with a fearful look still decorating his face. They both walked back towards him. "We can't see anything now."

PJ shook his head. "I'm not making it up."

"Nobody's saying you are. All I'm telling you is we can't see anything."

"I don't know why we needed this camp-out anyway."

"I told you, if we carried on in the dark, someone was likely to break their ankle or something."

"I'd rather that than get dragged back to Salvation."

"Firstly, if it was six people you saw—"

"I'm telling you it was."

"Okay, okay. What I'm saying is we don't know who they were. There's no reason to believe they were—"

"Cannibals. They could be those cannibals."

Dwyer's shoulders hunched. When the escapees had been recaptured, stories of what happened at the quarry had travelled around Salvation, gradually getting scarier and gorier with each retelling. "Say you're right. Say they're cannibals or say they're from Salvation's elite guard or say they're axe-wielding homicidal maniacs. There are only six of them. There are seven of us and we're all armed."

"They might just be scouts or something."

Dwyer let out an exasperated breath. "Okay, PJ. I tell you what. You stay up all night in fear of who might be out there in the dark, but I need to get some shuteye." He walked back around to the spot where he'd been sitting, laid his rifle on the ground and placed his head down on his rucksack. Revell did the same, and then Addy, leaving just PJ on his feet, staring out into the night.

The rest of the group had remained unconscious during the drawn-out conversation, exhausted from the journey and the stress of the day. This was something Dwyer was grateful for as a couple of them were just as jumpy and highly strung as PJ. He closed his eyes, hoping the quiet crackle of the fire would guide him into slumber, but there was a part of him that knew he would get little sleep. PJ was panicky, immature, highly strung, irritating, the list went on and on, but he was never someone prone to just making things up. As much as they had joked about it at the time, Dwyer was sure he'd seen something, and that opened up a whole load of questions, none of which he liked the answers to.

*

Marina hadn't drawn the short straw like the others. Instead, she'd volunteered to take the next watch. Dawn was breaking as she and three more former Salvation guards met on the road and began their journey up the hill.

"How was your first night's sleep as a free woman since entering Salvation?" Esme asked.

"Brief," Marina replied.

"Yeah. I get that. Maybe someone can fetch us a couple of espressos up when they start breakfast."

"I wouldn't hold your breath." People had already begun to stir across at the farm and fires were being lit to get breakfast underway. There was no hope for any of them to grab a bite to eat in the foreseeable future. "Drake will sort something out for us when he wakes up."

"I haven't seen him since we got here."

"He was talking with the settlement leaders even well after the official meeting had come to an end."

"About what?"

"Everything from work assignments to security, from what I gathered. I was around for a couple of the conversations, but I dare say we'll get a briefing today."

They carried on up the hill for several minutes until they reached the summit. "I thought they'd all be here, chomping at the bit to head down and get some sleep."

"Chances are the lazy bastards are nestled down catching some sneaky Zs already."

"This is a long ridge. They could have positioned themselves anywhere."

Marina put her hands up to her mouth. "CRIBBS. SURNOW. LANDIS. CHESTER. WAKE UP, YOUR RELIEF'S HERE!" Esme and the other two guards laughed. They waited a few seconds, but nobody materialised. "CRIBBS. SURNOW. LANDIS. CHESTER. BREAKFAST." The seconds dragged on to a minute, and the eyes of the four Salvation guards travelled along the ridge in both directions, but still there was no sign.

"If they are kipping, they must be hard on."

Marina shook her head. "I'd have thought at least one of them would have heard me. Come on, we'd better split up and look for them. Childs, Tapper, you head that way. Esme, you come with me. Be careful, okay? There are inlets, drops and ledges all over; it would be easy to put a foot wrong."

Childs and Tapper nodded before turning and heading west along the ridge.

"I don't think Drake will be too pleased if they are sleeping," Esme said as she and Marina began to head in the other direction.

"That's a bit of an understatement. He can't exactly have them up on charges anymore, but I'm pretty certain he can make them regret ever being born."

"Yeah. Drake has a special talent for that."

The pair carried on for a moment, carefully navigating the uneven rocks, looking for any sign of the other guards. "Maybe th—" Marina stopped in mid-thought as she saw three of the guards lying down on a jutting ledge up ahead. "Well, isn't that sweet? They decided to have a little nap together. Jesus. Drake is going to go spare."

"Are you going to—Wah!"

"What?" Marina turned quickly to see Esme on the ground.

"I slipped," she said, laughing a little at her own clumsiness. She started to climb back to her feet. "There's something wet here. I better not have fallen where those dirty bastards have taken a leak." She brought her hand up closer to her face. The light still wasn't brilliant, but she could see that whatever it was had a dark hue. "Err ... what the...." She sniffed at it. "Oh shit!"

"What?" Marina asked, sensing the concern in her friend's voice.

"It's blood."

Both women turned in unison to the three guards. "Cribbs? Surnow?" Marina said, starting to scramble towards them. "CRIBBS? SURNOW?" She shouted this time as Esme followed her. They both stopped as they reached the bodies. "Oh no, no, no, no, no. Oh shit! Oh

Jesus, no," Marina said, crouching down and checking each one for a pulse. "They're stone cold."

"Who's missing?"

"Landis. Landis is missing. Come on, he might be around here somewhere."

"LANDIS! LANDIS!" It was Esme who was shouting now. They travelled a little further along the ridge. "LANDIS!"

"Shit! Shit! Shit!" Marina hissed. "Okay. Okay. Let's just think a second."

"Do you think it was those Feral people?"

"Probably. Who knows? Um … right. Let's go get the others; then I need to tell Drake."

*

Drake had barely had three hours sleep, but as he stared down at the bodies of Cribbs, Surnow and Chester, he knew he would not be getting any more for the rest of the day at least. "Shit."

"Yeah," Marina said as another dozen guards continued the search for Landis.

"We're going to have to tell their families."

"Yep."

"Shit."

"Yep."

"I don't understand how they could have got the drop on them like this without a single shot being fired." There was enough light now to illuminate the trails of blood leading up to where the bodies had been laid out. "And why bother dragging them all to this spot? Why not just leave them where they killed them?"

"Maybe they didn't want to leave them in plain sight."

Drake shrugged. "I suppose but…."

"But what?"

"It just seems weird. It doesn't feel right."

"Well, course not. Our friends are dead. If that felt right, there'd be something very wrong, wouldn't there?"

"It's not that. It's—"

"Oh, Jesus!" Marina and Drake spun around to see Susan standing there.

"What are you doing here?" Drake demanded.

A bitter smile slowly bled onto Susan's face. "I saw a small procession of your people heading up the hill and I thought I'd find out what was going on. I hope you're not inferring that I don't have a right to do that. I hope this hasn't already become an 'us and them' thing after everything you came out with yesterday."

Drake closed his eyes for a moment. "No. I'm sorry. It's just that I'm still trying to come to terms with what's happened here myself. You took me by surprise, that's all, and I wanted a few minutes to figure this out before news of this spreads through the camp like wildfire."

"We had a visit from your Ferals," Marina said, turning back towards the bodies.

Susan walked up to join them. "You saw them?"

"Saw who?"

"The Ferals."

"No, but it's obvious, isn't it?"

"No, actually."

"What makes you say that?" Drake asked, peeling his eyes away from the bodies and looking at Susan once more.

"From the little that I've gathered and seen of them, they kill to survive, they don't kill for no reason. Your guards have still got their weapons, they've got their rucksacks, their boots, everything. Even if they were attacked by Ferals who weren't cannibals, they wouldn't have been left with any of those things."

"Maybe they were disturbed. Maybe Landis got the drop on them before they could finish what they'd started," Marina said.

"Okay, where are their bodies? Why didn't we hear any gunshots? Why were the bodies all dragged to this one place?"

"What are you saying exactly?" Drake asked.

Susan shook her head. "I'm just saying that I don't think you can just flat out say this was Ferals. It doesn't make sense."

"We need to find Landis and figure out what the hell happened here." He turned to Susan. "I'd appreciate it if you kept this quiet until I've had time to inform the families at least."

"Of course," Susan replied. "We'll be heading off soon anyway."

"Heading off?" Marina asked.

"Oh crap, I'd forgotten," Drake replied. "You're going to that Infinity place."

"Yes."

"I know I said I was going to make sure you had a significant armed guard, but given what's just happened, I—"

"We'd planned to head there before you showed up yesterday. We've got weapons. We'll be fine."

"But still, I want to send some of our people with you for extra security."

"Is it for extra security or are you wanting to keep an eye on us?"

Drake let out a small laugh. "I suppose your daughter said it well yesterday, didn't she? Trust is something that's earned. I don't want to spy on you. I want to make sure you're safe."

"Well, aren't you the sweetest?"

"It's nothing to do with being sweet. Phil Trainor is the single most valuable asset this place or any place has. I don't want anything happening to him."

"And there I was thinking you were worried about me."

12

Callie looked at the bowl in her lap. Variety was not something on the menu. "I wish you guys were coming with us," she said as she spooned another measure of stew into her mouth.

"Me too," Zep replied.

"I suppose it's quite an honour in a way to be asked to help organise things back here," Dani said. "They've got me and Mum heading the team to inventory all the food the new arrivals have brought with them, and Jason specifically asked for Zep to keep the momentum going with the building operations. But, yeah. I wish we were going with you. I'd like to see this Infinity place."

"Maybe next time. Like you said, it's quite an honour. Nobody asked me to help or take charge of anything."

"Well, they wouldn't, would they? You're Callie Bridges, action girl."

Callie laughed. "I don't think so somehow."

"How many are going anyway?"

"I'm not sure. Drake wanted to send a healthy

contingent of his people with us, so—"

A boom of gunfire made the air around them tremble and Callie, Zep and Dani jumped to their feet, dropping their bowls of food and sweeping their heads from side to side to figure out where it had come from.

A small group began running towards the stream, and in the absence of a better idea, the three of them followed. More people still came rushing out of the barn and the farmhouse as uncertainty descended on the settlement. A semicircle had formed on one of the banks and a female guard held her Q-Eighteen in her right hand, waving it in no particular direction as she shielded a young boy, presumably her son from his similar colouring and facial features. Blood was running down the side of his face and tears were streaming down his cheeks.

Five of the newly arrived refugees had paused their advance towards the woman and boy momentarily, but the tension continued to mount.

Callie was about to push forward to find out what was going on when she was beaten to it by John. "What is this?" he shouted angrily, positioning himself between the guard and her child and the mob.

"We were just washing," the guard replied, shielding her son behind her a little further, "and someone threw a stone at Tyler. The next thing I know, these pricks are heading towards us, so I fired a warning shot."

"Is this true?" John asked.

"They shouldn't be here. None of them should be here after what they did." The man who spoke had piercing brown eyes, and as the words left his lips, he continued to stare holes through the female guard and her child.

John searched his memory in order to be able to put a name to the face. "Caine. You're Caine, aren't you?"

The man finally broke his gaze with the woman and looked at John. "That's right."

"Yeah. I remember you. I remember helping your wife when she hurt her arm."

"Look. This is nothing to do with you. None of them belong here. If you think we're all going to live side by side in perfect harmony, then you're a fool."

"So what? You're just going to attack them when they're by themselves or with their kids?"

"You wouldn't even question this if you saw what I saw that night in the forest."

In the moments since this had begun an even bigger crowd had gathered around and several more uniformed guards had appeared. They stood with their compatriot; for the time being, their weapons weren't raised, but that could change in a heartbeat. And almost like a mirror image was forming right in front of him, an equal amount of former Level Three refugees bolstered the ranks behind Caine too. Some of them carried makeshift clubs or held small rocks in their hands.

Tania and Harper broke from the ranks of the crowd and went to stand by John's side, forming the start of a wall between the two factions. "Whatever happened in the past has to stay there," Harper said.

"That's easy for you to say. You didn't—"

"Screw you," Harper fired back.

Caine's face grew angry and he took another step forward, but this time in Harper's direction. "Who the hell do you think you're talking to, you little d—"

"You'd better be really careful about what comes out of your mouth next, pal," Zep said as he, Dani and Callie went to join their friends. "'Cause I saw Harper and a lot of other people get beaten half to death the night before we escaped Salvation. So, if you think for a second that she doesn't have a right to bear a grudge, then you don't know what you're talking about."

"Then why aren't you with us? Why aren't you joining us? You said it yourself. She got beaten half to death. We shouldn't be just letting these people in, all sins forgiven."

"Yeah," several of the expanding group behind Caine

agreed.

"Because we need to move on," Tania replied.

"No. They need to move on. There'll never be any peace while they're here."

"Says who?" John asked.

"Me, for one. And I'll be backed by about three thousand others."

"If you hate them so much, why did you accept their help to escape?"

"It wasn't like that. A lot of us didn't know. We were just told that there was a plan in place. We were told that people from Level Two were making a break for it as well. A lot of us didn't know the specifics until we were all out in the open and heading here."

"So, what's keeping you here?" Greenslade asked as he, Grace, Trunk and Libby joined John and the others.

Greenslade and Trunk carried rifles on their backs, and they each rested a thumb inside the strap in a leisurely manner but also as a not-so-subtle warning that they could grab their weapons at any moment.

"Now I've seen everything," Caine replied. "The crime kingpin of Level Three siding with the Salvation guards."

"Maybe he's not siding with anyone," Callie replied. "Maybe he just doesn't like thugs who attack a little kid while they're trying to get washed. Maybe he thinks there's something fundamentally screwed up with that."

"What are you, his fan club?" The others behind Caine all laughed.

"I'd explain it to you, but I'm not sure I know enough monosyllabic words for you to get the gist. Maybe if you get a few more of your hooligan friends together, you can work it out between you."

The smile left Caine's face. "You've got some cheek, you little bitch. I—"

Greenslade took a stride forward and he fixed Caine with a fierce stare. "I'll give you the gist," he said. "I'm pretty confident I can speak in terms you'll understand."

Even though there were growing numbers of people standing behind Caine and his cohorts, he seemed less sure of himself now as Trunk stood shoulder to shoulder with his friend too. "I … I'm done listening." He started to turn away, but Greenslade advanced further and placed a hand on the other man's shoulder.

"You're not going anywhere. I'm going to speak, and you're going to listen."

For the first time since arriving at the settlement, Greenslade revealed the man he used to be. There was menace in his tone and in his eyes, and although massively outnumbered by the refugees who had gathered behind Caine, he was the one who was in control. "Get off me," the other man protested, trying to shake his shoulder free, but Greenslade did not release his grip.

"You know who I was back in Salvation. I'm pretty certain everybody here does. John and the others knew who I was when I came to the settlement. They knew what I'd done, but they took me and my people in anyway. Do you know why?"

"B-because they're fools." Caine tried to sound belligerent, he tried to sound brave, but his voice quivered a little as he spoke and no one around him thought what he said was funny this time."

"In the past, I'd have agreed with you. In the past. But they understood what was needed to survive out here, and they still do. The planet has been virtually obliterated. It's going to take everything we've got as a species to hang on, and that means working together. The administration had us all at odds with one another. They thrived on conflict in the ranks. It created uncertainty and fear that made them look like the only constant, the only entity that could be relied upon. But they were feeding the fear and creating the division. Drake and the guards who broke everyone out yesterday did so at a huge personal risk to themselves."

"It was a risk for all of us."

"To an extent. But if you got captured while you were escaping, they'd probably just put you straight back to work. What do you think would happen to them and their families? They risked everything to be here. They could have fled by themselves, but they didn't like what was going on. They couldn't stomach what the administration was turning them into and they helped everyone escape. That took guts and, if nothing else, it gave them the right to breathe the same air as us and wash in the same water without being assaulted."

"You've got a short memory."

"I forget nothing." Greenslade tightened the grip on Caine's shoulder. "Nothing."

"So, we should just all play happy families?"

"I doubt that will happen anytime soon. But at the very least, just let them get on with their lives without interference." He finally let the other man go in the hope that the gesture would help the message sink in a little more.

John walked forward to join Greenslade and Trunk. "He's right. Look, you brought supplies with you, but they aren't going to last two minutes with this many people. We have real, tangible problems here rather than creating new ones. When you arrived yesterday, you all started with a fresh slate. We didn't hold it against any of you when you left with Preacher and we're accepting you back here now. This only works if we all do it together."

"And what if there are some of us who can't get past what happened?"

"Well, they can all fu—"

"Then we need to think of alternatives," John said, placing a hand on Greenslade's arm and stopping him in midstream.

"Alternatives?" Caine replied. "Like what?"

"The people from the quarry," John began. "Considering what happened there, we couldn't have them here, but we helped them set up another community. We helped them start again."

"You're saying that's what we should do with the guards and the Level Two people?"

"He's saying that's what we'd help you do," Callie said, finally joining the discussion.

"You'd have us leave rather than them?"

"No, you would be choosing to leave rather than working to live together. And even though there would be nothing in it for us, we'd be willing to help you set up somewhere else."

Caine's mouth hung open for a moment. He wasn't quite sure how to respond. "Well ... I think it should be them who have to go."

"Well, you can think what you like. These people are staying and you can either remain here and work with us to build something or you can go and try to build something else."

Caine broke his gaze from Callie and looked towards the guard who was still shielding her boy. "I never thought I'd see someone from Level Three taking the side of the Salvation guards."

"You still haven't got it, have you?" Harper replied. "They're not Salvation guards anymore. We're not Level Three inhabitants anymore. We're just people trying to find a way to survive in what is, quite frankly, a terrifying new world that bears little resemblance to the one we left behind when we walked into the bunker. We had a boy get attacked by a shark. A shark, for Christ's sake. You ever heard of anything like that in British waters? None of us knows what's going to happen from one day to the next, but I know I feel glad that I've got people around me, people with skill sets I don't have. People who share my fears and my hopes."

Caine shook his head. "I and many like me will never accept these people, no matter what."

"Then Callie made it pretty clear to you what to do, didn't she? But anyone who stays here gets treated the same as everyone else, no matter who they were or what they did in the bunker."

Caine exhaled deeply and his shoulders sank a little. He looked from Harper to Callie to Greenslade and the others and finally began to walk away.

"Hold it right there," Drake ordered, training his weapon on Caine while at least a dozen of his guards aimed their rifles towards his followers. Nobody knew how long he'd been standing there, but it didn't matter. He'd got the general gist of what had gone on.

Caine immediately put his hands up and he turned back to Tania and the others. "See? This is why we can't live together. It will always be us and them."

"This is nothing to do with us and them," Drake replied as Susan stepped up beside him.

"He's right," she added.

"What is this? What's going on?" John asked, first looking at Drake then to Susan.

"Err ... that whole bit about keeping this under wraps might be a bit tough under the circumstances," Susan whispered.

"Get everyone out of the house. We're going to need it to hold them," Drake said.

"Wait a minute," John protested.

"Now!"

"See. Y'see what's going on?" Caine replied. "They're administration through and through. You think any of us will ever be free while they're around?" Suddenly, the spectators who had not been involved in the initial fracas became agitated. "Déjà vu, anyone? How long before we're working in the fields under armed guard?"

Drake turned towards the forest. Marina and a couple of other guards had gone to look for the families of the men who had been on the night watch. He had wanted to wait until all concerned parties had been informed before talking about the dire events that had occurred the previous night, but as the tension mounted, he realised there was only one way to diffuse it. "Nobody will be working under an armed guard," Drake said, looking around at the others. "But when people are murdered in cold blood, there are going to be consequences."

"Murdered?" John asked. "What are you talking about?"

"The four guards who I placed as lookouts on the ridge last night. Three of them are dead and another is missing." Gasps spread through the crowd. Drake looked beyond the small sea of bodies to the young boy with the bloody temple. "Forgive me, but you don't need to be the world's greatest detective to figure out who the prime suspects are."

Caine suddenly looked panicked. "It wasn't us. It wasn't us," he said again, shaking his head.

Some of the refugees who had joined Caine when he was speaking out against the guards started to move away, but rifles were quickly trained on them and they were herded back with the others.

"The house is empty," called one of the guards as Paul and his family, along with a few other people, hurried out of the door. None of them were privy to what had gone on, but none of them questioned the demand to evacuate either.

"Okay," Drake said. "Get them all inside. Cover the doors and the windows so none of them can escape."

The men and women immediately stepped into action, corralling Caine and his group as he and they all protested their innocence.

"Look, I'm no fan of this guy," John said, walking up to Drake and Susan, "but there's no proof that they did this."

"I'm aware of that," Drake replied.

"Then why are you rounding them up like prisoners?"

"Because they need to be questioned. Given what they were prepared to do, given what they've just been talking about, you've got to admit it sounds like they had a bit of an axe to grind."

"Well, yeah, and no offence, but there are over three thousand people you could say that about. Are you going to question all of them?"

"Listen. I get what this looks like, and I'm not happy about the optics, not for a second, but what do you want me to do? You want me to just brush off the murder of my men and say, 'No hard feelings'?"

"He's got a point, John," Susan said.

"I mean ... it could have been anyone."

"That's why we're going to question them and see if we can glean any pertinent information."

"You realise this looks bad. It looks really, really bad."

"The fact that my people have been murdered or the fact that I want to do something about it?"

"Jesus! This never ends," John said, looking at Susan. "It's one thing after another and another."

"Maybe..." Susan began but then stopped herself.

"Maybe what?"

"Never mind."

"No," Drake said. "I'd like to hear too. Maybe what?"

"Maybe it's not just your people who do the questioning."

Drake's brow furrowed a little. "What do you mean?"

"Well, maybe, as well as a guard or two, there's a friendly face as well."

"Are you volunteering?"

"God, no. But I know someone who they'll trust, who's intelligent and will happily slap you down if you start getting too heavy-handed."

A crooked smile crept onto Drake's face. "Please don't tell me you want them to have a lawyer."

Now it was Susan's turn to laugh. "Err ... no. That really would be the end of the world if we brought them back."

"Who then?"

"Penny."

"And who's that exactly?"

"She led the survivors who escaped the mine. She's probably not your biggest fan either, but she's intelligent and fair, and she'll be someone your prisoners will relate to. If there's an intermediary, you might get a little further with your questioning."

Drake thought for a moment. This was a terrible situation. The last thing he wanted to be was heavy-handed just at a time when he was trying to prove everybody was on an equal footing, but at the same time, someone was guilty of killing his men and that had to be dealt with swiftly and justly. "Okay. If you think you can get this Penny to agree, we'll start straight away."

"I'm pretty certain she will. I'll go find her."

The crowd was slow to disperse, all of them casting concerned looks towards the house, Drake, then the other guards. Tyler's mother took the boy's hand and walked up to John and the others. "Thank you," she said, looking at each of them in turn and then nodding. She finally turned to Drake. "That could have got really ugly if these people hadn't intervened."

Drake nodded. "Then I owe you my thanks as well."

John shook his head. "Like I said, the only way this is going to work is if we all do it together."

"And how do you rate our chances?"

"What, without more fatalities? About zero."

13

Eventually, the crowd scattered completely and people went about their early morning routines of getting washed, fed and generally prepared for the day. The guard's presence around the house was significant and notable, however, and everyone knew things were far from normal.

"You're a hard woman to pin down," Susan said as she found Penny and Greta downstream with more than a dozen of the orphaned children. They were washing and rinsing out whatever extra clothes they had with them.

"There's a reason for that."

"You weren't interested to find out what was going on?"

"You really didn't need to be a genius to figure out that divisions would come to the surface sooner rather than later. I wanted to make sure the kids were as far away from it as possible. We were near the camp, but when we heard the gunshot, we moved further down. You could sense the tension in the air last night. I'm surprised something didn't happen then."

"Something did happen then."

Penny straightened up and moved away from the rest of the group, taking Susan with her. "What happened?"

"Three guards were murdered."

"Holy shit. Do they have any idea who did it?"

"Some."

"What does that mean?"

"A group of thugs attacked a guard and her kid, and they were about to really go to town on her before some of our people intervened. It's not a stretch to think they might have had something to do with it."

"It's a place to start, I suppose," Penny said, wiping her wet hands on her jeans. "Thanks for the heads-up. I'll be sure to keep the kids as far away from the farm as possible today."

"Well...."

"Well, what?"

"I was hoping for your help."

"My help? What do you think I can do?"

"I'm glad you asked. Let me explain."

*

"Drake! Can I see you a minute?" Marina said.

Drake was in a conversation with John, but seeing the concerned look on his friend's face, he brought it to an abrupt end and now the two of them headed out of earshot. "What is it? Have you told everyone concerned? Are they okay? Nobody's tried to do anything silly, have they?"

"We've informed Cribbs', Surnow's and Chester's families. They're devastated as you'd expect them to be. The other guards and their families are rallying around them and one of the doctors is on standby with a sedative if it's needed.

Drake nodded slowly. "Thank you for doing that. I'll go see them later, but I think the news would have been better coming from you." His brow suddenly furrowed as his mind processed the information he'd been given. "And Rachael? What about Rachael?"

"That's what I came to tell you. We can't find her anywhere."

Drake straightened up, leaning his head back a little as if seeing Marina at a slightly wider angle would make more sense of what she'd just said. "What do you mean you can't find her anywhere?"

"I mean she's gone. Everyone saw where she set up camp with Landis last night before he went on watch duty. Today, there's no sign of her. And what's more, Emily and Larch set up next to her. They're gone too."

"But that ... that doesn't make sense." Emily and Larch were husband and wife and both Salvation guards. When they weren't working, it was rare that you'd find either of them out of the gym. "For a few thugs to get the drop on all three of them at the same time, surely someone must have heard or seen something."

"Yeah, well. That's not the best bit. The cherry on the cake is that all their stuff's gone too."

Drake stared at his friend for a moment before his eyes drifted to the other people milling around the farmyard. "Just what the hell is going on here?"

*

"Callie!" Matt's call sounded almost panicked, and as he ran towards her, Dani and Zep, they could all see the concern on his face.

"What is it, Matt?" Callie asked.

He skidded to a stop about a metre away from them and they could all see the sheen of sweat on his face. "I ... I can't find Mum or Dad anywhere."

Callie looked out to the fields. Even so early in the day, it wouldn't be unusual to see Phil taking a walk. And today of all days, with the journey to Infinity to look forward to, he would surely be up extra early sharing his last pearls of wisdom with Wei before his departure. "Err ... have you checked—"

"I've checked everywhere. I've checked the fields, the stream, I checked with Wei, and I even went to the beach. I asked the people making breakfast if they'd seen Mum and nobody's seen them. What's more, I don't know if Dad came to bed at all last night. When I woke up this morning, neither of them was there. Mum was definitely there when I went to sleep, but I can't remember Dad coming in."

"Well, I saw him last night and he said he was just going to stop up a little while longer then turn in. Then I saw your mum, who I assumed had come to drag him to bed."

"Are you sure you've checked the fields, Matt?" Zep asked.

"I've checked everywhere. There's no sign of either of them. They're gone."

*

Within five minutes of the alarm being raised, a full-scale search was underway for Phil and Debbie. "I forgot to give you the official welcome yesterday," John said. "But welcome."

Drake only managed half a smile and shook his head despairingly. "I don't have a clue what's going on here."

"Then you're one of us already."

"Have Trainor and his wife ever gone missing before? Y'know, a quiet stroll hand in hand, a few peaceful minutes away from everything?"

"Phil's eccentric, distant, unapproachable, and generally unfathomable, but Debbie's a lot more down to earth. Even if he did go on one of his wanders, Debbie wouldn't go far without Matt. In fact, I'm not being fair to Phil. Neither would he."

"Then what is this? What's going on?"

"I really wish I could tell you, Drake. I really do."

*

A contorted expression of worry was etched onto Chloe's face as she and Nazya emerged from the small infirmary once more. Michelle had joined the small army of people who were looking for Phil, Debbie and, to a lesser extent, the other doctor and the missing guards.

"Callie!" Chloe called as her friend appeared from the back of the barn.

"Hi Chloe," Callie said without the usual warmth and enthusiasm.

"I feel selfish for even bringing this up, but we are still heading back to Infinity today, aren't we?"

"You're not being selfish," Callie replied. "Your dad must be worried sick about you. But, I don't think we're going anywhere unless we find Phil and Debbie."

"What's going on here today?" Nazya asked. "Everything seems ... off."

"Maybe it's the moon's cycle. Maybe it's the lousy food. Or maybe it's the fact that the population has grown by over three and a half thousand people in the blink of an eye and everything is turning to shit." Nazya's eyes widened and Callie let out a long, deep breath. "I'm sorry. I'm really sorry. It's just that, yesterday, I thought I saw a way to make this work. I thought there was an opportunity for us to flourish as a community, but today it's chaos. It's absolute anarchy. Murders, missing people, hostility between the different groups of survivors. It's like the whole world has imploded overnight and I don't know what to do to make it better other than find Phil and Debbie."

"They are lucky to have a friend like you."

Callie shook her head. "Even if I hated them, I'd want to find them. Everything depends on Phil. He's the difference between this place working or collapsing in on itself."

"Nobody is irreplaceable."

"I'd have agreed with you once. But then I met Phil and I realised that's not true. He's got a once-in-a-generation mind, and that's what we need right now. That's what we need as a community to survive."

"Maybe he's sloped off with his wife for a few minutes of peace and quiet," Chloe said, winking.

Callie replied with a weak smile. "I really hope you're right, but I've got a bad feeling about this."

*

"What's wrong?" Si asked, taking hold of Sasha's hand. They had barely been apart since the two had been reunited the previous day, but the look of elation that had seemed permanently etched on Sasha's face was gone for the time being.

"I've just heard some people talking."

"About what?"

"Drake and what they're doing with Caine."

"And?"

"Some people are talking about overthrowing the guards now, while things are so chaotic, before they can take a tight hold of what's going on. They're saying that if we let them carry on the way they've begun we're going to be no better off than we were in Salvation."

Si looked around. Everyone was caught up in the search for Phil and the others. Mayhem didn't even begin to describe what was happening. "What is wrong with people?" he muttered under his breath.

"They're talking about raiding the weapons cache. Enough of the civilians have guns to get the ball rolling."

"We need to tell someone, now."

"NO!" she said, squeezing his hand and pulling him back towards her. "These are our people, Si. They're my people. I told you this because I tell you everything. We can't betray them."

"Sash, I love you. But what do you think's going to happen if this place descends into civil war?"

"Don't you dare say anything."

"Sash, this is madness. With everything that's going on to be even talking about this is madness. It does nobody any good to create more conflict. We need to ease tensions, not escalate them. Look, I won't say anything to anybody, but let me speak to the person who's planning this."

"You promise? You promise you won't say anything."

He squeezed her hand. "I promise."

*

The first time Matt had walked through the forest that morning most people had still been asleep. The gunshot had woken a lot up and rumours were abound, not least of which that Phil Trainor and others had gone missing in the night.

This time, Callie accompanied him as he travelled, and as grateful as he was to have someone with him, there was a bigger part of him that wanted to be alone. All the hardships he'd faced in the past had been nothing compared to this because, in the past, he'd always had his parents there to guide him, to give him a shoulder to cry on. A shoulder to cry on was exactly what he needed now, but it couldn't be Callie, the girl who saved all those people from the quarry, the girl who saved Harry.

"We've pretty much got everybody looking for them now," she said as they weaved through the trees avoiding the makeshift cotton tents and remains of campfires.

"It doesn't matter."

"What do you mean?"

"I can feel they're gone."

Callie let out a small laugh then immediately wished she hadn't. "I'm sorry. That was insensitive. You can't know where they are."

"I can feel it, Callie. They're not here. They've always treated me with kid gloves. If they were going to go somewhere together, they'd have let me know. Something's happened, I can feel it."

"What do you mean something's happened?"

Matt turned to look at her and now she felt guiltier than ever as tears began to cascade down his face. He quickly brushed them away, but it was useless, he could feel more coming. "I don't know. I just know it's something bad."

*

Drake had remained in the farmyard with Marina. People had to know where to find him if he was needed, and this seemed like the perfect place. As the words, "Christ, what now?" left Marina's lips in an exasperated sigh, there was a big part of him that didn't want to look.

What if I say I'm going to join the search and instead grab my family, a rucksack of food, some seeds, and we just don't look back? Maybe we can find this Infinity place and trade some of the seeds. Maybe somehow we can eke out a living and find a new place to live. It was a nice daydream, and in those few seconds it felt like it might be a possibility, but being the dutiful leader he was, he turned to look at his friend and followed her gaze.

His eyes travelled to the long, steep road coming down from the ridge and the uniformed guard sprinting in their direction. "He's probably coming to tell us that the ground has opened up and hell is indeed about to swallow us."

"You think that hasn't happened already?"

"Actually, you make a good point."

"Seriously, Vad. What happens if we can't find Trainor?"

"As much as I want to find Landis and the others, Trainor's the important one. He had the plans in his head to make all of this viable."

"Are you saying we can't do this without him?"

"I'm saying that this needs more than someone who just has a passing interest in horticulture."

"Usually, I feel better when I talk to you."

"Sorry to disappoint."

"Do you think we made a mistake?"

Drake looked around. A small handful of people were still huddled by the ovens and grills. No one was in earshot, though, so he didn't have to worry about saying the wrong thing. Not that there was a wrong thing to say to Marina as she always held his confidence. The question was open-ended. It could mean did they make a mistake only leaving four lookouts on duty or was it a mistake to arrest Caine and the others? But Drake could see in his friend's eyes the true motivation behind the question. "Was it a mistake to leave our cushy lives behind in order to help the Level Three inhabitants and our families escape what would be generations of oppression at the hands of the same people who were pushing the planet towards oblivion before a different oblivion struck us?"

"In a nutshell."

He cast his eyes back towards the road. "I don't have all the answers. I wish I did. I want to think that coming here was the right thing to do for everybody, but it could be the biggest error of judgement I've ever made in my life."

"Yeah. About that whole talking to you to make me feel better thing; you're still coming up way, way short."

They watched in silence as the lone messenger continued his descent. By the time he reached the farmyard his face was red; after all, it was another mild morning. It took him a few seconds to catch his breath and then he finally blurted, "Dwyer."

"What about him?" Drake asked.

"We think we've spotted him and the others. It looks like all of them."

Drake cocked his head back and looked up to the sky, sucking in a lungful of air before blowing it back out again as if he was exhaling an expensive Cuban cigar. "Finally, something's gone right. When they arrive, send them straight to me."

The guard nodded before retracing his steps back out of the farmyard.

"Maybe this is where our luck starts to turn around," Marina said.

"Yeah ... somehow, I doubt that."

*

Jason sighed. "What are you thinking?" Zep asked.

"I'm thinking that everybody searching for Phil is a waste of time when we could be either heading to Infinity or working. And I'm pretty certain he'd say the same."

"Yeah," Dani said, but this is Phil. "Y'know, he's kind of important."

"Yes, he is," Nicola replied, "but Jason's got a point. The foraging teams should be heading out; the building teams should be getting to work; the farming teams should be tilling and weeding and planting."

"So, what should everybody do, forget about him and Debbie?"

"That's not what I'm saying," Jason replied. "Maybe a few groups go out and search areas in grids. I mean, hell, some of the guards must have had police experience or something before they got their jobs. They should know what they're doing with this kind of thing."

"Wait a minute," Dani said, pulling Jason around to look at her. "Search grids? Isn't that what you do when you're looking for a body?"

Jason cast a knowing look at Nicola before turning back to her daughter. "This is Phil we're talking about, Dani. We were due to head off to Infinity today. He wouldn't miss that for anything. I hate to say it, but given what happened to the soldiers last night, I'm guessing he and Debbie went off for a soul-searching walk before bed and ran into the same crowd that murdered those guards."

"I can't believe that."

"Well, you carry on believing whatever you want to, but it doesn't change the fact that we've got over three and a half thousand people here, and they need feeding and housing, and none of us can afford to waste time like this."

"Wow! Your compassion's overwhelming."

"I'm just telling you that you think things are bad now. Wait until you see what happens when people realise they're not going to have enough food to last beyond a couple of weeks. You'll realise there's more to life than compassion then."

*

Greenslade and Trunk had worked their way up the side of the hill, away from the road, making out that they were searching the scrub grass and behind the rocks for some hidden clue to find Phil and the others. In fact, they wanted to see the crime scene. They'd heard various accounts of what had been seen and what might have happened, but there were gaping holes in the theories. They each nodded respectfully to the guards standing on lookout duty at the summit and then carried along the ridge.

The bodies were still laid out as they had been discovered. Trunk put his hand over his nose as the smell of death had already begun to rise into the air. "What's wrong with this picture?" Greenslade asked.

Trunk may not have had smarts, but he did possess a degree of common sense. "They've all still got their weapons."

"Exactly," Greenslade said. "Even if Caine and the others didn't want to be seen with them, they could have stashed them. And the Ferals probably wouldn't have even left the bodies from what I've heard about them."

"So, what do you think happened, chief?"

"That's the million-dollar question, isn't it?" He cast his eyes to the road and saw the approaching group. A small smile appeared on his face. He remembered being suspicious of Drake when he had furnished him with directions to this place on faith, but now he had proof that his decision to trust him had saved lives.

"Looks like they got out then," Trunk said, following his eye line.

"Looks like."

"So, what do we do now?"

"We try to piece together a few more clues before this place explodes."

"What do you mean?"

"Can't you sense it? The whole settlement feels like it's about to erupt."

"But Caine's being guarded now."

"I'm pretty certain he's just the tip of the iceberg." Greenslade looked down towards the bodies once more. "And I'm pretty certain he was just some dumb prick with a gang of his mates trying to intimidate and assert himself a little. There's no way he did this. He's guilty of nothing more than being an idiot in the wrong place at the wrong time."

"Are you going to tell Drake?"

"Tell him what? He's got all the information we've got. He knows what we know. He probably thinks it's a long shot that they did this, but considering what they were doing this morning, they're the obvious people to start with. No. We need to find something substantive before we go to anyone with anything."

"But ... if there's a rebellion against the guards, would it be such a bad thing?"

Greenslade let out a laugh. They both still carried their cuts and bruises from the repeated assaults on them by Drake and his minions, and if anyone had grudges to hold, it was them. "As much as I hate to admit it, we're stronger together. I don't know about you, but I like the thought of having a well-trained army around, especially after hearing about the Ferals. And that's to say nothing of who else could be out there. No, Trunk. We need to douse any flames of insurrection before they get going; otherwise, this whole place will go up in smoke. Us, our families, everybody. There'll be nothing left, no future."

Trunk looked down at the bodies again. "Well, I'll do whatever you need me to, chief, y'know that. But piecing clues together isn't my thing." Greenslade smiled. There was a time when he would have been irritated by Trunk's self-deprecation, but now he was grateful for the other man's honesty and unswerving loyalty. "I mean, looking at the wounds, it seems to me like someone's just walked right up to them and gutted them. I mean there's got to be more to this because who'd let that happen?"

It was the first time Greenslade had even noticed, and given the rush to action by Drake and the others, they probably hadn't gone into forensic detail when looking at the bodies. All their heads were bloody, but that could have been due to crashing against rocks as they fell. Blood had soaked other parts of the dead men's clothing too, but there was plenty of it to go around from the wounds. Greenslade was oblivious to the smell as he crouched down and examined each of the victims a little more closely. "Bloody hell, Trunk. I think you've just figured this out."

"Eh? Figured what out?" Before he could get an answer, Greenslade was on his feet once more and heading back across the ridge. "Chief! Figured what out?"

*

"I have to tell you, I'm way out of my comfort zone with this," Penny said as Drake explained to her what needed doing.

"Why, because you think we're wanting to control you all as well?" he said, looking at her and then turning to Susan.

"No. Because it's going to put me at odds with a bunch of people. All I want here is a quiet life for my daughter and me. We've both been through enough."

"And the families of the guards who were murdered. What do you think they're going through right now?"

Penny's head dropped. "It's not that I don't feel sorry for them. It's just that people will see me as working for you, and let's face it, it's obvious from what's going on at the moment that you guys aren't the flavour of the month."

"Look, that's not what I want. I just want you in there as a witness during the interrogations. I want you to—"

"Interrogations?" Penny said. "Nice turn of phrase. Have you got a rack in there? Are you going to be waterboarding?"

Drake's shoulders sagged. "I just want to get to the truth."

"Uh-huh." Penny turned to Susan. "Look, I'm sorry, but I don't want any part of this for me or my daughter. Good luck."

"That went well," Drake said under his breath as he and Susan watched her walk away.

"Sorry. I thought she'd go for it."

"Back to square one then."

*

Callie and Matt were only a few metres from the edge of the tree line when Callie came to a juddering stop. Families and groups were camped all over the burnt-out forest and most of them had seemed faceless. Now, though, Callie's eyes were fixed on a single figure as he rifled through his rucksack.

"What is it?" Matt asked, coming to a halt too as he looked across towards his companion.

Callie didn't say anything; she just continued to watch the teenager who remained oblivious to everything going on around him. Eventually, he fished out the small sewing kit he had been searching for and looked up. It took him a second to understand it wasn't a nightmare and this was really happening. "Callie?" he almost gasped.

"Clive," she replied coolly.

"Err … I…."

"Clive, have you found that sewing kit yet?" his mother asked, coming out of the crude shelter they'd built with nothing more than a couple of blankets and a few branches. Seeing her son's hypnotised gaze, she looked up too. "Callie. How nice to see you."

"Hello," Callie replied with a forced smile.

"How are your mother and your brother?"

It was obvious by the tone and the greeting that she had no idea what her son had done, no idea of the betrayal and pain he had caused his closest friends in that one jealous action. "Soldiering on," Callie replied.

The woman took the sewing kit from her son. "Maybe we could all meet up later. Did Dani's and Jiang's families make it down here? It would be good for Clive to see you all. It's been hard since…." Her words trailed off and a look of sadness crept onto her face.

"I'll be in in a minute, Mum," Clive said.

The smile was gone from her face as her mind had visited a place she was doing her best to stay away from. "Yes. Okay, Clive."

She went back into the makeshift tent and Clive stood up, stepped away from the entrance and continued in a more hushed tone. "My dad died in the forest massacre."

"I'm sorry," Callie said and, to her surprise, she genuinely meant it.

"It's been hard since," he said, looking back towards the crude shelter.

"I bet it has."

Clive looked at Matt for the first time and nodded. "You look well, Callie. I'm glad."

Etiquette demanded that she should say the same thing, but she couldn't. Clive looked awful, even more thin, gaunt and pale than she remembered. His eyes were sunken marbles and his hair looked like it hadn't been washed in a month. Instead, she ignored what he said completely. "We're going to have to go. Two of our people are missing and we need to find them."

Clive's eyes dropped to the ground and he nodded. He didn't know if it was the truth or not, but it felt like an excuse. "Okay, Callie. Hope you find them."

Without another word, Matt and Callie set off once more. As they walked away, she could feel Clive's eyes following her. It was only when they were out of the forest and overlooking the cove that she turned back.

"What was all that about?" Matt asked.

"I'll tell you when we've got a free week."

*

"We're building something here. I know you've been through hell and I know you probably feel like there isn't a place for you, but there is, and it starts with us all working together." Si looked around at the faces. It was obvious that the like-minded group had deliberately set up camp together towards the north of the forest but away from the tree line, so there was less of a risk of prying eyes seeing what they were doing.

"Been through hell?" Austin replied. "You have no idea."

A bitter smile threatened to appear on Si's face momentarily, but he stifled it and looked towards Sasha instead. Sasha gave him strength. She calmed him when he needed it the most. "Look. You can't say that to me. You can't say that to either of us. We were imprisoned and, one by one, we watched our friends sliced into human bacon, knowing that our turn would come soon. What happened at the mine was horrific, evil.... I don't even have the words to do it justice, but don't tell me I don't know what hell is. Don't you dare."

Austin knew people who had been at the quarry and he had seen first-hand what the trauma of that experience had done to them. He nodded. "Fair enough. You know what hell is. But that means you should be supporting what we're talking about even more."

"How do you figure?"

"You escaped. What did you do to the people who committed those atrocities?"

Si suddenly realised that the bottom had fallen out of his argument. "Some of them were banished. We helped them—"

"I'm not talking about them. From what I gathered, a lot of them were victims just as much as you. I'm talking about the people in charge. You didn't banish them, did you?"

"Look. It's not the same."

"It is the same. How do we know some of the guards here weren't there on that night? How do we know that they didn't play a hand in massacring our people?"

"If they did, they'll have to live with that on their conscience. But they're here, aren't they? They didn't want to be a part of the administration any longer. They wanted freedom, and they could have just escaped themselves, but they freed you too. Isn't that worth something? Isn't that a show of intent?"

"It goes back to what you were saying about guilty consciences. Maybe they thought this one grand gesture would be a trade-off for all the shit they've done, all the families they've torn apart, all the lives they've destroyed."

Si looked around at the circle of Austin's followers. Many of them were armed with Q-Eighteens and Q-Thirties. Understanding the chances of a face-off with the guards loyal to the administration during the escape, Drake had insisted that some of the surplus weapons be distributed among them. In hindsight, this was a naïve show of trust, but at the time, it probably seemed not only logical but decent. "You just can't do this," Si said, shaking his head again. "You'll destroy everything we've worked for."

"We won't be destroying anything. This is a vermin control problem. And when we're done, we're all going to be able to build something together that's truly ours without the shadow of these people hanging over us."

"And their families?" Si said. "You going to kill them too?"

"We're going to take out the guards and anyone who raises as much as a fist to us. We're not cold-blooded murderers like them. We'll pack them off with some supplies and even some seeds so they can start again somewhere."

"Oh yeah, that'll really happen."

Austin shook his head. "I heard what Caine did. He's an idiot. He always has been. And I'll never defend some bastard who thinks he can justify hurting a little kid for something their parent might have done. But the guards locking him and the others up like that, it's not on. We're not their subordinates anymore. If punishment needs dishing out, and by the sounds of it, it does, it should be us who do it, not them."

"Three men were murdered last night. After what Caine did, it's not a stretch to think he and his pals might know something about it."

"Again. It's not up to the Salvation guard to do that. They've immediately turned it into an 'us and them' situation. Jesus, Si. Can't you see where this is heading?

We've been out of that place a day and look at what's going on. Open your eyes."

Si shook his head. "I won't let you do this. I won't let you spoil things here."

Now it was Austin who shook his head. He turned to Sasha. "Out of respect for you and your family, I did what you asked. I gave him five minutes. Take him," he said to a handful of armed men standing by his side.

Before Si even had time to react, firm hands grasped him as his wrists were bound with carefully torn strips of bedding. *Jesus, they were prepared for this all along.* "What are you doing? What the hell are you doing?"

"I'm sorry. When this is over, we'll let you go, but right now, we can't risk having you warn them."

Si turned to Sasha. "Don't let them do this. You can't let them do this."

"I'm sorry, Si. Austin's right."

Suddenly, it felt like all the bones in his body had turned to jelly. "Sasha...." He didn't know how to continue. He stared at her, and she stared back at him. *She's betrayed me.* He stopped struggling, and even when a gag was placed in his mouth and a blindfold was tied around his eyes, he did not fight back. He was pushed against a tree and he slowly slid down it. He felt another makeshift rope bind his feet while another longer piece tied him to the tree. He heard the crowd begin to move away, but it didn't matter now. Nothing mattered now. *She betrayed me.*

*

Ever since the extended gang who had assaulted Tyler at the stream had been bundled into the house, a vigil had been kept by a small group of agitated friends and relatives. The group had gradually got bigger and more vocal, and now there were over fifty men and women outside, facing up to the guards on the door, demanding that the prisoners be released.

"This is getting out of hand pretty quickly," Marina said as she joined Drake.

He had been watching the proceedings carefully. "They've got every right to protest. People used to be able to do that, remember?"

"So now you're a man of the people?" she replied with a nervous smile as she continued to observe the crowd. As well as the men and women guarding the door and windows, another fifteen had been positioned surreptitiously around the periphery of the farmyard and the other buildings. They weren't exactly hiding, but they weren't advertising their presence either.

"What are you going to do?" Susan asked, seemingly appearing out of nowhere.

"Well, unless you've found another unbiased mediator for the interviews, I think it would make sense for us to start questioning people. The sooner we do the sooner we can decide what to do next."

"Surely there's someone who'd be willing to do it," Marina asked.

"I've been asking around, but no one wants the hassle. Apparently, this Caine bloke's got a bit of a reputation and people are worried about it opening up a can of worms for them and their families."

Drake let out another long sigh. "Course they are. Why would anybody think that trying to maintain honesty, decency and respect in a society would require any sacrifice?"

"You sound bitter."

"Yeah, I wonder why."

"Hey. I think you need to let your prisoners go. Or at least the ones who didn't directly assault that kid," Greenslade said as he and Trunk walked up to where Drake, Susan and Marina were standing. All three of them turned to him with confused looks on their faces.

"Why?" Susan asked.

"Because I'm pretty certain it wasn't them."

"Oh, then who was it?"

BOOM! For the second time that morning, a

thunderous crack echoed around the settlement. Everyone froze for a moment until Trunk dropped to the ground like a lead weight.

14

The distant sound of the rifle crack reverberated over the fields, through the forest and beyond. Callie and Matt had only tentatively begun their search of the coastline down from the main beach when the noise carried to them. Without pause, they both set off at a sprint back in the direction of the farm.

*

Dani did not even consider finishing her sentence as the rifle's report reached her. She, her mum, Zep and Jason all turned for home, not missing a beat as they began to run faster and harder than they had in some time.

*

Si's head drooped further. The blindfold that had been secured around his eyes blocked out virtually everything, but in his mind's eye, he could imagine exactly what was unfolding. *Damn.*

*

Chloe ran across to the door of the small infirmary, slamming it shut and placing the primitive wooden bolt across. None of the occupants of the small building knew what was unfolding outside, but the tension and air of impending doom gripped them all.

*

Several seconds passed, and all Drake, Susan, Marina and Greenslade could do was look down at Trunk's body. Then, as if they had somehow been transported to the centre of a war zone, the sound of gunfire erupted all around them.

"Take cover," Drake shouted, grabbing hold of Marina's arm and charging across the farmyard as the sound of whistling bullets sliced through the air behind them.

Greenslade and Susan each grabbed one of Trunk's wrists and began to drag him towards the barn. A moment before, several people had been lingering in the doorway, but now they had all ducked inside for safety, hoping the walls would shield them from not just the bullets but the unfolding horror.

"They're not firing at us," Susan screamed.

"By all means, stay out here if you want to," Greenslade replied as they both continued to drag the big man towards the doorway.

*

Drake and Marina dived behind one of the large stone ovens. They were totally exposed to the west, but for the time being, there were no threats in that direction.

"What did you see?" Drake shouted over the continuing gunfire.

"I don't know. The piles of stones, the scrub grass on the way to the stream, behind the infirmary. I don't know. Could be none of them. Could be all of them."

The bullets continued to crash and chip at the oven as they remained crouched behind it. A scream sliced through the rumble of gunfire and Drake gambled a lightning-quick peek to see one of the guards falling backwards from his position at one corner of the house. He was clutching his leg as another guard took his weight and dragged him away from the danger area.

A sudden explosion of stone centimetres above Drake's head made him duck back once more. "Shit!"
"What is it?"
"Goldie's been hit."
"Shit!"

*

"Ugh! Chief?" Trunk struggled to speak as he was dragged over the threshold of the barn, but as his eyes flickered open, he saw his friend's face looking down at him.

"Trunk. Thank Christ. I thought we'd lost you."

Trunk's face contorted in pain as Greenslade and Susan finally let go. They had pulled him into one of the curtain-partitioned living quarters, whose exactly they weren't sure. "Where are you hit?" Susan asked, dropping to her knees.

He was wearing a baggy black shirt and, beneath it, a black T-shirt. No one had seen the bullet enter him; they had just seen him drop. Trunk slowly reached around to the back of his head and withdrew a bloody hand.

"That's just where you fell. You must have given your head a crack on the concrete," Greenslade said, finally spotting a hole surrounded by an expanding wet patch on his friend's shoulder. "Right. We need to apply pressure to stop the bleeding." He tore a section of Trunk's shirt away, scrunched it up and immediately pressed down on the wound.

"Agh!" Normal people would have howled in pain, but Trunk let out a barely audible grunt as his friend pressed down on his wound. The air still rumbled around them as the gunfire continued, but for the moment, they were out of harm's way.

"What do you think's going on?" Susan asked.

"I'm guessing someone doesn't like the new sheriff in town."

*

A bullet blasted a small hole in the door, and John, Chloe and Nazya all looked towards it with concern.

Michelle was holding Ollie as she squeezed Harry's arm with her free hand, desperate to try to make them feel a little less frightened. *These kids have been through so much. What now?*

"I hope to God Lilly and the girls aren't anywhere near what's going on out there," John said.

"Do you think it's those Feral people?" Michelle asked.

"I've never heard of them attacking a big camp like this before," Chloe said, reaching out to take Nazya's hand as more bullets crashed against the small building.

"As much as I'd like to blame the Ferals," John began, "I think this is all our doing."

*

With everything else that had been happening, Austin and his followers had arrived on the grounds of the farmyard unnoticed. The small mountains of stones that had been gathered for the building of more houses provided bountiful cover for them. To gain a fuller view of the yard and the guards scattered around the main house, members of the self-appointed freedom fighter brigade had covertly taken a few of the stones and positioned them behind wider tufts of scrub grass, creating mini turrets, protecting them from return fire.

Austin himself was ducked down behind one. His wife and loyalist follower, Clem, took cover behind the next. They had lost more than most that night at the mine. They had watched their children gunned down in cold blood by the administration's attack dogs and no amount of killing would ever satiate their hatred. The only thing that kept them going back in Level Three was their devotion to each other and the shared pain of their loss.

"How many have we got?" Clem.

"I think one, so far."

"No. We got that big guy straight off the bat, so—"

"He wasn't with them. He was one of us. Some bloody idiot must have seen he was wearing black, put two and two together and got five."

"Shit."

The bullets continued to fly, but other than split-second flashes as the guards or freedom fighters took their shots, there were no real targets to aim at.

"There'll be more coming soon. They'll come from the forest. Maybe we should have started there. Maybe that would have made more sense."

"No time for maybes now," Clem said before screaming as several chips of stone exploded above her. For the first time since that night at the mine, she feared for her life and that of her husband. All of this had seemed like a good idea when they'd been talking about it and urging others to follow them, but the reality was something different. "I love you."

Austin turned his head towards her, his cheek almost touching the ground as more bullets crashed against the stones he was shielded behind. "I love you too, Clemmy."

*

Tania and Harper had been helping Greta with the orphaned children when the gunfire had first erupted. The fear-filled screams of the youngsters had charged the already electrified air even further. Instinctively, the three adults had guided the crying and distraught group further downstream.

"We should be safe enough here," Tania said as they finally came to rest behind a tall rocky mound.

The children continued to wail and fret, and one little girl had lost control of her bladder, but nobody could blame her. "What the hell is going on now?" Harper asked as she, Tania and Greta stepped away from the rest of the group momentarily to look back to the farm. From the first round fired, people had fled, some into the buildings, some across the stream and towards the far woodland, others across the road and into the forest. On their own short journey, they had seen many cowering on the banks, not daring to raise their heads above the parapet.

"I don't know," Tania replied, "but whatever it is, we need to make sure the children are protected."

"Do you think it could be those Feral things?" Greta asked.

Tania and Harper glanced at each other. The thought had occurred to them too. "I don't know," Tania eventually replied. "Let's hope not."

"Shouldn't we try to do something?" Harper said.

Tania scoured the ground. Some of the children played King of the Castle around these rocks and it wasn't unusual for them to have blackened branches from the forest to use as swords. She grabbed one that came up to her waist, leant it against the rock at a slight angle and then kicked hard at the base. The wood splintered, leaving a jagged, spear-like edge. "What are you doing?" Greta asked.

"We don't know what's going on, but we do know these children only have us to protect them."

Harper and Greta suddenly turned a shade paler before they too grabbed similar branches from the ground and proceeded to weaponise them in the same way. "Oh, my God. My mum," Greta said, taking a few tentative paces back towards the farmyard before Harper reached out and placed a hand on her shoulder.

"Your mum's a smart woman. She'll be keeping her head down and leaving the guards to do their job. You need to stay safe here with us."

Greta continued to look towards the farm with concern then glanced at Harper before finally turning back to the crying children. Her shoulders sagged and her head bowed. "I really hope you're right."

*

A massive crowd had gathered at the tree line of the forest, sheltering behind the blackened trunks as much as they could. They could not see exactly what was going on at the farm, but the gunfire told them that, whatever it was, they were safer where they were.

The remaining Salvation guards had split into two groups and had begun an operation to slowly work their way around to the other end of the farmyard.

Callie had to virtually force her way through the lines of people as she made her way out of the forest. Matt paused briefly, hoping she would stop, hoping she would realise there was nothing she could do while a terrifying gun battle ensued, but his hopes were shattered as she continued running across the verge, across the road and towards the farm she and Phil had first laid eyes on a few weeks before.

"Callie. Callie, stop!" he shouted hopelessly. The mumblings from the massive crowd rose a little as he and his companion burst through their ranks. They continued towards the farm, adding a new dimension of curiosity to the vast line of fear-filled gawkers. "Callie, stop!" he pleaded again as he began to charge after her.

But if Matt could have seen her face at that moment, if he could have seen the bitter stinging tears rolling down her cheeks, he would have known that stopping was the last thing on Callie's mind. Sad, hollow whimpers left her mouth as she continued to tear towards the farmyard. Ever since that first day that she had met Phil, things had been hard. They'd been hard, but she had stayed strong despite all the terrifying trials they had faced.

The night when the lights went out. The thought of her mother drowning in the flooded tunnel. Getting captured by the Sanctuary guards and being left at the hands of that terrifying Micky creature. The battle at the quarry. Almost getting recaptured in Salvation. The near brush with death at the hands of the Ferals, first in the forest then again just yesterday morning. And now ... a full-scale battle taking place at the farm that was the foundation of the new settlement, their new home.

As she ran, she had no idea who the antagonists were. It could have been an attack by the Ferals, it could have been anyone, but all she knew was this one thing that kept going around and around her head. *This can't go on.*

*

"We need to get him to Nazya or one of the other doctors," Susan said.

Greenslade continued to apply pressure to Trunk's wound, but he looked up towards her. "None of us are going anywhere while the bullets are flying out there."

"Maybe I can head out the back way and work my way around." There were fear-filled voices whispering in the shadowy corners of the barn as the assault continued, but no one had any intention of moving, knowing to step outside would be to take their lives into their hands.

"That's not happening."

"No offence, but I don't take orders from anyone."

"I'll shoot you in the leg myself if you think about going out there."

"Why are you suddenly so bothered about what happens to me?"

"Because if anything happened to you or your daughter, then this place would collapse. You two have been the voices of reason. I've not always liked what you've had to say. I've not really enjoyed being called out for the stuff I've done. But you've been right from the start. You've been—"

"STOP IT! STOP IT! STOP IT!" A scream erupted from outside.

"Wh-what's that, chief?" Trunk asked weakly.

Greenslade closed his eyes and shook his head despairingly. "The voice of reason."

*

"What in Christ's name?" Drake hissed, edging out from his cover to watch the teenage girl running into the centre of the farmyard.

The gunfire continued for a moment before finally coming to a pause. "Oh shit!" Marina muttered, gripping her rifle tightly and hoping none of her people fired.

*

"Who the hell's she?" Austin asked, raising his head above the parapet a little to get a better view of the crazy girl who had just risked death by charging into the middle of what was essentially a battlefield.

"I think I saw her last night. Someone said she was the girl who'd helped us all escape from Salvation the first time," Clem replied.

"Has she lost her mind?"

"Well, she's not exactly an advert for good mental health, is she?"

*

Callie slowly turned. Tears were still streaming down her cheeks, but she could see enough to understand what was going on. It was a fight between some of the mine survivors and the guards.

"Callie?" The teenager turned to the barn to see her mother standing in the doorway.

She heard the sound of running feet behind her and looked to see Matt finally catching up. He came to a stop by her side and immediately began to turn in a full circle too to see what was going on. The tension in the air mounted further and it felt like the firing could start again at any moment.

"What is wrong with you?" Callie screamed, clenching her fists together by her sides. The tears continued to roll down her face, but now a deathly silence had fallen over the farmyard beyond the echoes of the young woman's shouts.

"Callie ... darling," Susan said, rushing towards her. "You need to—"

"No, Mum. I don't need to do anything." She gestured in the vague direction of the warring factions. "THESE PEOPLE ARE THE ONES WHO NEED TO DO SOMETHING. THEY NEED TO STOP. THEY NEED TO STOP!" More tears than ever were gushing from her eyes now.

"Callie," John said, appearing from the door of the small makeshift infirmary. "Calm down. This is—"

"This is what, John?" She had stopped yelling but was still speaking loudly enough to be heard by anyone who wanted to listen, which was pretty much everyone. "Crazy?

Is that what you wanted to say, John? Mad? Insane? You're damn right it is." Callie turned a full circle again, and her eyes picked out more and more guards and armed civilians. She pointed to the sky. "We were virtually wiped out. What don't you people get about that? We completely defied all the odds just by being here, and now you want to throw all that away."

Susan placed an arm around her daughter. She was convinced the shooting would erupt again at any moment, but if Callie was refusing to get off the field of battle, then so would she.

"You're just a kid. You don't know anything!" Austin shouted, kneeling up a little further. "Our children were murdered by these bastards. Our children and our friends and our neighbours. Thousands of them, and you just expect us to carry on with this hanging over us?"

Callie turned and focused on the man who had shouted out just as further figures blurred into the farmyard. Dani, Jason, Zep and Nicola weren't exactly sure what they were walking into, but they realised something had caused the fighting to stop and seeing Callie made the pieces fall into place.

Dani was the first to walk into the centre of the yard and join her friend. On seeing her, Zep, Nicola and Jason followed suit. "So, this is it?" Callie continued. "You want another war. You'll kill some of them, they'll kill some of you, and then you'll have even more loved ones to grieve for, more anger and hatred. And it will just go on and on and on."

"Then what are we meant to do? Just forget them?"

"No. That's the last thing you should do. You should remember them every day." Callie wiped some of the tears from her face. "You should honour them every day. There are children orphaned from that night who have nothing. There are widows and widowers who are trying to figure out if there's any point in going on."

"And what is the point?" the man shouted out.

"Building something. Building something not just for us but for future generations. We almost became a footnote in history, and hell, that still might happen. None of us knows what's around the corner and we've got plenty of tangible threats facing us without creating our own existential problems."

"Maybe some of us can't. Maybe some of us don't want to get past it."

There was a long pause before Callie wiped the remainder of the tears from her face. "Then your lust for revenge is damning us all. The loved ones you lost will have died for nothing, and—"

"They did die for nothing."

"No. They died because we all came to the surface to look for freedom in the first place. They died because Bucks and his people believe we are nothing more than property— pit ponies, or caged canaries, here for nothing but to work for them." She gestured behind her to the former Salvation guards. "They had no choice in what they did every day just like we had no choice working in the recycling plant or the farms or the water treatment works. They have even more to risk by doing what they did, but they're here because they couldn't take any more injustice. The only way any of this happens is if we all work together." Her eyes fixed on the man who was now kneeling up a little further still. "Your children ... make their deaths count for something. Make sure they didn't die in vain. They died as part of the struggle against Bucks and the others. Let's build something here together that will be their legacy; that will be a testament to what we can all do together."

Susan gripped Callie's hand tightly and the young woman turned to her mother. It was Susan who was crying now as tears of pride ran down her cheeks. Austin stood up, and everyone held their collective breaths for a moment. He stared at Callie for a few seconds that seemed to last an eternity then turned and walked away. Clem scrambled to her feet with a bewildered expression on her face and she paused too before running after him. One by one, the other self-appointed freedom fighters dispersed, and with each one that left, the tension around the farmyard diminished a little more.

"Can I get some help in here?" Greenslade shouted.

"Man down over here," another voice yelled. Suddenly, the farmyard became a hive of activity once again. Chloe and Nazya appeared from the doorway of what was fast becoming the permanent infirmary with the makeshift stretcher that Phil and Matt had made for Harry.

Several black-clad figures disappeared into the barn, and a few seconds later, Trunk was being helped out. Two guards bore his full weight as he held a bloody piece of cloth up to his shoulder.

"Dad, DAD?" Steph shouted as she and Libby ran towards him. Two more guards grabbed the stretcher from Chloe and Naz and ran across to where their compatriot had fallen with a bullet in the leg. More guards still gingerly wandered in the general directions that the fighters had been entrenched to make sure there were no snipers still lurking.

"That was quite something," Drake said as he and Marina walked up to the group in the middle of the farmyard. "I don't know if that was the bravest thing I've ever seen or the stupidest."

"It must have been hard to tell back there from your hiding place," Susan replied.

A smile appeared on Drake's face. "Well, thank you, anyway," he said, fixing his gaze on Callie. They all stood there for a moment, still dazed from the shock of the last few minutes. They watched Trunk and his family disappear into the small infirmary, followed by Nazya. Then two guards carrying a stretcher went in after them. "This could have been a lot worse if it wasn't for you."

"It could flare up again," Callie said. "There's a lot of bridge building to do on both sides."

"Yeah, I've kind of figured that. It's just knowing where to start."

"You can start by releasing Caine and the others," Greenslade said, walking up to Drake and the others.

"Blake!" He stopped and turned to see Grace and Theo running towards him. An unexpected smile lit his face. It was not so long ago that he wanted nothing more than to start again without them, to begin a completely new life, but now things were different. He had begun to cherish the time they spent together, and in the few seconds where bullets had been flying around the farmyard, his thoughts had not been for himself but for Theo and Grace. He held them both tightly as they rushed into his arms.

"I'm okay. I'm okay," he said, the smile broadening on his face as he locked eyes with Callie. It was this infuriating girl who had changed him so much. He knew it, and she knew it, and the slightest hint of a smile bled onto her face for a moment, cracking the dryness off her cheeks as the salty tracks had hardened.

"What do you mean release Caine?" Drake said, his mind finally drifting back to the conversation that had begun before the assault. "People are going to have to pay for their actions. Your friend got shot. One of my people got shot, and three others were murdered in cold blood while more are still missing. All that stuff just can't go without punishment. We'd be living in a perpetual state of anarchy. It would be like the Wild West."

"I don't think Caine did it."

"We caught him and his pals red-handed this morning attacking the child of one of my guards and, granted, the field of suspects for the murders has just got a whole lot wider in the past few minutes, but—"

"I think your guards were killed by someone they knew ... someone they trusted," Greenslade said. Drake fell quiet for a moment.

"What makes you say that?" Marina asked, taking over.

"Your guards were well trained. The men I saw all looked like they took care of themselves."

"And your point is?"

"They all had big knife wounds in their guts, suggesting that someone walked up in front of them. Now, that suggests to me that they knew the person and didn't perceive them to be a threat. They all still had their weapons too. Why would someone wanting to stage a rebellion leave them armed? And the bodies were dragged to one fairly tough-to-find spot. Why?"

"What are you saying exactly?"

"I'm saying that it doesn't sound like who you've got locked up."

Marina and Drake both looked at each other and their faces drained of colour.

"What is it?" Susan asked, immediately seeing the change in them both. "What?"

Neither of them could speak as their minds began to whir.

"I expected a warm welcome, but I didn't think there'd be fireworks," Dwyer said as he and the other escapees appeared. "What the hell happened here?" There was no response from either of his friends and he looked towards Greenslade, Susan, Callie and the others. "What's going on?"

"Yeah. What is going on?" Susan asked.

"I need a minute, okay?" Drake said, guiding Dwyer by the arm away from the small crowd. Marina and Revell followed.

"Oh, don't mind us; we've only been on the road for the last day and night. We'll just stand here while you all have your little chinwag," PJ shouted out behind them.

"Hey, weren't you listening to my daughter?" Susan asked, marching up to the four of them as they continued to move away. "We get through this together, no secrets, no—"

"Please," Drake said, "please just give me a minute." Susan looked into his eyes and a little shiver ran through her.

She reluctantly went back to the others and folded her arms. "What the hell do you think's going on?" she asked.

"Nothing good," Greenslade replied.

*

Drake shook his head slowly. "There has to be another explanation. I've had Landis and Rachael around to my house for dinner a dozen times for Christ's sake."

"Would somebody mind telling me what the hell's going on?" Revell asked.

"Like you said," Marina replied, "there has to be another explanation."

Drake shook his head again. "I was so eager to blame this on the Level Threes that I didn't even examine the bodies properly." He clenched his eyes together tightly as if suffering from the worst migraine of his life. "I still.... No, there's something we're missing. Rachael's a doctor; she does nothing but care for people. Landis is my friend. They...."

"Guys, guys," Dwyer said with a bewildered look on his face, pulling Marina around to face him in order to get her attention. The group of people they had left in the middle of the farmyard continued to cast furtive glances in their direction, but the strangers were of no consequence to Dwyer at that moment. All he wanted was some clue as to what his friends were talking about. "What's going on here? What's happening?"

Marina took a deep breath and finally focused on the man talking to her. "Last night, we stationed guards on the ridge; Cribbs, Chester, Surnow and Landis. We found Cribbs, Chester and Surnow dead this morning. We couldn't find Landis anywhere. I sent some men to find Rachael, but she'd disappeared too. So had Emily and Larch ... with all their gear."

Confused expressions crept onto Dwyer's and Revell's faces. "You think they're somehow responsible? That doesn't make any sense. Why?"

"Because they're not the only ones missing," Drake said. "Trainor and his wife are gone."

"Trainor?" Dwyer almost gasped. "But...." He couldn't finish the sentence. *But he's the one who made all this viable. He's the one who everybody's counting on. He's the one.... He is the one.*

"But I still can't believe it," Drake said. "There has to be another explanation."

"Ohhh shit!" Revell blurted. "PJ."

"What do you mean? What about PJ?" Marina asked.

"We thought he was just being his usual paranoid self. He went to take a leak last night and he came back all freaked out. We looked and we couldn't see a thing, so we just put it down to him being him."

"What are you talking about?"

"He reckons he saw people in the distance while he was taking a piss ... six of them."

"But...." Marina suddenly felt like the weight of the entire universe was on her shoulders, and for a second, it was like she wasn't in her body at all. She staggered forward and Drake reached out to grab her by the arm.

"Are you okay?" he asked. She looked at him with barely any recognition in her eyes until she finally took hold of her senses once more.

"No. No, I'm not."

15

Peter Shan was the youngest in a long line of troublemakers. His father had been in and out of prison and each of his brothers was threatening to follow in his footsteps. Like every bully, he demanded attention and a sycophantic following, and like his brothers before, he had got it.

"Trainor's pissed himself, Miss," he shouted out, causing his followers and the rest of the class to laugh as they all turned to look at the young boy lagging behind the rest of the group. There was a dark wet patch on his beige corduroy shorts and Phil's face was contorted as a pained expression of anguish and humiliation decorated it. He glanced around at the faces as they all stared back at him. Lindsey Kews, Robbie Tring, and Carla Hemp were just three out of the crowd he focused on. They all looked with mock disgust but equal amounts of delight as they pointed and laughed.

"We've only just set off from the visitor's centre, why didn't you go there?" Miss Carlton snapped angrily. The two teacher's assistants stood behind her, both trying not to giggle as the young boy just stood there looking down at his shorts.

It was a sunny day and Phil had been looking forward to visiting the ruins of the ancient abbey and the inevitable nature hike that would ensue afterwards. He'd hoped that it would be one of the other boys who would be the focus of Shan and his small gang of witless thugs, but it was not to be. He had made the mistake of dropping back to take a photo of a gymnopilus purparatus, a very rare red-capped mushroom. He knew his mum would be fascinated by it. Usually, it was the parents who feigned interest in the children's hobbies to develop a bond, but the lack of attention Phil received prompted him to make far more effort than a ten-year-old should have to.

It was only when he had caught up with the rest of the group once more that he realised Shan and his mob were between him and the small circle of safety near the teacher at the front. As a result, he had deliberately hung back, doing his best not to attract their attention, but in the end, he'd failed. It had all happened so quickly. Phil's eyes had been cast out over the green and pleasant hills in the distance, and the next thing he knew he felt something run down his leg. He turned to see Shan had squirted some of the contents of his water bottle in the direction of Phil's groin.

Phil could feel himself colouring up more and more each second, as the teacher continued to glare at him with chastising eyes, and virtually everyone else just laughed ... virtually everyone. There was a small group near the front who often fell afoul of Shan's antics whose gazes were solemn.

"It-it wasn't me," Phil protested.

"It wasn't you? You're saying someone else wet your pants, Philip?" This caused even more laughter from the crowd behind her. Phil glanced towards Shan to see a menacing look in the other boy's eyes. If he told the teacher what had happened, he'd get the beating of his life from Shan's gang and, in all likelihood, Miss Carlton wouldn't believe him anyway. "Is it, Philip? Is that what you're saying?"

I could run away. I could run back down the hill to the visitor centre and hide until it's time to go home. No. That would make everything a thousand times worse. I'd get called to the headmistress's office and there'd be the long march of dishonour through the teachers' lounge where they'd all be looking at me and laughing behind their hands. That's the boy who peed his pants then ran away and hid. "No, Miss Carlton. I'm sorry, Miss Carlton."

The teacher let out a long exasperated breath. "Well, look, we don't have any spare clothes or anything. You're just going to have to let the sun dry it out. It's a warm day. It shouldn't take long."

"But he's going to smell, Miss," Lindsey Kews called out. "Does he have to walk with us?" More laughter rippled around the crowd and Miss Carlton looked down at the patch on Phil's shorts with something approaching disgust. "Nobody's going to smell, Lindsey, and this doesn't concern you."

The young girl sniffed at the air in an exaggerated manner. "I can smell him already."

The teacher cast an angry glare towards the young girl. "Look. It's a beautiful day, and we've still got plenty to see before we head back to the bus. Let's all just carry on up the hill, shall we and mind our own business?" She glanced towards the two teacher's assistants, who picked up on her cue and started to lead the children up the hillside path once more. "What were you thinking, Philip?" she muttered under her breath.

Phil stared up at her and saw no compassion, no understanding in her eyes. "I'm sorry, Miss," he said once more and slowly began to walk away after the others.

*

"Hold up. Hold up, Trainor." Suddenly, Phil was torn away from his childhood reminiscences and firmly back in the present. His hands had been bound in front of him. It had taken two nasty falls to convince his captors that, at least this way, he could protect himself a little more should he trip again. Debbie's hands had been zip tied in front of her as well. Both of them were gagged and whatever they had been drugged with had left their mouths dry and their heads throbbing.

It had all happened so quickly. It had been dark and they had been taking a walk in the fields before finally turning in for the night. It was common for Phil to do this, especially after a busy day, and that day had been busier than most. The next thing either of them remembered was waking up on the ridge and seeing the bodies of guards. Then the march had begun. It had seemed like an endless hike until the terrain had become too dangerous to navigate by moonlight. They had stopped for a couple of hours, but there was always at least one pair of eyes monitoring them. They were on their way again before dawn, though, using what was left of the battery power for their torches.

Phil had refused to continue after a while and a knife had been put to Debbie's throat. Without hesitation, he began to put one foot in front of the other once more. Now the night was well behind them, terror had given way a little to weariness, sadness and resignation.

"Sit down there," another of their captors said, manhandling Phil and pushing him back. Memories of his childhood came rushing back to him once more before his buttocks found the solid support of a rock beneath him. "And you," the man said, forcing Debbie to sit down next to him. "We're taking a short break and then we'll be on our way again." The man handed them a bottle of water and pulled down their gags. "Don't get any stupid ideas, 'cause you know how they'll end up."

The guard walked over to where his three cohorts were standing and joined in their quiet conversation, occasionally throwing a glance back to his captives. It was the first time Debbie and Phil had been next to each other since their ordeal had begun, and both of them nestled up as closely as they could, touching shoulders and the back of hands, leaning their heads into one another. "Here," Phil said, offering his wife the bottle.

She took several gulps before handing it back to him. He did the same and then the pair just sat there, looking out across the patchy green and yellow fields that stretched off towards the coastline. "Matt's going to be scared to death. He's not going to know what's happening," Debbie said and tears began to roll down her face.

Phil turned towards her and his heart broke a little more if that was possible. "Matt's strong and he's got Susan and Callie and Tania and Harper and a lot more good friends who'll do whatever it takes to get him through this, to look after him."

"You don't really believe that. I can see it in your eyes."

Phil looked away. It was true, he didn't believe that, and more often than not, Debbie could see right through him when he wasn't telling the truth. "I want to believe it if that makes any difference. I want to believe that they're all going to be okay." Now it was Phil's eyes that filled with stinging tears.

"What's going to happen, Phil?" She looked across to their small group of captors at exactly the same moment one of them glanced at her. She broke eye contact immediately, feeling guilty for even daring to raise her eyes.

"I honestly don't know."

She let out a huff of a laugh. "Your powers of deception haven't improved even after all these years."

"I'm sorry, Debs," he said quietly.

"I need to know."

Phil turned towards her and his eyes were a little blurry, his face was long and drawn, and as he spoke, his voice cracked a little. "Nothing good, Debs. Whether it's to work in the hydroponics farms or to help them establish the crops for the new settlements, they're going to want me and my knowledge and they're going to hold the threat of hurting you over me constantly. That's my guess anyway."

"That doesn't sound like much of an existence." She leaned into her husband once more. "At least Matt will be safe." When no words of confirmation backed her up, she turned once more. "Phil. Matt will be safe, won't he?"

"I don't know, Debs." He nodded in the direction of their captors. "They know the location of the settlement now. I think it would be foolish to try to recapture their workforce, but I honestly don't know."

"Oh, God."

"How are you feeling?" Rachael asked, taking them both by surprise as their heads angled up towards her.

"How are we feeling?" Debbie asked with an air of indignation in her voice. "Like we've been kidnapped and torn away from our family."

What looked like genuine regret flashed on Rachael's face for a moment before it vanished again. "I mean physically."

"My head's throbbing," Phil said.

Rachael nodded slowly and reached into her bag. "And yours?" she asked, looking at Debbie.

"Yes, mine is too." The haughtiness was gone temporarily at the prospect of getting treatment for her headache.

Rachael tapped out two tablets from a bottle and handed one to each of them. They accepted the capsules with their still bound hands and took the small pills with a sip of water. Rachael looked at Phil's right temple, where he had cut his head after falling. "I'm going to clean that up a bit, okay?" Phil just shrugged as she reached back into her bag for some antiseptic wipes. "When we get back home, I'll be able to treat it properly."

"Why are you doing this?" Debbie asked.

"I'm sure all your questions will be answered when we get back to Salvation."

"Oh, I'm sure they will, but why are *you* doing this?"

"How about you just keep it shut and let her do her job?" one of the guards hissed as he walked over to join them. Debbie couldn't be sure, but she thought she'd heard the others refer to him as Landis.

"I was just asking why she was kidnapping us and taking us away from our family and friends."

Landis shook his head angrily. "The knowledge in your husband's head is valuable to the administration."

"Shame they didn't think that when they dumped us down on Level Three and left us all to die."

"Well, things change, don't they?"

"I'm guessing you haven't been able to achieve previous production levels," Phil said with half a smile on his face. "Amelia not up to the task?"

"Are you nearly done?" Landis asked Rachael.

"I'll just be a minute," she replied, continuing to dab Phil's head wound.

"Well, make sure you are. Five minutes and we want to be back on the road." He walked back to join the others.

"You're a doctor. You care for people. How can you be doing this?" Debbie asked.

"Despite what you might think, I believe the administration is our best hope for survival, everybody's best hope."

"And what about the thousands of Level Three people they killed outside the mine? Were they their best hope too?"

"That was rogue elements."

"That's what they told you?" Debbie said, laughing bitterly and looking across to the three guards. "For a doctor, you're not actually that bright, are you?"

"I understand you're angry and scared, and I'd probably be angry and scared too if I was in your position, but by you coming back, you're going to save a lot of lives. You're going to help found the new settlement, and then hopefully you'll understand."

"And our boy and our friends. What happens to them?"

"Are you done yet?" Landis shouted over.

Rachael dropped the wipe on the ground. "Yes. All done," she said, turning and walking away from the couple once more.

"It's just what you said." Debbie's voice was soft and Phil leaned across and kissed her cheek.

"We're together. You told me we could get through anything as long as we're together."

"I'm not sure we'll want to get through this."

A shiver ran down Phil's spine. Even at her lowest point, he had never heard her come out with something like that. He looked across at her. "Promise me you won't think about doing anything stupid. Promise me." She looked at him and tears started to roll down her face once more.

"Okay. Rest time's over," Landis said, snatching the bottle from Phil once more and placing it in his rucksack. He dragged the two prisoners to their feet and replaced their gags then pushed each of them as they began to put one foot in front of the other once more for the final stretch of the journey.

*

"We've got to go after them," Matt said as tears welled in his eyes. "I need a gun."

"Matt's right," Callie replied. "The sooner we set off the better. They've already got a big head start."

The pair began to walk away.

"Listen," Jason said, causing them both to stop and turn. "I get it, and if that was my family out there, I'd feel the same, but if they've been travelling most of the night, it won't be too long before they're back in Salvation."

"Well, we can't just do nothing," Matt replied.

Drake wasn't familiar with everyone's name's yet, but he'd heard Matt's mentioned a few times by Callie and Susan. "Listen, Matt. Your friend's right. Even if you knew exactly what route they'd taken and ran flat out, you wouldn't—"

"I'm not listening to anything you say. You brought these people here. How many more spies are there? Who will they kidnap next? I'm going to find my mum and dad and nobody's stopping me." Matt marched off and the expanded group in the middle of the farmyard all let him go.

"You're just making friends every way you turn today, aren't you?" Susan said.

Drake lifted his left hand to his head and his fingers slowly began to massage his temple. "Look. We need to prioritise. If what we think has happened has actually happened, then that means the administration knows where we are, or they will very soon."

"You're damn right we need to prioritise," Callie said. "You need to get some of your people together and we need to get on the road, now."

"Callie, you need to listen to us," Susan said.

Callie took a step back to look at her mother's face. "Mum, don't tell me you're siding with them."

"This isn't about sides, sweetheart. It's about listening to reason."

"Oh, and you don't think it's reasonable to go after one of our own when they're in trouble?"

"That's not what your mum's saying," John replied.

"So you think it's okay to let Phil and Debbie be kidnapped too?" she snapped, turning to him.

He put his hands up placatingly. "Nobody is saying that any of this is okay. What we're saying is—"

"You're too cowardly to do anything about it."

It was Greenslade who spoke now. "If I thought for a second that there was a chance we could catch up, you wouldn't be able to hold me back. But the chances are they'll be back in Salvation before we're even a quarter of the way there."

"So what then? That's it? Bye, bye, Phil. Bye, bye, Debbie. Thanks for everything, but y'know, it's a bit too risky coming after you, so tough shit."

"Risks? I'll take risks. I'll chance my arm and I'll overplay my hand, but I won't hand myself over to Bucks."

"He's right," Drake said.

Callie whipped around to face him once more. "This doesn't concern you."

"Funny. A minute ago, I thought you were telling me to put a rescue team together."

Tears began to stream down Callie's face. She turned from Drake to Greenslade and finally to her mother. "I can't believe this. I can't believe any of this," she said before running off.

Susan was about to head after her, but Greenslade put a hand on her shoulder. "She probably just needs a minute." Anger flared in Susan's eyes for a moment, but then it dissipated once more as she realised he was right.

A heavy silence fell over those who were left before John broke it. "Y-you don't think they'll come here, do you? You don't think they'll send an army?"

Drake looked at Marina. "It would be foolish. But I wouldn't rule it out."

"Oh, Jesus!" Nicola gasped and placed her arm around Dani a little tighter.

"So, what do we do?" asked Greenslade.

"Surely our priority still needs to be food," John said. "We need to get as many foraging teams out there as possible."

"And what about shelter?" Jason said. "We had three and a half thousand people camping in the woods last night. That's okay on a warm, dry night. But if we don't get a massive jump start on gathering more materials and building, what's going to happen if we suddenly get a cold spell or a wet spell or a wet season? Sickness will spread around this place like … well … a plague. It will be beyond a disaster."

"Somebody still has to escort Nazya and Chloe back to Infinity. They've already—"

"They've got work to do right now," Drake said, cutting John off. "They're going to have to stay another day at least. Yes, we need to keep the food coming in. Organise as many foraging parties as you possibly can. After this afternoon, though, tell them to stay south of the hills, okay?"

A slightly puzzled look appeared on John's face for a second before he nodded. "Okay."

"Jason," Drake continued, doing his best to remember everyone's roles and names from the previous evening, "you're the one who's responsible for the building projects around here."

"Well, not just me."

"Do you have a good deputy who can deal with all of this?" Drake asked, gesturing to the ongoing gathering of materials and gradual assembly of the houses.

Jason looked towards Zep. "I don't know about good, but I've got a deputy," he said with half a smile on his face. "But if I'm here, why does it matter if I've got a deputy?"

"Because you're not going to be here."

"Oh, and where am I going to be exactly?"

"You're going to be up there with us," he replied, pointing to the ridge.

"I know I'm going to regret asking this, but why?"

"Because we're going to turn this place into a fortress."

*

Callie could hear Matt's sobs long before she peeled back the curtain and saw him kneeling there with his rucksack. She stepped into the sheet-walled cubicle that was currently his home and knelt down too, placing an arm around her friend and pulling him close.

Matt's head flopped onto her shoulder and the pair stayed like that for over a minute. People had begun to come in and out of the large barn once more since the early morning's drama had come to an end.

"You've come to tell me not to go." The words struggled out of Matt's mouth as his crying continued. A single strand of saliva dropped from his bottom lip, and at that moment, Callie didn't see a teenager; all she saw through her own tear-blurred eyes was a little boy who had lost his mum and dad. It was not a million miles removed from how she was feeling. Phil and Debbie had become like family to her in the past few weeks and to contemplate life without them was devastating.

"I've not come here to tell you anything. I've come here to be with you, to tell you that, whatever happens, you'll never be alone." She kissed the top of his head like a mother would kiss a child.

"It's true what Drake said, isn't it?"

"Which bit?"

"That we wouldn't stand a chance of catching up to them."

Callie removed her arm and shuffled around in front of Matt taking his hand instead. "A thousand things could have happened on the journey up there that might have slowed them down, but in all likelihood, the chances of catching up to them are pretty remote, Matt."

She began to sob again and his head dipped further as more tears ran from his face onto his jeans. "But it's my mum and dad." Again, he said the words like a small child and more saliva dribbled from his mouth as he carried on crying.

"I know. And that's why even if you decide to go, I'll go with you."

He looked up at Callie. His eyes were red and raw, but he could see through the stinging tears that she meant what she said. "You'd come?"

"If you want to go after them, yes."

"Why?"

"Because I love your mum, and I love your dad, and there's no better judge of what is the right thing to do in this situation than you."

They continued to kneel, holding each other's hand for several more minutes before Matt broke his grasp and wiped the tears from his eyes. "My dad would never approve of me putting you in danger. He wouldn't approve of me going after him. It would defy the logic that he holds like a religion." He lifted his head to look at Callie once more. "What should I do?"

"I told you, I'm here to do whatever you feel you should."

"But ... I can't. Right now, I don't know, and I can't, and I just.... I just don't want to feel so lost, so useless, so ... sad."

Callie grabbed Matt's hand again. She had wanted to go after Phil and Debbie as much as he had. But with each second that ticked by, the reality of the situation dawned on her more and more. "This place," she said, gesturing out to the farm, "is your father's legacy. In the short time we've been here, he's done something amazing. He's inspired people; he's kept people alive; he's come up with plans for the future. I can't think of a greater way to honour him than to help continue what he started. Nobody's expecting you to do that today, Matt. I mean all this has just happened. But heading out there, heading into the unknown after your parents is dangerous. You'd be taking a big risk. We'd be taking a big risk. But staying here, helping to finish what he started, that would be a great thing to do. It would be a brave thing to do and it would help a lot of people now and hopefully generations into the future." She wiped more tears from her face with the back of her hand.

"But I don't have the knowledge."

"You have some of it. Think back to all the stuff Phil's harped on about endlessly in the past."

A sad laugh left Matt's mouth. "I've forgotten more than I've remembered."

"Then speak to people. Speak to Wei. Speak to Lanying. Speak to Tania and Harper. Speak to Dani and me. Read the notes he made on the backs of the plans. The information's here with us and you can help carry on where he left off."

"He was talking a lot about that irrigation system. The Duji-jan or whatever it was."

Now it was Callie's turn to laugh a sad laugh. "The Dujiangyan Irrigation System. Yeah. That's my point. It was Wei who told him about that. The knowledge is here, Matt. You can be the curator. You can help keep your dad's vision going."

"But I'm not him."

"No. You're you, but you're his son and there's no one who'll take the job as seriously."

Matt pulled his hand away from Callie once more and looked across to the pages gleaned from Tania's journal, which were all bound together with a piece of string. "I'm not going to put you in a position where you have to follow me back to Salvation. But I think I'd like a little bit of time alone."

"Of course. You take as long as you want. Nobody will be expecting you to do anything right now. But Matt, I'm always here if you want to talk." She stood up and went to leave.

"Callie." She stopped before she reached the sheet curtaining the front of the small cubicle.

"Yeah?"

"Thank you."

Callie smiled. "Just remember what I said." And with that, she left.

*

"I never got to welcome you to our settlement properly," John said.

Drake couldn't help but laugh, as did Dwyer, Revell and Marina. "That's very kind, thank you. I have to say that the warm reception we've received so far has been overwhelming."

"I've got my people organising foraging groups. After what happened to Callie and Dani yesterday morning, I'm making sure the adults are armed just in case they come across more Ferals. I think Jason's already headed up to the peak with a team and Zep's gone into the forest to round up more labourers. I know for a fact we had all sorts of skilled workers in Level Three, so finding people who know what they're doing shouldn't be a huge ask."

"Well, I suppose I'd better go in and talk to the prisoners. Ask them all to play nice."

"We're just going to let them go?" Marina asked. "And the people who shot Trunk and Goldie?"

"I can't say I'm happy about it, but given the new information, and given what's facing us, I think we need to put everything else on a back burner."

"Our people aren't going to like that."

"Yeah, well, they can get in line to hate me."

"I'll go in with you," Susan said, nodding towards the house where Caine and the others were held.

"All things considered, I'll let you." He turned to Marina. "Keep twenty of our guards here. The remainder will go out with their families in the foraging teams. John was right. We can't risk these Ferals becoming an issue again today with everything else that's happening."

"Okay," Marina said, and she, Dwyer and Revell began towards the forest.

"You ready?" Drake asked, looking at Susan.

"Always." The yard, the fields, the forest and all the surrounding area was bustling once again. It was almost as if the armed confrontation hadn't occurred. And as they reached the front door of the house, Susan paused. "It's the smart play."

"What is?"

"What you're doing. I think if someone had died, you'd be forced to play it differently, but putting any retribution, any justice on hold for this moment is the only way to go."

"Well, if I'm still alive by tonight, I'll give you my judgement on the matter."

"You're making it sound like you regret coming here."

"I don't know what makes you think that. I'm having the time of my life."

Susan smiled and opened the door. They walked along the short corridor of blankets and sheets to the larger end room, where Caine and his cohorts all sat with their backs to the wall.

"You survived then?" Caine said without the hint of a smile on his face.

"Look—" Drake began, but Susan took over.

"Look," she said, glancing around the room and picking out the odd vaguely familiar face before fixing her gaze on Caine. "You might think you've got scores to settle and axes to grind, but let me tell you this; we think Phil's been kidnapped by the administration. That means we've lost the one man who knew what he was doing with the crops, and even more disturbing is it means that the administration knows exactly where we are."

Concerned murmurs rippled around the small audience before Caine spoke. "We can't go back there." All the cocksureness and aggression from before were gone now. He shared the same look of abject fear that the others in the room had on their faces.

"Yeah. I think we're all pretty much on the same page there. So, you and your people, and I'm not just talking about the ones in this room but anyone who feels the way you do, have a decision to make. You can carry on thinking Drake and the others are the enemy." She pointed to the Salvation guard. "The one who got you all out of there, I hasten to add. Or you can accept that we're all in this together and we need to work together to survive."

"But if Bucks sends an army down here, we'll be slaughtered."

"Actually, we won't," Drake said. "But we'll have to fight. We took a good supply of weapons and ammunition with us when we left. We have over seventy trained guards and I know there are plenty more among you who can use the guns with a minimum amount of training. As of right now, I've got groups working on the ridge to build turrets. I doubt if Phil and his abductors will have even reached

Salvation yet, which means we've got a good day at least to get ready."

"Do you really think they'll come after us?" Caine asked.

"I genuinely don't know, but at the same time, I think it's better that we're prepared if they do, don't you?

The colour had drained from Caine's face in the past minute and he nodded slowly as he considered the prospect of all-out war with the administration. "Yes," he said, eventually.

"Yeah," Susan replied. "So, what are you going to bring to the table?"

"What?" Caine asked, a little confused.

"What?" Drake echoed.

"So far, you've shown up here. You've managed to injure a little kid and cause no small amount of dissent. What are you going to do now to help?"

Caine looked around, a little unsure of what to say. "I can't do a lot from in here."

"When I walk out of this place, you'll be walking out with me," Drake said.

"You heard him. So, what are you going to do to help?"

"I'll … I'll talk to people."

"You'll talk to people? Bloody parrots can talk to people, Caine. We need to recruit people. We need to make them understand that the problem isn't in here, it's out there and it's coming for us."

Caine gulped and nodded. "Yes."

"That group who attacked the guards this morning. You'll be able to find out who they are quickly enough. Start with them. There's a lot of work to do and not much time to do it. That's the case today. It's going to be the case for a long, long time to come. We've got enough challenges and difficulties facing us without creating new ones."

"O-okay," Caine stuttered.

"That's all I've got to say. The rest is up to you."

"Okay," he said again, nodding once more.

Susan shrugged. "Well, what are you waiting for, a horse-drawn carriage? Piss off and get to work."

Without saying another word, Caine headed out and, one by one, the rest of his group followed. Drake stared at Susan for a moment. "You're not really someone I should mess with, are you?"

Susan laughed. "There was a time when I let people walk all over me, but those days are gone now. This place has to work for my family, for my friends, and I'm not above ruffling a few feathers, bruising a few egos or punching a few faces to make that happen."

Drake laughed. "Thanks for the warning, that's good to know." The pair headed out of the house and no sooner had they made their way through the doorway than Callie rushed up to them.

"Mum. Do you know where Si is? I haven't seen him anywhere."

"Have you tried looking behind you?"

Callie turned around to see Si heading into the farmyard from the direction of the forest. "I think that's the first time I've not seen him glued to Sasha since she arrived."

Susan smiled. "He's in love. Trust me; you'll be the same when you find someone."

"Somehow, I doubt that."

Si looked up and Callie and Susan both waved. He reciprocated, but rather than heading across to them, he disappeared into the barn. "Uh-oh. Looks like trouble in paradise."

"I'll go see what's up."

"No. Don't pry, Callie. Sometimes, people just need a little time alone. He'll talk to us if he wants us."

Callie shrugged. "I suppose."

"Anyway, I think we've got our work cut out today, don't you?"

16

Phil only had a handful of what he could call friends in school. Of those, Purnit was his closest. He, too, was often a target for the bullies and it only took him seconds to realise what prank Peter Shan and his mates had pulled to humiliate Phil.

Now their mission was accomplished, Shan's gang didn't linger at the back of the short procession anymore; instead, they moved forward to join Lindsey Kews and her friends. As they did, Purnit dropped back, careful not to rouse any unwanted attention.

"Are you okay?" he asked as he joined his friend.

"I hate those people so much," Phil replied under his breath.

"I know. Me too."

"I just wish…." His words trailed off and Purnit looked across at him. Up until this point, Phil had maintained his composure despite everything, but now a single tear rolled down his cheek, which he quickly brushed away.

"Wish what?"

"I just wish I had the guts to stand up to him. Every time he does something, I promise myself I won't let anything like that happen again, and then it does, and they make a fool of me."

"I know it is little consolation, but my brothers say it is us who will have the last laugh. He will probably end up unhappy in life in a dead-end job with no future. We are destined for something else."

Phil sniffed and wiped his nose with the back of his hand. "Do you really think that? Do you really think we'll be happy or will we always be victims to people like this?"

"It is hard to see sometimes. We are in the top sets. We get the best grades. This makes some jealous and angry."

"I think it will always be like this. I think people will always be jealous and angry."

A roar of laughter went up from Shan and the others and there was a part of Phil that knew he was the butt of the joke. Purnit glanced and saw his friend's face grow a little sadder. "The assistants should have been back here. It is not right that they let this happen."

"They don't care about us. Didn't you see them? They were laughing too."

Now it was Purnit's head that dipped. "I'm sorry."

Phil sniffed again. "I swear, the next time he does anything, I'm just going punch him as hard as I can. He won't bother me again after that."

There was a pause before Purnit spoke again. "I think that would be bad. I think that would do the opposite."

Phil balled his fist. "It would feel good."

"Until he and his friends hit back."

"I don't want to be like this anymore. I don't want to dread every second. I don't want to feel like this."

"My brothers say—"

"Your brothers aren't here. Your brothers didn't have water thrown over them to make the rest of the class believe they peed themselves."

Purnit leaned forward a little and looked at the patch of dampness on Phil's shorts. "It is drying already. Soon you won't know it was there at all."

Phil looked across at him. "I'll know it was there. You'll know it was there. Miss Carlton will. All of them will," he said, gesturing to their classmates, "and probably the rest of the school will by tomorrow."

Another laugh went up from the boys and girls around Shan and the two friends looked towards them. "Who knows, something else may happen before then, and all this will be forgotten."

*

"As long as you don't cause any trouble, they said I could take your gags off," Rachael said, first removing Debbie's then dropping back and taking Phil's off. "Please don't make me regret it."

It was another very warm day and the heat and physical exertion were enough to deal with without having to contend with having gags on too. Phil shook his free and stared at Rachael with something approaching contempt. As the doctor walked back up to join the other two, Debbie muttered, "Thank you."

"You're welcome," Rachael replied.

Phil looked behind him. The fourth member of the quartet – Larch – was a little shorter than Phil. He was unremarkable to look at other than his eyes. They were the darkest brown Phil had ever seen. From a distance, one could be forgiven for thinking them black, almost like giant pupils that saw everything. He strode along, holding his Q-Thirty just like the ones they called Landis and Emily. There was no mistake that if he or Debbie tried to run, it would end badly and painfully. "Thank you? You're thanking them now?" he hissed as he turned back around to their direction of travel.

"What do you want me to do, Phil, spit at her?" They kept their voices low enough not to be heard by the others as they carried on their own conversations.

"I wonder if we'll ever see this again."

"Don't talk like that."

"You can't tell me you haven't thought the same."

"I said don't talk like that. It doesn't do anybody any good."

"You're scared I'm going to go into another funk and go off the rails again? Ha! I think it's a bit late for that."

Debbie turned her head to look at him. "Phil, please."

His heart broke at that moment. Debbie's eyes were the saddest he'd ever seen them. Sometimes during the period on Level Two when they had been at odds with each other, he had thought she had looked dead behind her eyes, but never anything like this. "I'm sorry, Debs," was all he could say.

She turned back around once more and continued forward, one foot in front of the next. Phil had suffered from depression in the past, but the funk he was referring to was something completely different. That was when he'd had his breakdown. What he was feeling now wasn't quite like that. There were elements of it, but there was something else too, something darker, something that he thought had been buried way, way down inside him many decades before. He could feel it coming back to the surface and it scared him. Because if that showed its head again, there was a very real possibility that it would stay around forever this time.

*

"I still can't believe what's happened," Dani said as she and Callie walked side by side down the long road that ran parallel with the farm. They had agreed to head one of the groups of foragers. It was made up of half a dozen or so of Penny's people and more than fifty of the newcomers. Two Salvation guards and their families were with them too, but they weren't the only ones who were armed. Callie carried a Q-Thirty, Dani had a Q-Eighteen, and two of the people Penny personally vouched for had firearms too. The rest all carried makeshift spears or clubs.

Their group was one of the biggest heading out. There were twenty foraging troops in total. They had decided to go to one of the larger beaches to the south, where they would demonstrate the difference between the types of seaweed, which ones were best for what, and, most importantly, how to harvest them. If any of them still had room in their rucksacks afterwards, they would head into one of the many unexplored fields or patches of woodland to see what they could find there for the supper pot.

"No. Me neither. I don't think I want to believe it."

Dani looked across to her friend and saw fresh tears gathering in her eyes. "Nobody would blame you if you stayed back at the farm, y'know."

"There was part of me that thought about it. But I think it's better that I keep busy with you. I'm glad you ended up foraging and not on inventory duty."

"Yeah. Me too. From what I gathered, the idea of asking people to hand over what they'd carried from Salvation was something of a point of friction."

"Can't think why."

"I know, right? Did you get to see Matt before we set off?"

"I saw him soon after we found out and had a chat with him. I looked for him before we set off, but someone said they'd seen him walking by the side of the stream, so I thought I'd just leave him to it. He probably needs to get his head around all this."

"And how are you feeling?"

"What do you mean?"

"I mean you were pretty close to Phil. Well, we all were, but you more than most."

Callie let out a long, deep sigh. "Like I said, I just want to stay busy. I want to occupy my mind so I don't have time to think about it. I think there's still a part of me that thinks when we arrive back at the farm, Debbie and Phil will both be there, waiting for us."

"And when that doesn't happen?"

Callie reached out and took her friend's hand. "Well, then I've got you to cheer me up, haven't I?"

Dani smiled. "You'll always have me."

*

Wei, Jiang and Lanying had avoided all the drama from earlier. Other than taking cover temporarily when bullets were flying and confusion reigned, they had been out in the fields, not the ones already tilled and planted but the new ones that Phil had discussed preparing. There was an army of familiar faces helping them, but today there was an extra one.

"Your father talked about this yesterday before the arrival of our new friends," Wei said with a little chuckle. "He wanted to plant wild crops and make sure we had enough prepared land to rotate the potatoes."

Matt looked down at the notes in his hands. "He talked about all this with you?"

"Not so much. Phil speaks, but he does not always talk. Sometimes he speaks to himself and you just have to listen to know what is on his mind."

"Yeah. That's so true." Matt was realising he should have listened more. He had cried himself hoarse once Callie had left then gone for a walk by the stream. It was only when he'd seen Wei, Jiang and Lanying working in the fields that he decided being out there would help him feel a little closer to his dad.

"Your father is possibly the cleverest man I have ever met. We are lucky to have his knowledge to help us."

"Had," Matt said sadly. "We had his knowledge."

Jiang looked around at the hundreds of people who were beavering in the fields off into the distance. They only had a few tools to share between them, but many had grabbed pieces of slate or other sharp bits of stone to dig out the weeds and scrub grass in order to ready the land for tilling. It was backbreaking, arduous work, but despite everything that had gone on and everything that was hanging over them, there was optimism in the air.

"No. Your father is alive somewhere. He is alive, Matt, and we must believe that we will see him again one day soon. He is resilient and clever. But more than that, he lives on around us. In the fields, in the plans he left, in the knowledge he gave, he is here with us, and we must continue his great work."

Matt turned slowly and watched the countless bodies digging and hacking at the ground with whatever instruments they had to aid them. "I think that's why I came out here. Somehow, it makes me feel closer to him. It makes me feel like he'll show up at any minute to check on everyone's progress." He tried his hardest to smile, but instead, he broke down in tears once more.

Wei reached out and placed a hand on the teenager's shoulder. "Maybe it is better that you take a rest from everything today."

Matt sniffed and wiped his eyes. "I'm sorry. I keep crying, no matter how hard I try not to."

"This is nothing to apologise for. This is natural."

"I think I'd like to stay out here with you, if you don't mind."

Wei smiled. "Of course. If that is what you wish. I see a lot of your father in you."

"You do?"

Wei smiled. "Yes. It is obvious you are his son." He bent down and picked up a fistful of soil, slowly letting it run through his fingers. They both watched as it fell to the ground. "If you treat the land kindly, then it is kind to you in return. Your father knew this. I think this is why he spent so many hours a day out here, even when the work was done."

"And now they're going to lock him away in that bunker again."

Wei tapped his head. "A man like your father can see without seeing. He will be able to picture the crops growing in his head. He will be able to taste the fruit of his hard work without it ever touching his tongue. Let us make sure that the next time he lays eyes on these fields, they are what he pictured in his mind. That way, it will feel like he was never away at all."

Matt didn't know if Wei really believed Phil would return or whether he was just saying it to make him feel better, but being out with him in the fields felt far better than being in that small curtained cubicle. "Thank you, Wei."

"There are no thanks needed."

*

"I thought you'd be off with your daughter," Drake said as he and Susan climbed the road to the ridge. Dwyer, Revell, Marina and Greenslade followed behind them.

"I don't know if you noticed or not, but my daughter has a habit of putting herself in the centre of situations. Considering the simmering tension around here, I think it's best that she's as far away from the place as possible right now."

"Yeah. It's baffling where she gets it from really." Susan smiled. "And why are you glued to my side again exactly?"

"I've decided to make you my project."

Drake laughed. "Project?"

"Yes. I'm challenging myself to get you through the day without being murdered."

"And how confident are you?"

"Depends how much you talk. The more you speak to people the less confident I become."

Drake laughed again. "I see."

"Seriously, I think it's important that people don't see all the Salvation guards together all the time with no interaction from the rest of us. The best way to prove that there's no us and them is if we show there is no us and them."

"And do you believe that?"

Susan carried on walking for a little while before she answered. "Pretty much right up until the last day or so in the bunker, I was dependent on alcohol. I was working stupid shifts to keep my family afloat after my husband died and I thought that was enough. I thought putting food on the table was enough and I disengaged."

"I'm not sure I understand."

"I wasn't there. I wasn't there for my son or my daughter. Most nights, I'd zone out in front of the TV with some black-market hooch. Then I'd be out of the door for work in the morning before Callie had even got up for school. If truth be told, I doubt I can recall maybe five conversations I had with my kids in all that time."

"Okay. So, what happened?"

"Callie. Seeing what she did turned me around."

"Yeah, kids can do that."

"No, not like this. Seeing her inspired me. It was like I didn't really know who she was ... who she'd become until everything turned to crap. Then I watched her, and she was amazing. She'd built this life completely unbeknown to me. People were in awe of her and the same thing happened to me when I opened my eyes and saw her again. She has this ability to bring people together, no matter who they are or what they've done in the past. She's more than a voice of reason; she's a voice of hope. And that last day ... that day I quit drinking, that's what I saw. It was like a revelation. I hated myself for being missing in action so long because this girl who I'd been sharing a house with was just ... amazing." A tear ran down Susan's face, but she wiped it away just as quickly.

"From the little I've had to do with her, she certainly seems formidable."

"Ha!" Greenslade said, coming up behind them. "You can say that again. Talk about a right pain in the arse." Drake laughed. "But Susan's right. There's something about her that cuts through everybody's bullshit, that makes them realise they're just tiny cogs in a giant wheel, and the wheel spins a whole lot better if they're all moving in the right direction."

"I didn't think I'd ever hear praise for anyone coming out of your mouth, Greenslade."

"Yeah, well. I save it for those who deserve it. She's young, but this place wouldn't have happened without her."

"Duly noted. Suddenly, I feel honoured to be in the presence of her mother."

"So," Susan said, taking over once more. "To answer your question, yes, I do think we can make people believe there's no us and them anymore."

They all carried on walking and finally came to a stop on the brow of the hill. At least a hundred men, women and older children were working along the ridge. Guards had laid down their weapons and were labouring alongside their families to help move stones and build the turrets. "What are you, the supervisors?" Jason asked with a smile on his face as he laid down the stone he was carrying and walked over to join them.

"Somebody's got to make sure you're not slacking off," Susan replied. "Seriously, how's it going?"

Jason wiped his forehead on his shirt sleeve. "It's going well. We're getting a little short on materials, so I've got people with trolleys gathering more. He pointed down towards a wall. "Up until now, we've not had anybody collecting stones from the north, but since we've got something approaching transport, there's a huge supply that we can tap into. It's a complete ball ache having to cart it up the hill in what are essentially shopping trolleys, but we've gotta do what we've gotta do. We've got one of the turrets about a third of the way complete if you'd like to see it."

"Already? I most definitely would," Drake replied, looking to the other guards.

They followed Jason along the ridge until it narrowed a little. "Be careful here," he said, stepping down onto what would once have been a flat, open ledge but was now the first of their defences. A semicircle of stones three layers thick had been built up to thigh height. The stones had been packed with earth to make them sturdier and more secure.

"This is good," Marina said.

"This is great," Drake replied. "How many do you think you'll have done by the end of the day?"

"I don't know. Getting the materials is the slow part. Maybe half a dozen, maybe more," Jason replied.

"I'm officially impressed."

"Unless they've got heavy artillery, there's no way they're going to get your people in here."

"Our people," Susan said.

"Our people," Jason corrected himself.

"We can probably find a few more bodies to help."

"Bodies aren't the thing. The people who are putting them together know what they're doing; it's just getting the stones up here. I was too generous with the trolleys this morning. I told a few of the foraging groups they could take them. I thought we probably needed a quick and big influx of extra food more."

"You're not wrong. Unsurprisingly, the newcomers have been reluctant to give up what they carried down here on their own backs. We've got the stuff that was brought down in large bindles and in the trolleys, but that's not going to last long."

"Can't you force them? Can't we seize it or something?" Jason asked, looking at Drake and the other soldiers.

"I'm not convinced that would do anything for public relations," Greenslade said.

"No, on second thoughts, you're probably right."

"If there's one thing you can always rely on, it's the fact that people will never fail to let you down."

"That's a bit of a dim world view," Marina said.

"Remind me, where's Phil exactly?"

"Point taken."

*

In total, there were around eighty people in the foraging group that Tania, Harper and Greta took out. All of the orphaned children from the night at the mine were glued to Greta's side and a number of men and women who refused to allow their own kids out of their sight were with them too. In addition, there were three former Salvation guards and their families to beef up the security a little. Every adult and teen carried a weapon of some description. After the events of earlier in the day, no one was prepared to take any risks.

They arrived at the edge of a meadow and the large group all gathered in a circle around Tania and Harper, who stood in the middle.

"Well, it's a long time since I've had such a big class to teach," Tania shouted out, and in return there was a small ripple of polite laughter. "I know I've come out with a handful of you before, but just act like you've forgotten if I tell you something you already know. As you can see, this field looks a lot healthier than some we've passed. There are areas where the plants and weeds are really starting to take hold again. Now, I know that doesn't sound very exciting to a lot of you, but some of these plants we can eat, drink and use as medicines, so it's good that you learn to identify them." She turned in a full circle to make sure she had her audience's attention then continued. She pointed down at the ground. "Okay, who can tell me what this is?" she asked, virtually ignoring the adults and instead looking at the younger children.

"A dandelion," a small black-haired girl replied.

"That's right, very good, it's a dandelion. And does anybody know what we can use dandelions for?"

"Vase," said one of the smaller boys this time, putting up his hand at the same time.

"Vase?" Tania replied.

"We can put them in a vase."

"Well, yes, I suppose we can. But we can do much more than that with them too. What if I was to tell you that we can eat the leaves of dandelions? We can use the petals as sweeteners too. We can roast the roots, and when we do, they taste quite a lot like parsnips, and best of all," she said, straightening up and turning full circle again, this time looking at the adults, "we can make coffee." Laughter rippled around the men and women present this time.

"Yeah," Harper said. "And apparently, they're good for your liver. I could have done with knowing that when I was spending my life in the Dublin pubs before I ever came over here."

More laughter circulated, and suddenly, the audience that was so diverse in background and age seemed to relax and feel more comfortable with their teachers and one another. Tania and Harper went on to show the other varieties of plants and weeds that they were looking for and how to extract each one from the ground. They did it slowly and expertly, doing their best not to patronise their audience. After fifteen minutes, they set their class free. They stayed with Greta and the orphans while the parents split away with their own children.

"You guys are so good at this," Greta said as they watched the younger children. They had been out the day before and some of them seemed to be dab hands now as they levered plants out of the earth with whatever makeshift tools they carried.

"We've done it enough times since getting here," Harper said.

"No, it's more than that. It's not just what you say; it's how you say it. You're natural communicators."

"Well, I don't know about me, but this one's been a teacher all her adult life."

"That's what I wanted to be."

"From what I've seen, it's what you are," Tania said.

"No, y'know, I mean a proper teacher."

"So do I. Just because we're not in a classroom, it doesn't mean we can't teach. And y'know, when we get more established, when the crops come in, when the houses get built, I've got every intention of starting classes again, proper classes I mean. I can't do it all by myself. I'll need others who are willing to help me."

"I'd love to help, but what do I know?"

"One thing I've learnt is that knowledge is only a small part of the job when it comes to teaching. Communicating, that's the big part and the hard part, and you seem to be great in that department. The kids love you."

Greta looked towards the children she had been looking after since the night at the mine. "I love them too."

"You're sounding more qualified by the second."

"But what would I teach?"

Tania let out a short laugh. "We'll worry about that later. I'm sure between us we can create a few lesson plans. But for the foreseeable future, I think what we're doing now is the best thing to learn and pass on."

"I suppose you're right," Greta said, nodding. "Well, I'd better get back to my class."

Tania and Harper stood watching for a moment. The last few days had been beyond turbulent, and the past twenty-four hours even more so, but as they surveyed the entire group working in unison, mothers, fathers, children, and strangers, a feeling of happiness rose inside them. Harper reached out and took Tania's hand, squeezing it tight.

"I think we're going to be okay. Despite everything, we're going to be okay."

No sooner had she said the words than her eyes fixed on one of the former Salvation guards. Trott was his name, and they'd been introduced briefly before setting off, but she didn't really know anything about him. He was staring, stony-faced, straight at them, and for the briefest moment, she thought it was because he disapproved of their open display of affection. After all, same-sex partnerships had been prohibited in Salvation. But as she continued to stare back, he turned towards the woodland at the far end of the sprawling meadow. Harper's eyes followed his gaze, and suddenly she saw what he had seen.

"What is it?" Tania asked, sensing the immediate change in Harper.

"Shit, Tan. I think we're being watched." Trott went across to his colleague, who was crouching down with her daughter, helping her uproot one of the dandelions that had now become such things of wonder to the whole group after Tania's talk.

The second guard straightened up and the pair of them edged over towards Tania and Harper doing their best not to cause any alarm as children and adults happily got on with the task at hand.

"What do you think?" Tania asked as the pair reached them. The guards looked back to their families, and although their children were still happily hunting the plants and weeds that Tania had taught them about, their partners were staring at them with concerned looks.

"I think there are at least half a dozen of them," the guard replied in as low a tone as he could while still being heard.

"Shite," Harper hissed. "What do we do?"

"We don't know what this is. It could be anything."

"There's a hell of a lot more than half a dozen," the second guard suddenly blurted.

"Talk to me, Moppy."

Moppy was in her early thirties. A moment before, she'd had a broad smile on her face as she'd shared the same euphoria as the others in the field, but now her demeanour had changed completely. She peered towards the forest and the warmth of before was gone. She was a guard again now, and with her family at stake, she had never been more serious about doing her job.

"Look about fifty metres to the south of where they're standing." The other three all followed her eyes, and there they could see at least ten more figures. "Then keep following the trees."

"Oh crap," Trott said, doing his best to maintain his composure and not raise his voice.

"That's one word for it," Tania replied.

"What do we do?" Harper asked.

Trott turned towards her. "I don't really think we've got that many options. Do you?"

17

The ruins of the abbey were much like the ruins of every abbey they had seen before. The vast majority of the pupils were uninterested in anything other than using it as a climbing frame. They took selfie after selfie, despite the teacher and teacher's assistants doing their best to stop them. It was hazardous and all it would take was one slip and someone would be heading to hospital. Phil hoped beyond hope that Peter Shan would be that person, but he knew in his heart that he wouldn't be so lucky.

Normally Phil would have loved a day trip like this, but there was nothing to love about today. While the others continued to play the fool, he sloped off even though his teacher had commanded them all to stay together. There was a maze of decrepit walls for him to get lost in. His trousers had almost dried now, so he was no longer in physical discomfort, but the psychological one would be something he would not be able to shake off.

He strolled along, hands in his pockets, kicking the ground as he went. He didn't understand why things had to be so challenging all the time. He didn't understand why people targeted him. All he wanted to do was get on with his life. Was that too much to ask?

He stopped suddenly as he laid eyes on a striking chunk of white marble lying on the ground next to the remains of one of the walls. What it was doing there he had no idea. He picked it up in his hand and marvelled a little at its smoothness. Maybe some other outcast had found it in the stream at the bottom of the hill. Maybe they had been entranced by it too.

For the first time in a while, a small smile appeared on his face. People rarely made Phil smile, but nature, even something as simple as a rock, could give him peace and a feeling of serenity.

"Here he is." And in that instant, the happiness and serenity were gone. Phil had hoped he wouldn't hear Shan's voice again, but now he realised he would find no respite.

There were seven other boys and girls behind Shan and Phil silently prayed that Miss Carlton or one of the teacher's assistants would appear around the corner at any moment to rescue him. As the seconds ticked by, though, he knew this was not to be.

"Will you sign this for me, Phil?" Lindsey Kews asked, handing him a pen and a notepad. The others laughed, Shan louder than most.

"I ... I don't understand," Phil replied.

Lindsey pretended to look confused, but somehow Phil could tell it was all part of another set-up to humiliate him. He looked behind the small group again, willing someone to walk around the corner, but when it didn't happen, he focused back on Lindsey as she pulled her phone out and revealed a picture of Phil with Miss Carlton standing over him. The wet patch on his trousers had been circled and the writing underneath read TRAINOR GETS AN F IN BLADDER CONTROL. "You're famous. You're trending all over, Phil. I want your autograph; it could be worth a fortune someday." Lindsay and the others all burst out laughing again, but all Phil could do was stare.

THE BURNING TREE: BOOK 4 - ANARCHY

He could not break his gaze from the small screen as dozens of laughing face emojis appeared. "Yeah, you've gone viral, Trainor," Shan said, laughing louder than any of them.

"No." *This can't be happening.* "No. No, no, no, no." He whispered the word disbelievingly over and over again. *Surely no one can be this cruel.* He raised his eyes from the screen and looked from face to face as they all took joy in his humiliation. "No," he said again softly. Of all the things that had been done to him, of all the injustices he had suffered, this was by far and away the worst.

He felt himself beginning to shake and tears cascaded down his face blurring his view of the ugliness that cut and hacked at him like some hell-born threshing machine. *You've gone viral. You're trending all over. You're famous.* The words sang a devastating song in his head as the chorus of laughter scaled up and down in deafening accompaniment. *Will you sign this for me, Phil? I want your autograph. You're famous. You're famous. You're famous.*

Phil had never felt like this before. He continued to shake, and as well as everything else he was feeling, fear gripped him as well now. It wasn't unusual for any animal to tremble in fear, but this wasn't just some slight tremor. He looked down at his hands, and no matter how he tried, he could not steady them.

He blinked, releasing another torrent of salty heartbreak and prompting another round of callous, hate-filled laughter from the crowd who seemed to be gradually trying to encircle him. Their faces magnified in his head, burning permanent impressions into his brain. With each tear he shed, the gang's joy seemed to elevate to a new level. They were feeding off his misery like lions feasting on a captured gazelle. With each bite they took, he died a little more inside.

"Don't let it get to you, Trainor. Lindsey's little sister's still in nappies. She says she can fetch some with her tomorrow so you don't have to worry about doing the same in school," Shan said, causing another explosion of raucous laughter.

"Yeah, no problem. Don't worry, Phil. I'll look after you."

It doesn't matter that none of this is true. It doesn't matter that he threw water on me. All that matters is perception. All that matters is that single meme and the sway of public opinion. Truth means nothing. Loud-mouthed bullies can say what they want and they'll always drown out the voice of truth because the lies are so much more entertaining.

Phil looked again at his trembling hands, noticing that he still held the white chunk of marble that had brought a smile to his face just a few minutes before. Suddenly, it looked less miraculous now. It didn't seem as white. It didn't seem as smooth. Phil wondered if anything would look the same to him again after this. He felt a poke against his chest and realised the barrage of taunting and humiliation was just a precursor to more pain as Shan glared down at him with a cruel smile turning the corner of his lips. Pure malevolence beamed from the bully's eyes like lasers and Phil staggered back a little as he was pushed again. He felt two more hands on his back, ushering him into the fray.

"I think you should thank Lindsey, don't you, Trainor? I think it's good of her to—"

"RAAARRRGGGHHH!" The roar came from the very depths of Phil's soul as he brought his hand around with sledgehammer force. A crack, like the sound of a cricket ball being hit for six, brought an immediate end to the laughter.

Shan's eyes rolled back in his head, but the split second before he collapsed to the ground, a fountain of blood sprayed from his temple. His gang just watched in silent disbelief for a moment before Lindsey and two other girls began to scream at the top of their voices.

Phil's hand was perfectly still as he looked at it now. His eyes became entranced by the drip, drip, drip of blood as it rolled over the surface of the once white stone. He was deaf to the screams, deaf to the cries of horror. He was at peace again, no longer the centre of attention as all eyes looked to the figure lying on the ground.

"You've killed him. YOU'VE KILLED HIM!" one of the boys shouted. There was no anger in the tone, only fear. The shoe was on the other foot now and the circle around Phil widened as it gradually dawned on them what this was.

Phil remained aloof as if all this was just a dream and he hadn't smashed the small rock against Shan's temple. "What have you done? WHAT HAVE YOU DONE?" Miss Carlton put her arms out, urging Lindsey and the others to stay back, almost as if she was protecting them from a rabid dog. "What have you done, Phil?" she asked again in wide-eyed horror as she looked down at Shan. More frightened screams sounded from behind her as the teacher's assistants and several of the children appeared, eager to see the cause of all the excitement.

Phil blinked once, twice, three times, and finally came back to his senses. He could still feel the tear tracks as they dried on his cheeks, but there were no fresh ones for the time being. He looked from Miss Carlton to the bloody stone in his hand and finally down to the body on the ground. Then, suddenly, everything went black.

*

"I'm going to take the longest bath of my life when I get back home," Emily said and the other three laughed.

"I'm going to have an ice-cold beer," Landis replied. They were on a wide stretch of road now, and their two prisoners, still bound but ungagged, walked along by their sides. Neither Debbie nor Phil had spoken for the last couple of miles as they slowly resigned themselves to the fate that lay ahead.

"How much farther do you think it is?"

"Can't be more than an hour or so. If we hadn't stopped to rest for a while last night, we'd be there now," he said, casting a chastising glance towards Rachael.

"Hey, look, I'm sorry. But I can't remember the last time I slept properly."

"We'll be able to sleep plenty when we're back. Hell, we'll be able to sleep for a week."

"Provided we don't get shot first."

"Will you shut up, Rachael?" Landis snapped. "I told you. By the time we get back there, everyone will know about Paris's plan. We had to make sure there were no leaks. We had to make sure everything looked as authentic as possible. It was—"

"And the guards who died?"

"Their families will be looked after."

"Course they will."

He stopped and grabbed her arm, turning her to face him. "You keep going," he said to Emily and Larch. The other two guards continued with the prisoners. Landis waited until they were out of earshot to continue. "You stop this. You don't embarrass me. You don't publicly make people question our loyalty to the administration."

"We couldn't have that, could we? Not for Paris's little golden boy."

"I'm warning you, Rachael. Do you realise what we're doing here? We're securing the future for the people of Salvation. Trainor made an agreement when he came into the bunker with his family and he needs to fulfil it."

"I'm sure that's what drove you to do this."

"It's one of the things," Landis said as a smile appeared on his face. "But I have to admit, a move up to Level One and becoming a member of the elite guard was pretty enticing too." His demeanour mellowed a little more and he eased his grip on Rachael's arm. "And just think about it, babe. You're going to be a doctor on Level One. We're going to be living a life of luxury until the settlement's established, and then we'll have a proper home. Maybe then we can think about having a family. Maybe when you can see the future I see in my head right now, you'll want the things I've wanted all along."

Rachael let out a long sigh and nodded. "Maybe. But what about the others? What about Drake and Revell and all the people we've left down there?"

"What about them? They get to live the lives they wanted."

"You don't think the administration will go after them?"

They began to walk after the others once more. "It's not up to me, but I seriously doubt it." It was a lie. Not the biggest he'd ever told, but big enough. They needed a workforce; that was the reason they'd rounded them up in the first place. But whether the administration did or didn't go after the Level Three escapees was not something that had a bearing on their current situation and he would say whatever he needed to in order to keep Rachael moving.

"Why?"

"Because it would be a huge expenditure of resources for no tangible benefit. Yes, they stole food and seeds and equipment, but we've got more of all of those things. To go to war over a few scraps would be foolhardy. We're taking back what they wanted—Trainor."

"If they hadn't cast him down to Level Three in the first place, none of this would be happening now."

It was Landis who sighed this time. "Yeah. That was bad judgement. They put too much faith in Banner and it turned out she was nothing more than a glorified administrator. She didn't know a fraction of what Trainor did, despite her protestations otherwise. She just saw a fast track to Level One being waved in her face."

"So, you really think the others will be safe?"

Landis reached out and took Rachael's hand. He really was crazy about her, and her big heart drove him mad sometimes, but at the end of the day, it was probably one of the main reasons he loved her. "Trust me. Bucks is a businessman, first and foremost. He'll measure manpower, resources, time and risk against the potential gain and realise there's no benefit whatsoever in going down there. And besides, we've got what he coveted more than anything," he said, gesturing towards Phil.

"But their boy."

Landis' shoulders slumped. "Look. When the settlement's established, when more people are trained, who's to say they won't be freed?" Another lie.

"You don't really believe that."

"Listen, Rach. I believe that, without Trainor, there's a very real danger that thousands of people might starve to death and the settlement will never get built. Whatever doubts you're having, weigh them up against that."

"You're right," she said softly.

"I never get tired of hearing that." Rachael let out a sad laugh. "I love you, Rach."

"I love you too."

*

Their vigil of the figures in the woods had dragged on from seconds to minutes. "Whatever we do, we don't want to start a panic," Trott said. "We need to make an excuse to head back to the farm."

"That's about two miles away," Harper replied. "They could take us all out one by one before we walked a hundred metres."

"Well, it's not like we're in a position to take them on, is it?" Moppy said, looking around at the foragers, young and old, who were still oblivious to what was going on.

"Everybody! Everybody! Can I have your attention, please?" Tania said, clapping her hands and getting everyone to look towards her. "Y'know what. I've made a big mistake. I'm so sorry about this, but I just remembered that we were meant to be beach foraging today. We've already got a few teams out in the fields."

"Oh yeah, that sounds so plausible," Harper said under her breath.

"Well, we're here now. Can't we just carry on?" one of the women asked as she placed a freshly uprooted elderflower into her rucksack.

"Err.... Look, we have a plan each day and we should—"

"We're too late," Trott said, slipping the rifle from his shoulder as he saw multiple figures emerge from the blackened woodland.

"Oh crap," Tania replied, pulling the Q-Eighteen from her backpack.

A collective scream erupted from a few of the children and adults alike as they saw the two of them draw their weapons, but then as they turned to the forest and witnessed the close to thirty figures heading in their direction, the panic ratcheted up a notch.

"What do we do? What do we do?" one of the parents screamed.

"Who's got a gun?" Trott demanded. Besides Harper and Tania, seven men and women stepped forward. Four were carrying rifles and the others withdrew Q-Eighteens.

"Dammit. We should have thought this through," Tania said. "I didn't think they'd risk approaching a group as big as this. We should have stayed closer to home or headed south. This was reckless. I just wanted to—"

"Should haves aren't really our concern now," Moppy said. She turned to two of the men armed with rifles. "Start heading back with the kids now."

"What?" one of them replied. Many of the children were crying as the panic from the adults became more palpable by the second.

"You heard me. We'll try to stall them as long as we can."

"What, nine of you?"

"Just do what I say."

The pair looked from Moppy to Trott to Tania and then finally back at the small army heading out of the woods. It would be some time before they were in range and vice versa. "This is mental," one of them mumbled.

"Mummy!" a little girl cried, running up to the female guard.

"It's alright, darling," Moppy said, getting down on her knees and hugging her daughter. There was a man behind her. Concern was etched on his face as he looked down at his wife and child. "Make sure she's safe." She broke her embrace and stood, throwing her arms around her husband. Cries and screams of anguish continued to circulate around them and some of the families had already begun to retrace their steps through the meadow.

"Shouldn't we all stick together?" the man asked.

"Just take her, Rich. Just get her out of here, please." At that moment, they both wanted to cry, to say a thousand things that had gone unsaid in their time together, but they both knew it was too late now.

"Come on, sweetheart," Rich said, taking hold of the little girl's hand. "Your mum will meet us back at home."

Moppy's heart broke a little as she watched the pair of them walk away.

"Hold up!" Harper shouted out, and everyone turned to her. The army from the forest was still well out of range, but they had stopped their advance, all barring one lone figure who now continued towards them with a white flag raised above his head.

"Wait!" Trott shouted and gradually the fleeing figures slowed, conveying the order further down the line of escapees. "What the hell is this?" he asked under his breath.

"Well, there's only one way for us to find out, isn't there?" Tania said, placing the pistol back in her rucksack and starting towards the lone envoy.

"Wait a minute," Harper said. "We don't know what this is. We don't know what's going on. It could be some kind of trap. It could be a trick to stall us. There might be more of them encircling us right now for God's sake."

"I don't think so," Trott replied. "If they meant us harm, I think they'd have charged by now. I think they'd have done something other than sending one of their people towards us with a white flag."

"He's right," Tania said.

"I really don't like this," Harper replied.

Tania started out. Her heart pounded harder in her chest with each stride she took, but as Harper, then Moppy and finally Trott joined her, her nerves eased a little. The two guards shouldered their rifles once more and Harper reluctantly returned the Q-Eighteen to her rucksack. She glanced behind her to see some of the escapees returning while others stood their ground, unsure whether they would have to start fleeing once more.

It took several minutes for the two parties to meet and the flag bearer looked more nervous than the four of them felt when they finally saw him up close. "What do you want from us?" Trott asked, cutting straight to the chase.

"I didn't mean to scare you. We were trying to figure out who you were."

"Figure out who we were?" Tania asked.

"We've run into a few bands of Ferals since we set off yesterday morning. They've spread further west than we anticipated. We weren't sure what the situation was at first, but then we saw the children."

"Ferals?" Tania said. "You call them Ferals?"

"Yes. Wild people who—"

"Who are you?"

The man stared at Tania then the others before casting his eyes behind them. There was still a part of him that was a little wary. He, after all, had made the gesture of peace by heading out with the white flag to greet these strangers. "My name's Eric. I come—"

"Eric?" Tania asked.

"Yes."

"You're Chloe's dad."

"Yes. You've seen Chloe?"

"She and Nazya are back home."

Eric began to cry. "Oh, thank God. Thank God," he said. His legs buckled beneath him and he managed to avoid falling but instead went down onto one knee.

"Are you okay?" Tania asked, crouching beside him and placing a hand on his shoulder.

"I am now. I thought I'd never see her again. I know she and Nazya went after your friends, but neither of them really appreciate how dangerous it is out here."

"How did you know where to look?"

"I didn't really. I knew you lived somewhere near the sea and I got a vague hint of where your people were looking on the map. Like I say, we set off yesterday morning and we've done a lot of backtracking. We got into some scrapes, but thankfully, we didn't lose anyone. We were going to head to the coast and just follow it down; zigzagging inland in the hope we'd see something. It was a long shot, but she's my daughter. I couldn't just do nothing. When we saw you, we thought we were going to have to backtrack again, but the longer we watched the more we figured out what was going on. I'm sorry again for scaring you. All of us shouldn't have advanced from the woods like that. It was stupid."

"Well, you certainly had us worried," Tania said.

"You can say that, again," added Harper.

"So, Chloe and Nazya are both okay?"

"They're both fine."

Eric let out a long, deep breath and finally climbed to his feet. "The more time passed the more I became convinced that I was never going to see my little girl again."

"Well, we'll take you to her now. She and Nazya have achieved heroine status with our people. They saved a boy's life."

"The one who was attacked by the shark?"

"That's right."

"Well, I suppose me ageing forty years in the past couple of days was good for something then."

"Come on," Tania said, smiling and climbing back to her feet. "Let's go see your daughter."

18

A small whimper left Debbie's mouth as the hillside came into view in the distance. It wouldn't be long before they were entering the mine once again and all the hopes and dreams they'd shared in these past few weeks would become nothing more than memories.

Phil looked across at her. The road had narrowed once more and he and Debbie were walking side by side behind Landis, Emily and Rachael, with Larch bringing up the rear. He brushed his arm against his wife. He couldn't remember the last time they had spoken, even though the gags had been taken out of their mouths. He was feeling more disconnected than he had in a long time and wanted nothing more than to ease her pain, but he feared anything he said would only make things worse.

Debbie began to cry, causing Rachael to throw a glance over her shoulder. A hint of regret flashed in the doctor's eyes even though she knew everything they were doing was for the greater good.

"Don't cry, Debs," Phil said.

"Don't cry? Do you have a better idea?"

"Shut it, you two," Landis barked. "I allowed the gags to be taken off so you could breathe a bit easier; I can easily put them back on again."

"What's wrong with you?" Phil said, causing Landis to stop dead. The others halted too and Landis walked back to his prisoners.

"There's nothing wrong with me. I just want to be able to have a conversation without hearing you chirping away and your wife bleating like some lost little lamb."

"Don't you have any compassion? Don't you realise what you're doing to us, what you've done to our family? Can't you comprehend why she's upset?"

Landis faced up to his prisoner. There was a cruel smile on his face and he poked his captive in the chest. Suddenly a thousand childhood memories came flooding back to Phil and hate flashed in his gaze momentarily before he blinked and took a breath.

"Listen to me," Landis said, pushing him this time and making Phil stagger back. "You're nobody now. Less than nobody. You won't have people looking up to you and following you around like you're some big I am. You're going to do the job you were paid to do, the job that got you and your family into Salvation in the first place. And this," he said, taking hold of Debbie's jaw in a vice-like grip, "this crying shit stops now."

"Get your hands off her."

Landis immediately let go of Debbie and stepped towards Phil once more. There was fury in his face as he spoke. "What did you say to me?"

Phil did not waver for a second. He was only a few centimetres shorter than Landis, but where the guard had probably spent all his free time in the gym, and he had the frame and muscles to prove it, Phil was slight. "I said get your hands off her."

Landis continued glaring at the other man for a moment before he burst out laughing. He looked to Larch, who started laughing too, and then back towards Emily and Rachael. The female soldier giggled, but there was an increasingly forlorn look on the doctor's face. Landis suddenly unleashed a powerful punch and Phil brought his bound hands up to his stomach before collapsing to his knees and then onto his front. His cheek scraped against the ground as he hit the rough tarmac, his body half on the road, half on the verge. The laughter continued behind him as more laughter erupted, causing another flashback of freeze-frame images to strobe in his head.

"Phil!" Debbie cried out, starting towards him.

Landis grabbed her roughly by her bound wrist and pushed her back to where she was standing a second before. "He can get up himself."

"Phil!" she called out again as a fresh torrent of tears flowed.

Phil remained on the ground as sadness and despair pinned him down. *You're nobody now. Less than nobody.* All his life, he'd been sought out, targeted. *All my life. You've gone viral. You're trending all over. You're famous. You've gone viral. You're trending all over. You're famous. You're nobody now. Less than nobody. You're nobody now. Less than nobody.*

"Get up. There's not far left to go and I'm already fed up of the sight of you. I'm just glad you gift-wrapped yourselves for us. We thought we'd be in for a long haul down there, waiting for just the right moment. Didn't think it was going to come on the first night. Just as well. I don't know how long I could have stomached that place." Phil continued to lie on the ground. His eyes were open, unblinking, just staring at the small tufts of grass by the roadside. "Get up I said."

Then he saw something that mesmerised him for just a moment. It was a jagged lump of almost black granite roughly the size of a grapefruit. He remembered back all those years before and how he had marvelled at that white piece of marble, how smooth it had been, how pure. What he was looking at now was just the opposite. It was not smooth or clean or white. It was black and jagged and painted brown by the earth it sat on. The white marble had probably lain on the bed of a stream for years, decades, centuries, millennia and hundreds, thousands, millions of gallons of pure water had washed over it in that time, giving it its form.

This dirty, uneven chunk of rock had not been so lucky. He had no idea how long it had been in its current position, but it had witnessed the end of the world. It had probably been trodden on and kicked a thousand times by those escaping the mine. There was nothing charmed about the life it had led, and now, as it stared back at him, like some dying creature, he saw himself. *This is how far I've come.*

From that day at the abbey to here, there had always been people trying to bend him to their will, push him around, bully him, mock him. In all that time, nothing had changed. He had always tried to push the pain deep down inside, hiding it away, burying it so nobody could witness the weakness he felt sure it portrayed. But it had taken its toll. It had grown inside him like a cancer—hard, solid, malignant.

"I said get the hell up," Landis growled again, this time giving him a not-so-gentle kick in the side of the ribs.

Phil's body jerked a little from the pain and he scrambled on the ground a little, shuffling to his knees and finally climbing to his feet. He looked blankly towards Landis as the guard stared back with a victorious smile. His intent had been to humiliate Phil, to prove who was the alpha male, who was the boss. He'd succeeded. Or so he thought.

Phil's hands blurred upwards and what smashed Landis' chin was more than flesh and bone. A grunt of pain left his mouth and he stumbled a little before Phil swung around again with lightning speed, and this time, the jagged lump of rock smashed into Landis' temple just as that piece of marble had crashed against Shan's all those years before. And just like Shan had collapsed, so Landis did now.

The attack was so fast, so brutal that no one actually realised what was happening until a fountain of blood sprayed through the air like a small volcano erupting. Phil pivoted and leapt back towards Larch, who only now understood what this was. He attempted to slip the rifle strap from his shoulder too late. Phil brought the rock down like a hammer, utilising his body weight to maximise the force. There was an echoing crack as it connected with the other man's skull, but Larch did not go down straight away. A stream of blood rolled down his forehead, causing him to cross his eyes comically before he staggered across the verge and fell.

"NOOO!" Emily screamed. She had watched in horror, forgetting she was a guard, forgetting everything except that she was married to the man whose skull had just been cracked open.

Phil turned, leaping towards her, and only then did her senses kick in. He dived, knocking her off balance before she could bring her weapon up. She crashed to the ground with Phil on top of her. The lump of granite flew from his hands with the force of the impact, but it didn't matter. Instead, he grabbed hold of her head as she desperately tried to throw him off balance and scramble away. But it was no good. One, two, three, four. He smashed the back of her skull against the ground over and over and over again. Each time, there was a little less understanding, a little less recognition in her eyes until, finally, the lids closed. But still, he continued again and again and again.

"Phil! Phil!" It was a familiar voice. It was the only voice that could drag him out of this insanity. He looked up. "Phil," Debbie said again, more gently this time. There she was, standing with her hands still bound together but with a large hunting knife held up to Rachael, whose wide eyes were stretched open in terror.

Only seconds had passed since the first assault had begun, but in those seconds, their entire world had changed.

Phil looked down at the body he was straddling and realisation finally caught up with him. He shuffled off her, scrambling awkwardly to his feet before going across to join his wife. Tears were streaming down Rachael's face as her eyes moved from Emily to Larch then finally to her husband. What had been Larch's knife teetered just a few centimetres from her chest, but that was the last thing on her mind. She struggled to comprehend the horror that had unfolded in the last few seconds.

"Here," Phil said, offering his bound wrists to Debbie. She quickly cut through the zip tie and then Phil took the knife and freed her before they both turned to Rachael once more. The doctor didn't move an inch, clearly still in complete shock.

Silence reigned over the scene for the best part of a minute until Debbie finally broke it. "What now?"

Phil's hand shot out with the knife still in it. The blade disappeared into Rachael's stomach and the horror and bafflement that had been engrained on her face magnified a hundredfold. Her hands instinctively went up to the wound as the weapon was withdrawn once more. Blood spurted out in a rhythmic pattern staining first her T-shirt and then her jeans as it spread. She watched, unable to move, unable to react until, finally, a hopeless gasp left her mouth and she staggered back then fell.

She continued to lie there, the blood still pumping through her fingers, her eyes wet with tears of pain and sadness until finally they closed. Phil turned towards Debbie, who looked back at him in bewilderment. This was not the man she had known all these years.

A grunt sounded from behind them as Landis began to rally once more. "You don't need to see any of this, Debs. Close your eyes and cover your ears. Please."

She did as he asked and, one by one, Phil walked to each of the guards, starting with Landis, and slit their throats, ensuring that if there was any life left in them, it would drain away. He removed their rucksacks and took two of the rifles then dragged the bodies to the side of the road before walking back over to Debbie, who was sobbing once more.

He gently touched her arm and she flinched a little as her eyes opened. "This is a nightmare, isn't it? I'm going to wake up by your side back at the farm any minute."

Phil handed two of the backpacks to his wife and shuffled the other two over his shoulders. "It was a nightmare, Debs. Just not the kind where you wake up in bed."

She looked across to the verge and the bodies. "Did you…." She couldn't finish the sentence. She could barely believe the whole thing had even happened.

"I made sure they're all dead."

"No," Debbie said, turning to him once more. "Did you have to kill that doctor?"

He looked over to the bodies as well then turned towards the imposing hill that housed the entrance to the mine. "I didn't have a choice, Debs. Even if she didn't want to, she'd have been forced to tell them where the farm is."

"It was like I didn't know who you were. It was like you were someone else. I've never even seen you raise a fist in anger."

"Let's not talk about it. Let's head home."

*

When Shan fell to the ground, there was not a soul watching him who was not convinced he was dead. A fresh panic had risen in the air emanating from Miss Carlton more than anyone. It had spread as more and more of the children had gathered around the scene despite protestations from the teacher's assistants for them to stay away.

He did not die though. He went to the hospital with a concussion and he had to receive stitches, but he did not die. Phil was expelled from school, however, and was very nearly sent to a young offenders' institute—ultimately a prison for children. After testimony from a number of his teachers and the evidence that was given regarding the events that led up to the incident, it was deemed more appropriate for him to receive counselling.

The sessions were at three-thirty every Thursday afternoon. The counsellor was a young woman called Teresa, and right from the outset, Phil felt comfortable talking to her. The counselling was nothing like what he had expected. It seemed more like an informal chat. Teresa didn't make notes in the sessions, but once, Phil had to go back into the office for his school bag and found her frantically typing away on a computer. She seemed a little ill at ease to have been caught out, but Phil was just grateful that in their sessions he was never made to feel uncomfortable.

"So, how was school today?" Teresa asked, more like an older sister than a court-appointed counsellor.

"Fine."

"The workload's still manageable? I mean you did miss a few weeks. I can talk to them about easing the—"

"It's fine," Phil said. "I like schoolwork."

"Okay. That's good. And the other children?"

"I don't know whether they enjoy it or not."

Teresa laughed and the corner of Phil's mouth curled up into a smile. "I think you know that's not what I meant, Mr Trainor."

The smile didn't stay on Phil's face for long and his eyes drifted to the window. They were on the second floor and he could see the leaves of the old oak in the car park outside shimmer in the breeze. It felt like they were almost whispering to him. There was something about plants, trees, and the natural world that made him feel comfortable and relaxed. It had been that way for as long as he could remember. It was like they understood him and vice versa. "They're nice."

"That's it? That's all you've got to say?" she asked, still smiling.

"Nobody's picked on me yet. Nobody's made fun of me."

"Yet? You make it sound like there's an inevitability that they will."

He looked towards her. "All past evidence points to it being likely."

Teresa flashed her teeth this time. "You're funny. And say that does happen. Say someone starts picking on you or making fun of you or bullying you. What will you do?"

He straightened up in his chair. "I'll tell Mum and Dad. I'll bring it up with them as soon as it happens so I don't fall back into a victim cycle."

Teresa cocked her head. "Y'know, it's funny. That's pretty much a perfect word-for-word answer for that question. It's almost like it's been rehearsed."

Phil smiled again. "I will though. If anything starts happening, I'll talk about it. It didn't feel like I could before. It never felt like Mum and Dad were listening, but since … since that day, they've been different."

Teresa nodded. "That's good. And that day, Phil, we've touched on it a few times, but we've never really talked about it properly, have we?"

Phil turned to look out of the window once more. "I don't remember much," he said distantly. It wasn't true. He remembered every second, every word, every gesture, every sound, every smell. He remembered everything about it. He always would. But saying he didn't, treating it as some heat-of-the-moment aberration never to be repeated, made answering questions like this a lot easier. His parents had grilled him about it time and time again and pretending not to recall, pretending to get upset when he was asked to do so, was an easy option. "A lot of it's just a blur now."

Teresa looked at him long and hard. "I want you to sit back in your chair and close your eyes."

Phil did as he was asked. It was a strange chair for a modern office. It was old-fashioned and the design was some kind of tapestry. He rubbed his fingers over the surface, and in some places, it felt almost like braille. But it was comfortable and that was the important thing. He rested his head back and took a deep breath. "Now what?"

"Think back to when they showed you that picture."

Phil felt his eye twitch and he silently chastised himself. He'd done his best to brush the whole experience off as something in the past, something forgotten, but that one tick was a betrayal to his thoughts. "Okay," he replied.

"How did it make you feel?"

"Upset."

"Okay. You've been coming here long enough to know I'm not going to settle for that as an answer. Keep your eyes closed; relax, concentrate on your breathing and tell me how it really made you feel."

Phil felt his body slump a little. He was going to have to give her something. "I felt sad, humiliated, angry."

"Okay. Let's talk about that. What was it that made you feel sad?"

Phil kept his eyes closed and thought. "I was sad because, no matter what, I never fitted in. I tried in that place. I tried to be nice to people, but I was never accepted. I was always an outsider."

"Okay, Phil. And you said you were humiliated too. You didn't actually wet your pants. It was a prank that was pulled on you. Why did you feel humiliated?"

"Because it didn't matter that it was a prank. Everybody in school ... in fact, not just in school, everyone in the local area who knew me and was on social media would see that picture and that's all that would matter. I was made a laughing stock, the punchline to someone's stupid joke. I was powerless to do anything about it, just like I'd been powerless a hundred times before in a hundred different situations."

"But you did do something about it this time, didn't you, Phil? You said you felt anger, and you did get angry, didn't you?"

Living the scene out again with Teresa's comforting voice guiding him somehow seemed to help. He relaxed a little, and for all the walls to the outside world he'd put up inside his head, he opened a door for her to peek inside just for a moment. "Yes."

"What went through your mind at that moment?"

"I wanted it to stop. I wanted it all to stop. The teasing, the taunting, the bullying; I wanted it all to stop." Phil didn't realise it, but he was no longer sitting back in the chair and his hands were gripping the arms. "There's only so much someone can put up with. There's only so long someone can be a victim." This time, he said the word without any awareness. "I was sick of it. Sick of all of it. People trying to take away my happiness, trying to … to make me less."

"Make you less, Phil. What do you mean?"

"Chip away at me like I'm some block of wood. Wear me down. Break me."

"What did you want to do? All this time, you've been coming here and you've never told me the truth about this." Phil's eyes flicked open. "What did you want to do?"

"I wanted to kill him."

"Peter Shan?" she said, looking down at the table next to her.

Phil watched and realised for the first time that even if she didn't make notes, she had some kind of crib sheet hidden behind the small potted plant she kept on the small table next to her chair. "Yes."

"Go on."

"I wanted to kill him and the others. I wanted to stop them laughing. I wanted to make it so no one would ever laugh at me again, so no one would ever bully me again, so no one would ever try to hurt me again."

Teresa sat forward in the chair. "And do you think a single action like that can stop all those things?"

Phil looked down at his fingers as they clawed into the fabric of the chair and suddenly realised he had revealed way more than he wanted to. He turned to Teresa. "There's something wrong with me, isn't there?"

It was time for Teresa to sit back in her chair. "Why do you think that?"

"Because … because of what I just told you."

"They did a horrible thing to you, Phil. And every emotion you felt was understandable and completely justifiable."

"But—"

"I haven't finished. Everybody gets angry, and I dare say you've got angry a lot in the past, but this time, you just couldn't control it anymore. This is why you were sent to me. This is what we're here to do. We're here to make sure that you learn how to handle your emotions if you're ever in a situation like that again."

"Do you think you can help me?"

"I'm sure I can help you, Phil. Don't worry about anything. It's all going to work out just fine."

19

Tania, Harper and the others were still about half a kilometre from the outskirts of the farm when they came across the first roving patrol. It was made up not just of Salvation guards but former Level Three citizens too.

"I was never great at maths, but I'm pretty certain that there are more of you coming back than went out. How does that work?" Revell asked as Tania and Harper came to a stop.

Tania replied, nodding to the gun. "Don't we get in without the secret password?"

Michelle suddenly appeared from the back of the group. "I wouldn't let this lot in. Way too much trouble," she said, smiling. "Who are your friends?"

"This is Chloe's dad and these are some of the guards from Infinity."

The humour was suddenly gone from Michelle's face and she stepped forward, shouldering her rifle and shaking Eric by the hand. "Your daughter saved my Harry's life.

She's fast become one of my favourite people in the world." She paused, realising it was the first time she had ever referred to Harry as hers.

"That's very kind of you to say," Eric replied.

"I thought you'd be with Harry," Tania said.

"It was getting crowded in our infirmary after this morning. He's propped up playing cards with Ollie at the moment, so I thought I'd come out and get some exercise with this lot." She gestured to the rest of the squad.

"And what is this lot exactly?" Tania asked.

"We've got four roving patrols made up of guards and civvies."

"Okay," Tania said. "This is new."

"Yeah. I know you haven't been gone long, but I'm guessing you're going to notice quite a lot of changes since you left."

"Whose idea was this?"

"Susan suggested it. She thinks integrating the Salvation guards and the rest of the Level Three people into a kind of joint security force is a good idea. I think she's on a crusade to show that the only differences between us are the ones that were created by the administration."

"And Drake went along with it?"

"I've known Drake a long time," Revell interjected. "Despite what any of you might think, power is the last thing he's after. All of us integrating, working side by side is all that he hoped for when the idea to escape Salvation was first hatched."

"So, that's it? Susan has an idea, Drake seconds it, and suddenly it's a thing?" Harper asked, looking at Michelle.

"I don't think anything's cast in stone, but with the attack by the Ferals yesterday, and the situation with Phil, I think it's a pretty good idea to keep our eyes peeled, don't you?"

Harper put her hands up. "Don't get me wrong; I think it's a grand idea, but I'm a little concerned about just two people possessing the power to put something like this into place."

Michelle raised an eyebrow. "Well, I'm sure you can raise it with them when you get back."

"So, are we allowed through then?" Tania asked with a smile on her face.

"As you've got Chloe's dad with you. Otherwise, I'd have second thoughts. Some of these little 'uns look like they could be trouble." Michelle narrowed her eyes and peered at some of the children gathered around Greta, who all laughed.

"See you a bit later then," Tania said as the group set off once more.

"What do you think about that?" Harper asked in a hushed tone as she walked up alongside her partner.

"I think it's a good idea."

"And?"

"Yeah … I'm with you. I don't like the precedent either. If one or two people just start making decisions like this, things are going to get even more out of hand than they already are."

They carried on walking and, gradually, more and more of the settlement came into view. They finally entered the farmyard itself to find another of the dome-shaped stone ovens had been erected and at least thirty people were busy working away in what was essentially a large open-air kitchen. Pots clanged and trays rattled as they were removed from the fiery apertures.

Tania turned back towards the foraging group. "Empty your bags over there," she said, pointing to a small mountain of produce that had already been dumped by another of the groups. Tania slid her own rucksack off and handed it to Harper then looked towards Eric. "Stay here a minute. I'll make sure she's not giving more blood or something."

It took every gram of self-control Eric possessed to stay put. He felt the eyes of everyone in the yard staring at him and the small army of strangers who had arrived with him, but he didn't care. He didn't care if people stared and talked behind their backs. All he cared about was seeing Chloe again.

It had been a long journey to find this place. Every minute away from his daughter had felt like an hour. While the others in his group took in their surroundings, Eric just stared towards the doorway of the small building, silently praying that this was not some dream. He did not have to wait long for confirmation.

Chloe stepped out into the sun, and then he saw the smile that he had longed to see ever since she'd left Infinity. Tears were running down his face before he began towards her, and suddenly, the fear, the hopelessness, and every other emotion he'd experienced in the last couple of days washed away.

"Dad!" Chloe ran to him; tears poured down her face too and the pair fell into a tight embrace as they met in the middle. "I'm sorry," she said as she buried her head in his chest.

"It's okay, pumpkin. It's okay. I'm just so happy you're alright."

The pair clung to each other for well over a minute, just standing in the middle of the bustling yard like a pair of statues. It was only when Nazya appeared in the doorway that their embrace broke and Eric extended his arm for her to join them.

"The boy's going to be okay then?" Eric said eventually, releasing his grip on the two women and stepping back a little.

"Yes," Nazya replied, nodding and wiping away a tear of her own.

For the first time since arriving, Eric began to look around the rest of the place. "There are a lot more people than I expected."

"Yeah. A lot's happened in the last twenty-four hours," Chloe replied. "A lot."

"Oh?"

"Yeah, Dad. There was another escape from Salvation, but then some people kidnapped Phil; y'know, the guy who set all this up."

"Kidnapped him?"

"Yeah, and yesterday, there was an attack by the Ferals."

Eric's eyebrows arched. "We discovered a few tribes of them on our way across here. They seem to be spreading out a little."

"Yeah, so, to say things have been crazy is a big understatement."

"So it would seem."

"Hey, look, I'm sure you guys have a lot of catching up to do," Tania said. "We can't exactly offer you a roof over your head, but you and your people are welcome to stay the night and eat with us."

Eric nodded. "I'd appreciate that. We had to spend one night in the wild and I can't say any of us slept much."

"We were going to head back to Infinity today, but then everything spiralled."

"Well, we can all head back tomorrow."

Chole took hold of Eric's hand. "I love you, Dad. I'm sorry."

"I love you too."

*

"The tide's starting to come in. We should probably think about heading back," Callie said.

"Yeah," Dani replied. There were dozens of rock pools enclosing the beach and the foragers had reaped a bountiful harvest. The sun was beating down and the turquoise sea looked welcoming, but after hearing the horror story about Harry, nobody had dared so much as to dip a toe.

Within an hour, they were back in the farmyard unloading the rucksacks. "You've been busy," Susan said, coming up to greet them.

"Hi, Mum," Callie replied, hugging her. It was the first time they'd held each other since Callie had stormed off and it felt good for both of them.

"Are you okay?"

"Yeah, why?"

"We haven't really spoken properly since...."

"Since I had a meltdown and made a prat of myself?"

"You didn't make a prat of yourself at all. I was very proud of what you did. I mean we haven't really talked since Phil disappeared."

Callie turned and looked towards Dani, who was directing the others. "I'm okay, Mum."

"Somehow, I don't believe you."

"What do you want me to say?" she asked as a tear appeared in the corner of her eye. "Phil was my friend and I'm never going to see him or Debbie again. But it's not like I can just sit back and feel sorry for myself, is it?" she said, gesturing around her.

"I think people would understand if you did. Phil and Debbie meant a lot to everyone, but he had a special bond with you."

Callie wiped her eyes. "I think it's just best that I stay busy."

"I understand, sweetheart."

"Where's Si?"

"Ugh!"

"What does that mean?"

"He's broken up with Sasha."

"What? But they've only just got back together. What the hell happened?"

"He refuses to talk about it."

"I'll go talk to him."

"Err...."

"What?"

"I think sometimes it's best if people are just left alone for a while in situations like that. I tried talking to him and he was pretty adamant he didn't want to discuss it."

"I suppose you're right. It's not like I can impart any nuggets of relationship advice, is it?"

Susan laughed. "I think you've got a few potential suitors around here. I'm sure it won't be long. On the subject of which, Matt was looking for you earlier."

"Why?"

"I don't know."

"Where is he?"

"I think he was with Wei for most of the morning, and about an hour ago, I saw him heading into the forest."

"I'll see if I can track him down."

"Track who down?" Dani asked, walking up to them.

"Matt."

"I just spotted him and Si heading upstream with a load of wood."

"What?" Callie asked. "What were they doing?"

"Carrying a load of wood."

"Yeah, you said, but why?"

"I don't know."

"Oh, and before I forget," Susan said, "guess who Tania and Harper ran into when they were out foraging."

"Not more Ferals?" Callie replied with concern.

"Eric."

"Eric? But how?"

"He was looking for Chloe. He was with a big group. They're in the fields at the moment, getting the grand tour."

"I'll have to go say hi when they come back. In the meantime, shall we go find out what Si and Matt are up to?" Callie asked, looking at Dani and then her mother.

"I'm going to find Zep," Dani replied, disappearing as quickly as she had appeared.

"I need to get back to Drake."

"Err ... why?"

"Long story."

"Okay."

Callie stood there as she watched her mother walk away and a feeling of pride gripped her. It was only a matter of weeks ago that Susan was just a hollow impression of the woman she had once been, of the mother she had once been, but now she had become one of the leading figures of the new settlement, someone who made a difference every day. A small smile appeared on Callie's face, but as she turned and caught sight of Matt and Si continuing up the hill by the side of the stream, the smile vanished.

She looked around the busy farmyard. Several groups were sorting the different food that had been foraged. Others were preparing it while more still manned the ovens. Drake and the new arrivals had brought a lot of kitchen equipment with them, including large stock pots from some of the restaurants. At least a dozen of these were now simmering away.

Callie turned and headed out of the busy farmyard. She walked towards the stream and it didn't take her long to spot Matt and Si, who were both now perched on a rock just a little way up the incline of the hill.

When she arrived, she saw several piles of branches and boughs. None of them was less than two metres in length, and although blackened, like everything else that had survived through the asteroid, they looked sturdy and heavy. "You come to help us?" Si asked before taking a drink from a collapsible bottle and handing it to Matt.

"Well, that all depends on what you're doing," Callie replied.

Matt took a drink and placed the bottle down before reaching into his back pocket. "I was looking for you earlier," he said, pulling out a piece of paper.

"Mum said. What for?"

"I found this." He handed the paper to Callie. The writing was tiny and there were various diagrams and sketches on the right-hand side of the page.

"What is it?"

"It's Dad's plans for the irrigation system." He sniffed deeply as just the mention of his parents still made him catch his breath. *I can't believe they're gone.*

"Okay, and?"

"I figured that if we at least made a start on building the framework then people would begin to realise that this is something we can do that will benefit us, rather than just being an idea on a piece of paper. It would be like my dad's legacy or something," he said, gulping and doing his best not to cry. He had succumbed to tears several times already and Si had been there to help him. After all, he'd had first-hand experience of losing a parent. Earlier in the day, Matt had spent time with Wei before heading back to his quarters in the barn and sobbing himself to sleep. When he woke, it was like a black void had opened up inside him, but the physical exertion of collecting the wood from the forest had somehow managed to numb some of the pain he was feeling.

"Yeah," Si said, taking over and letting his younger friend gather himself once more. "It's actually pretty simple but pretty brilliant at the same time."

Callie looked from her brother to Matt and then back again. "And what, you two are going to build this thing just like that, just the two of you?"

"Like I said, we could do with some help if you're offering."

"And what's all the wood for?"

Si stood and grabbed two of the pieces, crossing them about three-quarters of the way up. We bind these together and plant them firmly in the ground and they become our piers. Y'know, like on a bridge or—"

"An aqueduct," Callie said.

"Yeah, so the pipe sits in the V shape up here and voilà."

"Okay, but you still haven't said how you're going to get hold of the pipe. I mean Phil was talking about trading with some of the people at Infinity, but—"

"But people won't take us seriously," Matt said, having gathered himself once more. "I know Dad had to do a lot to convince Jason and John that this was a good idea, and I know they were concerned that it would tie up a lot of resources and cost us a lot in trade." Matt looked down towards the farm. "Especially now, with everything that's happened in the last couple of days, they're probably going to be less inclined to take risks than ever, but on the other hand, having a proper irrigation system would make a huge difference to our ability to grow more crops." Callie let out a small laugh. "What?" Matt asked, a little hurt.

"You sound like your dad."

Matt smiled. "Thank you. But it's true, with three thousand plus people, we need this more than ever."

"You don't have to convince me. I think it's a great idea. I just think you're going to have a job convincing others."

Matt and Si looked at each other. "We've got a plan B in place if we can't get John to agree to trade," Si said.

"Oh?"

"We'll salvage the stuff we need ourselves."

"What?"

"We saw the remains of a few towns on the way back from Crowesbury, didn't we?"

"Yeah, and there's a reason we didn't go anywhere near them. They could have been swarming with Ferals for all we knew."

"Well, I'm not proposing we go by ourselves, not to a town, but if we can get more people together willing to help, I think it would be doable. But failing that, there must be hundreds of smaller villages and things that wouldn't offer anything for the Ferals that maybe we could pick apart."

"Yeah, and newsflash, most of them will have been turned to ash."

"That's possible, but remember the buildings in Crowesbury? Some of them weren't that bad on the inside, and Woody and his people have managed to find plenty, haven't they?"

"Okay, time out. I need to talk to you for a second."

"I thought we were talking."

"I'm sorry, Matt," she said, turning to him. "I just need to have a quick word with my brother."

Matt nodded. "No problem. I'll head back to the forest," he said, looking at Si.

"I'll catch up with you in a minute," he replied.

They both watched Matt walk away before Callie turned to her brother. "Mum told me you split up with Sasha. What happened?"

Si looked uneasy for a moment. "I don't want to talk about it."

"Okay. But do you think this," she said, pointing to the wood, "is a knee-jerk reaction to that?"

"What, helping Matt?"

"It's a bit more than carrying a few pieces of wood, isn't it? You're talking about starting a salvaging team. I'm just worried that you're not thinking straight, that's all. And the last thing Matt needs right now is for someone to follow him down the rabbit hole. I'm just barely hanging on, Si." Her voice trembled as she said those last words. "It's taking me everything I've got not to just scream and cry and run away. And it's going to be ten times worse for Matt."

"Look. I know what you're saying, but I've been keeping an eye on him. And yes, I wanted to throw myself into something to forget, just like he did, but this is a really good idea. It will mean fresh running water for everyone without trailing to the stream. It will mean water for the crops. Ever since I came back from the quarry, I haven't been able to find a place for myself, Cal. I've helped a bit in the fields, I've helped a bit with the building, but I've not been able to really contribute. This could be it. What Phil came up with was a great idea."

"I know what he was wanting to do, I just worry that you immersing yourself in this is a way of not dealing with—"

"I love you, Callie. But I know what I'm doing. You don't need to worry about me. I'm going to work on this,

I'm going to keep an eye on Matt and be there for him when he needs it, and we're going to build something for the community. Now, are you going to help us or not?"

Callie looked at the pile of wood, shook her head and shrugged. "Well, someone's got to keep an eye on you two, haven't they?"

20

Phil and Debbie both felt exhausted. Even when they had stopped to rest in the night, they had not really rested. They had merely contemplated what horrors were ahead of them. Now they were on their way back home, they could feel the heat of the sun blazing down and every step felt like a mile.

"Phil."

"Yes?"

"What happened back there?"

He just carried on walking for a while but eventually stopped and turned to her. "You saw what happened."

"Yes, but ... it wasn't really you, was it?"

"It was and it wasn't."

"What does that mean?"

"Sometimes, something snaps."

"This is what I'm talking about. I'm worried about you."

Phil took his wife's hand. "You don't need to worry about me having another breakdown if that's what you're concerned about."

"I just need to know that you're going to be okay."

"Listen. Those people, they were going to put us back in that prison, and this time, there would never have been an escape. They'd threaten you to get to me, and...." Tears started rolling down his face and Debbie wrapped her arms around him, pulling him close.

"It's alright. It's alright."

"I couldn't allow that. I couldn't allow them to lock you up, to hurt you. I couldn't allow them to take us away from our boy, Debs. I-I didn't want to kill her. I didn't want to kill any of them, but they pushed me into a corner. I—"

"Sh. Sh," she said, stroking the back of his head as she continued her embrace. "It's all okay. You did the right thing. I just need to know that you're alright. That's all."

He pulled away and she could see the sadness in his eyes as the tears continued to fall. "As long as I've got you. As long as I've got my family."

"You'll always have me, Phil." She brushed away his tears with her fingers. "You'll always have me."

*

Campfires began to light up the forest as night fell. So much had happened in the last twenty-four hours that many people had been left shell-shocked. There were a few who were fearful of what the night may bring, but most felt reassured by the four roaming squads of enforcers and an expanded band of lookouts on the ridge. Things had moved quickly, and to expedite proceedings, only a few had been involved in the decision-making processes, which was why now a meeting had been called by the ones chiefly responsible for founding the settlement and a few newer key figures.

It was a warm evening and they held it outside near the stream as a show to people that there were no secrets, no us and them. As it turned out, most people were more interested in feeding themselves and setting up camp for the night. A fire blazed away in the centre of the circle, giving them enough light to see whoever had the floor at the time.

"Okay," John began. "I realise things have been a bit chaotic in the last twenty-four hours, so I've called this meeting in the hope that we can make the next twenty-four a little less so." He looked towards Drake and Marina then across to Austin, Clem and Caine. "Thank you for coming. We've got a lot to discuss, and first on the agenda is the security force." He turned to Tania. "I believe you wanted to say something about this."

"Yes," she said, glancing towards Harper before continuing. "I just don't think a decision like this should have been made without the kind of discussion we're having now. If people are going to establish armies without consultation, then what next, a police state?"

"Exactly," Caine agreed. "It will be like Salvation again before we know it."

"Just a minute," Susan began. "I was just trying to come up—"

"What's wrong with you?" Greenslade boomed, and everyone fell silent. He stared towards Tania and then at Caine, making the other man feel an inch tall. "Two of our people were attacked by Ferals." He pointed to Callie. "Thankfully, they picked on the wrong girls, but it could easily have gone the other way. We know there are hundreds more out there somewhere. There are an undetermined number of hostile guards from the quarry too. In addition, Phil and Debbie were kidnapped, the administration probably knows by now where we are, and for all we know, we could be attacked at any minute."

"Yes, but—" Tania was cut off by him this time.

"Today, Susan and Drake asked for volunteers for an armed force to add to the guards we've already got so we can have twenty-four-hour security. It's a two-to-one ratio of Level Three inhabitants to Salvation guards. It's not to impose a police state, it's to protect us from whatever the hell else is out there, and hopefully it will be able to stop us from killing one another too," he said, this time looking at Austin and Clem. "If any of you have got a problem with that, I refer to my earlier question, what the hell is wrong with you?"

There was a pause before Tania spoke again. "It's not that we have a problem with the idea. It's that we have a problem with decisions this big being made without a wider discussion."

"Right. We're all here now. Does anybody object to a security force that's made up primarily of Level Three inhabitants to make this whole place safer?" The seconds ticked by and the only sound to be heard was that of the crackling fire. "Excellent. So, it is written. So, it is done."

"I never thought I'd see the great Blake Greenslade talking about the value of a security force," Austin said.

"Yeah, well. Times change and people change." He sat back a little and looked across at Callie, who had the start of a smile on her face.

"Okay, staying with security," John began, "the turrets," he said, looking towards Jason.

"We completed work on eight today."

"Eight?" John asked, surprised.

"Yeah," Drake said. "They're quality as well. They did a great job. We're going to identify further strategic points to the south and the east. Jason's agreed to put a few more in place for us."

"But Salvation's in the north," John said.

"Yeah, but as Greenslade said, we don't know who else is out there. It can't harm having something in place just in case."

"So, we have lookouts to the south and east?"

"We've got the roving patrols. When we've identified suitable positions for the lookout posts, we're going to be able to permanently station two of the four patrols there. That is providing nobody has any objections," he said with half a smile.

"Okay," John said. "The farm." He looked across to Wei. Matt was sitting by his side. It was obvious he'd been asked as a sign of respect to his father, but despite all his enthusiasm earlier on in the day, he was perturbed by the gathering. Callie was sitting next to him and she reached out a hand, squeezing his arm a little.

"We cleared twelve fields today and—"

"Twelve?"

"Is your hearing okay, John? You seem to be asking people to repeat things a lot," Susan said, and a small wave of laughter rippled around the group.

John laughed too. "Twelve just seems like an awful lot, that's all."

Wei nodded. "We had a lot more willing helpers today. Whole families worked side by side, pulling weeds and clearing ground. Tomorrow, we will clear more and begin tilling the ground already cleared."

"That's impressive, Wei. Phil would be over the moon," John said, smiling fondly and looking towards Matt, who cast his eyes down to the fire.

"Actually, if you're talking about the farm, Matt's got something to raise too," Callie said, kneeling up.

"Oh?"

"No, it's okay," Matt said, looking decidedly embarrassed.

Ignoring him, Callie continued. "He found the plans for Phil's irrigation system and he's started work on them. He and Si."

"Si?" Susan asked.

"Yeah."

"Err ... that's great, Callie," John said, "but I think we need to take a breath and get everything fine-tuned before we take on such a massive project, don't you?"

"No, actually."

Her words were greeted with silence until Greenslade broke it. "Tell us why you think that."

"We've got the best part of three and a half thousand people here now and no Phil to guide us. Twelve fields is a good start, but we're going to need a lot more. That's going to take time and work, and how many people do you think it will tie up having to manually fetch water from the stream? Matt and Si are right. We need this irrigation system. Phil knew we needed it for the handful of fields he had planned. What do you think he'd be telling us now if he was sitting here?" She'd lost count of how many times she'd cried that day, but now tears flooded her eyes once more.

"But, Callie, it's not just the building of it," Jason said, "it's all the materials too."

She wiped the streaks from her face with her sleeve before continuing. "Si wants to form a salvage team."

"What?" John said.

"What?" Susan echoed.

"It's something we've talked about briefly, but now we've got the manpower, and now everything is changing so fast and it's so critical to get things right, don't you think it makes sense?"

"What is it with your children?" John asked, looking at Susan.

"Don't blame me. They take after their father."

"No, actually. They take after you," Greenslade said. "I think this is a good idea."

"What?" John asked.

"What?" Susan echoed.

"It makes sense," Greenslade continued. "Think about it. After what I've heard about this Infinity place, having a salvage team will mean we can help scrape together the things we need and trade any excess. It's the next sensible step."

"Okay," Susan said. "Well, firstly, are you forgetting about what's just been said about security and all the people out there who present us with a threat?"

"No. That's why if we do this, it can't be half-hearted. We need a big team with security. I'm not talking about just a small group heading out. I'm talking about a decent-sized team with an equally decent armed force to guard it."

"And what about the foraging? What about the farm? What about everything else?" John asked.

"I...." Caine began but stopped himself.

"You what?" Callie asked.

"It doesn't matter."

"It does. What were you going to say?"

"I used to work in demolition and reclamation. It was our family business."

Everybody stared at him for a few seconds before Matt continued. "It's like Callie said earlier today. We have to work together. It's the only way we're going to survive. Whatever happened in the past is in the past. We need to farm and forage and build and fight together; otherwise, they've won."

"Who've won?" It was Clem who spoke this time.

"The administration. All they ever wanted was to sow division, to make us believe we're all different, but, in truth, we're all the same. People just want to get on with their lives and think their families are safe." His eyes teared up once more at the mention of family. "What happened this morning ... we can't let that happen again. If we do, we'll tear ourselves apart and all this," he said, reaching into his back pocket and holding up his father's notes, "all this will have been for nothing. Everything my dad did and planned will have been for nothing."

"Some wounds don't heal that easily," Clem replied.

"But they do heal," Callie said, taking over. "Your children, they had friends, yes?"

"Of course."

"Don't you think you'd be honouring their memory a little better if you did something to help them and the people of this community rather than live in the past and wallow in your own hatred?"

Clem was taken aback by Callie's words. She stared at her for a few seconds then began to cry.

"You make it sound so simple," Austin said in a shaky voice.

"When you think about it, it is. You can either choose to make this work or choose to tear it down. Those are the only two options. We need everybody to be on board. We need all their skills, all their knowledge. We're starting again from scratch. No books, no computers, no information recall at the touch of a button. Everybody has something to contribute, everybody. Everybody is vital to this community thriving. Everybody. Now, what are you going to choose?"

There was a long pause and all eyes watched Clem and Austin intently. Eventually, Austin broke the silence. "I think maybe the salvage team is a good idea. I think maybe our people spending the days away from this place and gradually acclimatising to us all living together might be a good thing."

"Okay, but everyone is our people now. That's the whole point."

Austin stared at Callie for several more seconds. "Yeah, well, I dare say we'll all need to acclimatise ourselves to that too."

"So, you're in?" Si asked.

"Aye. There'll be a few more besides me to add to your list too."

"Good. We'll meet here at sunrise."

Austin and Clem climbed to their feet. "We'll see you then, I suppose," and the pair walked away without turning back.

"I know a few lads and lasses who'd want to do this too," Caine said.

"Bring them all. Bring as many as you can find," Si replied.

"Alright then. I'll see you tomorrow." They all watched him go too and then turned towards the fire once more.

"Well. Sounds like we've got another early start tomorrow," Greenslade said. "I'm going to drop in to see how Trunk's doing; then I'm going to get some shuteye."

One by one, the other members of the unelected council disappeared until there were just Susan, Si and Callie left. "I think I'll come with you tomorrow," Susan said.

"No," Si replied sharply.

"You don't want me to join you?"

"No, Mum."

Susan suddenly looked hurt. "Okay, I understand."

"No, you don't. It's not that I don't want you with me. In fact, I do. It's that things are volatile here and they're going to be like that for some time to come. This is our home and there are only two people I trust. One of them is Callie and one of them is you. You need to keep an eye on things here. You need to make sure there are no more rifts or confrontations." He turned to Callie. "It's true what you said. They are all our people now, but it's going to take time and patience for everyone to realise that. We need someone here who's strong ... a leader. That's you, Mum."

She let out a short laugh but then realised he wasn't joking. "I'm not a leader. I'm just ... me ... your mum."

"Si's right, Mum. John's a nice guy and a good mediator, but he's not strong, and right now, the people need strength. You went through hell after Dad died. Then, when all this happened, you became like this ... superwoman."

"Give over, Callie. I've just been getting on with it like everybody else."

"No, Mum. You were the first into the water in that tunnel. That took real guts."

"I did it for you."

"I know. And that's why I know if you do this, it will be for us too. It was a really good idea to stick with Drake today. It was a good idea for the security force made up primarily of Level Three inhabitants with a few guards thrown into the equation. Those are the types of decisions that are going to make a difference between this thing working and not. Si's right. You're needed here. You're the glue that will hold this place together."

"Stop it. You're going to make me cry."

"It's the truth."

"It is, Mum," Si said.

"Come here. The pair of you." The two siblings went across and sat by their mother's side. She first kissed one then the other. "I love you two so much."

"We love you, Mum," they both replied in unison.

EPILOGUE

Drake woke with a start. The campfire was still crackling away and it took him a few seconds to focus on the figure who had gently shaken him.

"Dwyer? What is it?" he whispered.

"You wanted to know if there was anything to report."

Drake sat up, careful not to wake his wife, who was still nestled by his side. "What?"

"There are two figures approaching from the north."

Drake's brow furrowed a little. "Could they be spotters?" he asked, climbing to his feet and grabbing his weapon.

The pair began walking away but kept their voices down so as not to cause alarm if anyone overheard them. "If they are, they've got a weird way of going about it. They're on the road."

The two men left the forest and started up the hill. "Maybe they're messengers. Maybe they're coming to give us a warning. Surrender now and we won't obliterate you and everyone you care about."

"Good to see you've woken up in a cheery mood."

"Well, what else could it be?"

"I mean, from what I've heard about that Infinity place, there are a lot of survivors out there."

"And they just happen to show up the night after the architect of the hydroponics farms and his wife get kidnapped and taken back to Salvation. Tell me again, how did you pass the IQ test?"

"I copied Marina's answers."

"I can believe that."

The two men finally arrived on the ridge and the guard holding the binoculars handed them to Drake. "Where did we get these from?" he asked, looking at them.

"Greenslade."

"He just gave us them, no strings attached?"

"Yeah."

"That man is completely unfathomable. He worries me."

"Why, because he gave us some binoculars?" Dwyer asked.

"No. Because I can't figure out what he's thinking."

"Well, whatever he's thinking, he's not really our concern right now."

Drake lifted the binoculars up to his eyes and followed the moonlit road until his gaze fell upon the two figures walking side by side. "They're armed."

"Yeah, we saw. The rifles are slung, though, and like I say, they don't actually look like they're going to make a charge towards us. What do you want to do?"

"What do I want to do? I want to go back to bed and get a few hours' sleep before another complete shitshow of a day starts, but that's probably not going to happen now, is it?"

"You asked me to wake you."

"I know, I know." Drake let out a long sigh. "We wait until they get closer."

"And then what?"

"We see what they want."

"You don't want to head them off before they get closer?"

"To what end? Just to have to walk all the way back up here with them? Let's see who they are and figure it out from there."

"What's your gut saying?"

"It's saying we're about to get a message from our friend Bucks and it's not going to be 'I miss you, please come back, all is forgiven.'"

"And if that is the case? If they're messengers and they're here to tell us there's a war coming if we don't surrender?"

Drake lowered the binoculars from his eyes. "Then we give them a war."

The three men waited on the road. There were other guards along the ridge, some in the turrets, some out in the open, watching the two strangers approach.

It was several more minutes before the pair of figures made it to the bottom of the hill. When they were roughly fifty metres away, Drake raised the binoculars once more. "You see anything?" Dwyer asked.

"Like what? Like a glow-in-the-dark sign saying, 'We come in peace'? We'll find out what they're doing here soon enough and then—you've got to be kidding me."

"What? What is it?" Dwyer asked, sensing the surprise in his friend's voice.

"It looks like ... Trainor."

"Trainor?"

It was another minute or so before they finally reached the three men. "No champagne? No fireworks? No offence, but I expected a little more for our triumphant return," Phil said.

It was bluster, all bluster. Their journey had been a long one and they had barely spoken for most of it. Phil wouldn't admit it, but the events of the morning had left him scarred, and that terrified Debbie. She was the only one who would see the true Phil. She was the only one who knew what signs to look for if he was on the verge of another breakdown. *A breakdown when there are hospitals, drugs and psychiatrists around to help is one thing, but one out here. Shit. I don't even want to think about it.* She couldn't think about it. She was physically and emotionally exhausted.

"What happened?" Drake asked eventually.

"We never got to Salvation if that's what you're asking."

"That was part of what I was asking. And the others?"

"They didn't get to Salvation either."

The three men looked at Phil for the longest time before Drake spoke again. "And there's no chance of them reaching it in the future?"

"None."

Dwyer had flicked a dynamo lantern on and Drake could see the expressions on the new arrivals' faces. He knew not to push things any further. "Well, I can't tell you how good it is to see you back."

"We can't tell you how good it is to be back," Debbie replied.

"A lot's happened since you've been gone."

"Yeah, that happens here. You get used to it," Phil said. "We'll catch up later, but right now, we just want to see our son."

*

Matt hadn't been able to sleep. He thought he was tired enough, but when he put his head down, all he could think about was his mum and dad. He left the confines of the barn and went to sit outside. A fire still burned in the centre of the farmyard where a few had gathered to while away the hours before bed, but now he was the only one left.

He sat with a piece of wood ready to throw on and feed the flames if he thought they risked dying. His eyes stung and he wasn't sure if it was the heat or the threat of more tears that was the cause. He sniffed loudly and a second later felt two streams run down his cheeks.

He was full of regret and sadness. *Why didn't I talk to Dad sooner when we moved down to Level Two? Why didn't I tell him I missed him? Why didn't I spend more time with him when he was here? Why didn't I tell Mum I loved her more? Why did I always switch off when she started to tell stories about the old days, about their honeymoon, about the good times they enjoyed together?*

"I'm sorry, Mum. I'm sorry, Dad." He said the words in little more than a whisper before wrapping his arms around his legs and burying his face into his knees. "I'm sorry." He began to sob louder and louder. Up until now, he'd done his best to remain strong, to occupy his mind, but in the dead of night, with no one around to see him, he could grieve, grieve the way he had wanted to grieve all day. "I'm sorry," he rasped as more tears than ever ran down his face. "I'm sorry, I'm sorry, I'm sorry."

"Son?"

"I'm sorry, I'm sorry, I'm sorry."

"Son?"

He kept hearing his father's voice in his head, but that was only natural under the circumstances. He'd relived a thousand conversations with his mum and his dad during the course of the day, so hearing them now, in the wee small hours, was no surprise.

"Matt?"

He looked up with blurry, tear-filled eyes and saw two familiar figures heading across the farmyard towards him. *Now I'm seeing things too.*

"Son ... Matt."

He raised his head a little further and used the heel of his palm to blot the tears. A shiver of fear ran through him as he saw his parents standing there. *I really am seeing things. Am I losing it?*

"Matty!" Debbie said, shrugging off two rucksacks and a rifle before dropping to her knees and throwing her arms around her son.

Still, he couldn't believe it. As he heard another rifle and two more rucksacks clatter to the ground, realisation jolted through him. *This is happening. This is really real.* "Mum?"

"It's all okay, Matty. It's all okay, darling. We're here. We're back with you and we're never leaving again."

"Mum?" he asked again, gripping her as tightly as she held him.

He felt a kiss on the top of his head as Phil knelt at his other side and put his arms around him too. "It's all going to be okay, Son. We're back now. We're back."

Matt started crying again, louder than ever now, but this time, they were tears of happiness. "Please tell me this is real and I'm not dreaming," he managed to say through shivering breaths.

"This is real, Matt. This is real and we're here with you. I can't even imagine what it must have been like, Son. But we're back now and neither of us is going anywhere ever again."

"You promise?" The words came out not from the teenager who had been doing everything he could to act like a man for most of the day but from the small, vulnerable voice that lies in the heart of every son or daughter irrespective of their age.

"I promise."

The End

A NOTE FROM THE AUTHOR

I really hope you enjoyed this book and would be very grateful if you took a minute to leave a review on Amazon and Goodreads.

If you would like to stay informed about what I'm doing, including current writing projects, and all the latest news and release information; these are the places to go:

Join the fan club on Facebook
https://www.facebook.com/groups/127693634504226

Like the Christopher Artinian author page
https://www.facebook.com/safehaventrilogy/

Buy exclusive and signed books and merchandise, subscribe to the newsletter and follow the blog:
https://www.christopherartinian.com/

Follow me on Twitter
https://twitter.com/Christo71635959

Follow me on Youtube:
https://www.youtube.com/channel/UCfJymx31VvzttB_Q-x5otYg

Follow me on Amazon
https://amzn.to/2I1llU6

Follow me on Goodreads
https://bit.ly/2P7iDzX

Other books by Christopher Artinian:

Safe Haven: Rise of the RAMs
Safe Haven: Realm of the Raiders
Safe Haven: Reap of the Righteous
Safe Haven: Ice
Safe Haven: Vengeance
Safe Haven: Is This the End of Everything?
Safe Haven: Neverland (Part 1)
Safe Haven: Neverland (Part 2)
Safe Haven: Doomsday
Before Safe Haven: Lucy
Before Safe Haven: Alex
Before Safe Haven: Mike
Before Safe Haven: Jules
The End of Everything: Book 1

The End of Everything: Book 2
The End of Everything: Book 3
The End of Everything: Book 4
The End of Everything: Book 5
The End of Everything: Book 6
The End of Everything: Book 7
The End of Everything: Book 8
The End of Everything: Book 9
The End of Everything: Book 10
The End of Everything: Book 11
The End of Everything: Book 12
Relentless
Relentless 2
Relentless 3
The Burning Tree: Book 1 – Salvation
The Burning Tree: Book 2 – Rebirth
The Burning Tree: Book 3 - Infinity

CHRISTOPHER ARTINIAN

Christopher Artinian was born and raised in Leeds, West Yorkshire. Wanting to escape life in a big city and concentrate more on working to live than living to work, he and his family moved to the Outer Hebrides in the northwest of Scotland in 2004, where he now works as a full-time author.

Chris is a huge music fan, a cinephile, an avid reader and a supporter of Yorkshire county cricket club. When he's not sitting in front of his laptop living out his next post-apocalyptic/dystopian/horror adventure, he will be passionately immersed in one of his other interests.

Printed in Great Britain
by Amazon